Man of the Desert

Man of the Desert

A Western Story

By

ROBERT J. HORTON

Skyhorse Publishing

Skyhorse Publishing books may be purchased in bulk at special discounts for sales promotion, corporate gifts, fund-raising, or educational purposes. Special editions can also be created to specifications. For details, contact the Special Sales Department, Skyhorse Publishing, 307 West 36th Street, 11th Floor, New York, NY 10018 or info@skyhorsepublishing.com.

Skyhorse® and Skyhorse Publishing® are registered trademarks of Skyhorse Publishing, Inc.®, a Delaware corporation.

www.skyhorsepublishing.com

10 9 8 7 6 5 4 3 2 1

Library of Congress Cataloging-in-Publication Data is available on file.

Print ISBN: 978-1-62873-627-4
Ebook ISBN: 978-1-62873-984-8

Printed in the United States of America

Chapter One

The desert road led up a long acclivity toward the mesa. On either side the grotesque branches of the Joshua trees, resembling long, green, bristle brushes, were tipped with clusters of white blossoms. Between clumps of juniper and yucca, among patches of gray sage, little red and yellow flowers peeped forth in radiant bloom, lending an unaccustomed flow of color to the saffron-tinted earth. The sun swam in a cloudless, high-arched sky of blue, and struck fires of brilliancy from the green and crimson stains on mineral rocks. A breath of wind laved a land of desolate, unending distances, cooling and soothing in subtle mockery of the inferno's blistering blast soon to come. It was the brief season of the desert spring.

The road was a cushion of dust in which the wheels of a buckboard, drawn by two sturdy grays, moved noiselessly. But the familiar sounds of slow travel were audible—creak of harness, squeak of floor board, the crunch of hoofs. And there was dust, and noonday heat, and the scent of sweating horses. In the buckboard were two people, a man, who was driving, and a girl. The man was short, slender, with prominent knees and a stoop, but displaying a wiry strength in his movements that belied a first impression of frailty. He was not young. There was an intricate network of wrinkles at the corners of his eyes, his neck was seamed and lined, and gray hair showed under his headgear. His neck and gnarled hands were burned a deep brown, but his face was of a lighter shade, almost rosy. His eyes were of a washed-out blue, and constantly twinkling. He wore faded blue overalls,

1

riding boots, flannel shirt, a hat with a medium brim, undented high crown, and adorned with a narrow, fanciful band of leather.

The girl was a blonde with laughing gray eyes that were frequently serious, rather full-lipped and soft-cheeked, but not enough so to be merely pretty, or really beautiful. Her face and smile indicated a likeable personality; her eyes mirrored a certain strength of character while frankly flashing a question. She seemed cool, radiant, composed, glowingly healthful in a neat blue suit and snug blue turban. The wisps of hair that peeped from beneath the turban were the color of spun gold in the dazzling sunlight.

"You say, Mister Crossley . . . but I believe you told me you wished me to call you Jim?" She favored the man with a smile that caused him to catch up on the lines with a jerk.

"Jim it is, Miss Farman," he said. "It's what most of 'em call me. My name's Crossley, all right, but Jim's easier on the breath an' the ear, I reckon."

"Very well, Jim." The girl laughed lightly, easily, reassuringly. "Jim, what did you say was the name of my uncle's place?"

"Rancho del Encanto," Jim recited with a lingering accent.

"Spanish, of course. And what does it mean, Jim?"

"Means 'Ranch of Enchantment' or something like that." Jim reached for the plug of tobacco in his hip pocket, remembered just in time, and sighed. Hard luck, this, hard work driving a team without the comforting taste of strong tobacco. But wasn't Miss Hope Farman a lady? And wasn't she a New Englander? He didn't know exactly what a New Englander was, although he knew they came from the East, but the housekeeper had warned him to be careful when he had left the ranch the day before to go to the distant railway station. Well, he would play safe; he would forego the chew.

They were nearing the mesa and the girl looked back over the gray and yellow expanse of desert. Rancho del Encanto—enchantment in this wild and lonely desolation? Perhaps the wife of her uncle, Nathan Farman, had so named the ranch. Perhaps she had found enchantment there; surely she had found love. Her uncle never had remarried after his wife's death. He had written of her often. He had sorrowed long and deep after he had lost her. It was one reason why Hope Farman had decided to visit him and spend the summer on his ranch.

The girl looked long and wonderingly at the desert. It seemed so empty! It was so utterly devoid of life. Even with its scant vegetation, it appeared bare. The green grass and trees of her native Connecticut! The contrast was so vivid, had been brought about so suddenly after her long journey, that it left her numbed by its very reality. She found it hard to adjust her mind to the new order of things inanimate. But it interested her, as did Jim Crossley, who handled the horses so easily that he appeared to drive by instinct.

"Do you know, Jim," she said suddenly, "do you know . . ." She hesitated.

"Nope, I reckon I don't, ma'am."

"I don't believe half what I've read and heard of the West," she said boldly.

"Don't blame you a bit, ma'am. There's liars in all countries."

She looked at him quickly. He had subtly turned the edge of her point. If his reply was a sample of the dullness of the desert breed, it occurred to her that she had been misinformed in a quarter she had not suspected.

"I mean, Jim, that I'm minded to think some of the things that have taken place out here have been exaggerated," she explained.

"Mebbe so," he considered. "An' I reckon half ain't been told about some of 'em."

The horses pulled up a last stiff piece of grade and came out upon the mesa. Then the wind hit them. It was a chilling wind, sweeping down the great trough east of the foothills of the Sierras. League on league the desert stretched northward and eastward, rimmed by jagged mountains, naked save for a veil of blue haze.

3

Hope Farman caught her breath at the stupendous sight. Gone were the fantastic Joshua trees, the junipers, and the yucca, gone were all the beautiful flowers.

"Why, it's changed!" she exclaimed.

Jim shrugged, made another false move toward his hip pocket, and shook out the lines. "Yep, she's a tough proposition from here on in," he announced. "Nuthin' but greasewood an' sage till we get pretty close to the ranch. We come on it sudden like . . . off there." He pointed toward the northwest and the foothills.

"Is it all like this at the ranch?" she asked with a feeling of revulsion.

"Nope. There's trees there, an' water."

She smiled at him gratefully. That was it. Water! It was the water she missed so acutely. There was so little of it. They were carrying it in bags. They hadn't passed a single water hole or spring since leaving the small town at the railroad. It was good to know there was water somewhere in that barren country.

"Are there any towns . . . places of interest . . . near here?" she asked.

Jim motioned eastward. "Bandburg's off there. Mining town. Ever hear of a glory hole? Bandburg's got one. They're scooping the gold out of the mountain like it was soft coal! They've gutted the hill five million dollars' worth already."

Hope was thrilled. She always had associated the thought of the desert with gold. Here was evidence that it was not a fallacy that the two words were synonymous.

Jim was pointing again, northeastward this time. "Death Valley's up there. Can't see it. Too far away an' the Slate range shuts it off. Panamint's on this side an' Funeral Mountains on the other."

She had heard of it, a dreaded sink in the desert, sometimes white as though covered with the dust of powdered skulls, glowing with color at sunset, practically waterless, below the level of the sea.

"How did it get that name?" she inquired.

"Bunch of Mormons, headed for the gold fields, tried to cross it an' died there," Jim replied. "Plenty has died there since," he added as an afterthought.

Slowly the significance of his laconic speech dawned upon her. It was the water. It made her thirsty, and she said so. Jim drew a drink from one of the water bags.

Refreshed, she again scanned the far-flung reaches of desert. The mesa was a long tableland and the horses were taking it at a jog trot. In the north it sloped down into a great basin. The wind had freshened and Hope took her coat from the back of the seat and put it on. She saw what appeared to be a dark, filmy cloud in the basin. She pointed to it and remarked about it.

"That's dust, ma'am," said Jim readily. "We skirt the basin on the west an' mebbe we won't get much of it. It's mighty dusty in here when it blows."

They rode on in silence. Jim, on such short acquaintance, was naturally reticent. Hope was turning over in her mind the many remarkable things she had read and heard of in this new land, in which she intended to stay several months. The nature of the landscape seemed to inspire silence. But Hope had been bred where conversation is a habit. Besides, she was curious. After all, it was an astonishing adventure—this change from the soft, æsthetic beauty of her native New England to the forbidding, sinister land that lay spread out before her. That it held a menace, she sensed, rather than knew; the thing she did not realize was that she had yet to learn the inexorable nature of that menace.

"We never see anyone," she complained suddenly. "There isn't a single living thing in sight except a few wandering birds, and I feel that they have gotten here by mistake."

"There ain't much travel in this direction," Jim commented. "Your uncle's is the only ranch in here. If we was to see anybody sloping this way, I'd be curious."

"Why? They might be going to the Rancho del Encanto."

"They might," was Jim's matter-of-fact rejoinder.

"There's a certain element of mystery in your replies, Jim," said the girl in a tone that hinted of severity. "Has there been any . . . is there ever any trouble at the ranch?"

"Hasn't been any all winter, ma'am." Jim was giving the horses closer attention.

"I believe you are trying to intrigue my curiosity," she said reprovingly. "Next thing you will be telling me there are outlaws in the country." She had read of outlaws and she awaited his reply with amused interest.

"Mendicott's still here somewheres," he said with a drawl, favoring her with a side glance.

"Mendicott? Who is he?"

"An outlaw just like you mentioned, ma'am."

"But, what kind of an outlaw?"

Jim's right hand got clear into his hip pocket and was closing on the plug of tobacco before he recollected his decision. He withdrew it reluctantly. "He's the regular kind, ma'am." His drawl was now pronounced.

"But what does he do?"

"He does a general outlawin' business, ma'am. Takes what he wants an' don't bother 'bout receipts."

Hope Farman's chin tilted a bit. "I suppose it's impossible to catch him," she observed, mildly sarcastic.

"Has been so far," answered Jim cheerfully.

"Do they . . . the authorities . . . know where he is?"

"They think they do," replied Jim, grinning.

"Then why is it that they don't go in force and capture him?" the girl demanded.

"He throws a wicked gun for one thing," drawled Jim patiently. "Then he usually ain't where they think he is, an' it irritates him an' his gang to be follered."

Hope's chin went up another degree and she regarded the little driver coldly. "Then I am to assume that the authorities cater to the whims of this desperado?"

"They sure do, ma'am, most of 'em bein' men of family."

"Humph!" It was a prim exclamation, but the girl managed to put considerable feeling into it. "Do you know what I would like to see, Jim?"

"People, probably," Jim conjectured.

"Yes, and one . . . ah . . . character in particular."

Jim looked at her speculatively. "An outlaw?" he ventured.

She shook her head a bit disdainfully. "No, I can't say I am particularly interested in that class of misguided humanity. I'd like to see one of these famous men of yours, the specimen that is tall, broad-shouldered, slim-waisted, and tanned a beautiful brown, that can ride the wild horses, and throw a lariat without ever missing, and draw his revolver and fire it and hit the mark before you can wink an eye, and . . . and all that. What do you call them . . . buckaroos? Are there any buckaroos on Rancho del Encanto, Jim?"

"Nope, I reckon not," Jim confessed slowly.

"I thought so!" exclaimed the girl with a note of triumph.

They had reached the north end of the mesa where the road turned westward in descent. The force of the wind had increased as the afternoon wore on, and now it flung blinding clouds of dust in their faces. The horses snorted and tossed their heads, straining in the harness so that Jim had to keep a tight rein. Hope drew her coat closely about her and buttoned it tightly. The air was growing colder with the approach of sunset. The foothills loomed close ahead through the dust veil. As Jim had said they would come upon the ranch unexpectedly, she felt a growing interest. Suddenly she gripped Jim's right arm and cried out in excitement.

"There's a man on a horse down there!" She pointed eastward into the basin. He looked quickly, nodded, and again gave his entire attention to the horses.

They came to the rolling ground on the west side of the basin and started north at a brisk trot. The dust swept down upon them. Jim drew a blue bandanna handkerchief over his mouth and nostrils, while the girl buried the lower part of her face in her coat collar for protection. She shielded her eyes with an arm. To the left she saw an opening in the foothills, and through this opening came rolling clouds of dust, riding fiercely on the wind.

Jim turned to her and shouted: "That's live dust, ma'am!"

She looked at him queerly, as if she suspected an awkward jest.

"I mean it's kicked up by something that's alive an' movin'," he called. "There! Just what I thought. It's cattle that's kickin' up that fog!"

Her eyes widened as she caught a glimpse of tossing horns through the dust. The bellowing of cattle came to her ears on the wind. She caught her breath sharply as the horses lunged under Jim's whip. The buckboard careened as they dashed wildly ahead.

Chapter Two

Hope held up her left hand in a futile effort to shield her eyes while she clung to the seat with the other. The road led down for a short distance and then cut straight across in front of the opening. Although she was far from experienced in such matters, the girl realized that the little driver intended to try to cross in front of the onrushing cattle before the maddened animals could reach them. It was the only course left to him. He could not turn around in the narrow road, lined with boulders and rock outcroppings, and to stop would mean merely to await the inevitable in the path of the herd. She heard him swearing, and the words—"Lost Cañon"—came to her. She assumed that it was the name of the opening in the hills.

The dust stung their faces and nearly blinded them. Hope closed her smarting eyes for a few moments. She opened them when Jim yelled: "They're drivin' 'em!"

A rift in the dust clouds enabled her to determine what he meant. For, at a distance up the cañon, she descried the dim, swift-moving forms of horses and riders. There were men with the cattle. Very likely the herd had gotten away from them. She remembered what she had read of stampedes, and shuddered. Terror seized her, left her white and shaken, clinging to the seat of the swaying buckboard, as Jim flung away the whip he no longer needed.

The horses were galloping madly and they made the turn at the foot of the grade on two wheels. The buckboard came down with a jolt, bumped and swerved, and again the world was blotted out by a solid wall of dust through which the dying sun shone obscurely in a dull, yellow opaqueness. The effect was weird, uncanny, and added to the terror inspired by the danger of being run over by the oncoming herd. The air was filled with the thunder of pounding hoofs, and the raucous bellowing of the cattle. Jim braced his feet against the dash, leaned forward on the lines, but gave the horses their heads. Then the vanguard of the stampede loomed directly ahead, so close that they could see the wild, red light in the eyes of the frightened animals.

Jim pulled in on the lines, shouting to the horses, causing them to slacken their pace a bit. Over they went to the right, the buckboard tipping to a dangerous angle, the right wheels nearly buckling. They left the road just ahead of the cattle, now almost upon them, and started down the steep grade into the basin. It was impossible to mark their course any distance ahead because of the dust. The girl was choking, and she saw the wind strip Jim's hat from his head. The horses plowed through clumps of greasewood and sage; rocks jolted the buckboard until it became a twisting, writhing thing, with no balance of motion, in imminent danger of overturning.

Hope's gaze seemed riveted on the flying ground under the light tongue of the vehicle. She dared not look up; she could only hold on with all her strength in the effort to keep in the seat. She glimpsed a streak of gray under the tongue; one of the horses stumbled, recovered; there was a shock as the front wheels struck an obstruction. The right side of the little buckboard was lifted high. She was thrown heavily against Jim. Then came a confused moment and something struck her on the left side and head. It was some moments before she realized she had been thrown.

She lifted herself and cried out in horror. The buckboard had overturned. The horses were dragging it, and behind it she saw a bobbing object on the ground. It was Jim, still holding to the lines! The dust closed in and shut off the sight.

She rose from the ground, pains shooting through her left shoulder, a queer tightening in her throat. She saw the gray ledge of rock that had caused the catastrophe. She looked at it dully. A loud bellow sounded above the thundering rumble of flying hoofs and instantly she was aware of her peril. She started to run, stumbled in the sage, fell. In that moment she felt it was no use; she could not hope to escape; the herd was plunging down upon her to pound her to death. And suddenly she was cool. It was as if her mind could not fully grasp the horror of her predicament. It had all happened with such suddenness that it seemed unreal—impossible! In swift retrospect her well-ordered life—calm, punctilious, devoid of thrills, exact—flashed before her in kaleidoscopic review. She felt the hard, sun-baked earth shake under her. The sensation reminded her vaguely of her danger. She gained her feet and a red-hot iron pricked at her right ankle. A sprain! Her temples throbbed. It was almost dark in the swirling dust—so dark she could hardly see the shadow that suddenly loomed over her. She closed her eyes.

But, instead of the impact of horns or hoofs that she calmly awaited, she felt herself caught up, rudely, unceremoniously, held tightly within an arm, and pressed against leather under which was the feel of playing muscles. Then came motion. She swayed, but the arm held her securely. She recognized the motion. She was on a horse. She opened her eyes, red and smarting, and looked up into the face of a man. Then darkness descended upon her and she was drifting—drifting—slowly out on the tide of oblivion.

* * * * *

From a distance, a great distance, it seemed, she heard the ripple of water. It became more and more distinct, closer and closer. It seemed good to hear the water. Gradually she became aware of a luxurious sense of lassitude. It took possession of all her body, and she reveled in it. She felt a soothing coolness on her forehead, her face, her hair, her hands—at her temples. Then a twinge of pain in her right ankle and a dull, aching throb in her left shoulder, and she abruptly regained her normal senses. Her thoughts flashed back to the long, tiresome ride, the wind and dust, the bellowing of the stampeding cattle, the crash of the buckboard, Jim being dragged on the ground, the sprain, the shadow above her.

She opened her eyes with an effort to see a man leaning over her, applying a wet handkerchief to her temples, holding a canteen in one hand in which water gurgled. She looked into gray eyes—gray eyes, shot with brown. She saw regular features, strong, clear-cut, and a bronzed skin—hair a shade darker than the color of copper against the gray of a big hat, pushed back from the forehead. She saw white, even teeth, a neckerchief of blue, dark blue silk, perhaps.

"Here, drink some of this." The voice was a modulated bass, musical in its varying inflections. He held the canteen to her lips and she drank eagerly, watching him the while. When he drew back the canteen, she tried to grasp it, then pouted.

"In a minute," he promised. And then: "If I had any whiskey, I'd give you a shot of that, but I guess you don't need it."

She knew she was lying on the ground, but she felt something cushioning her head. She twisted about and saw that it was a coat. His coat, of course. She saw a big, bay horse standing with bridle reins dangling. She had been on that horse, and so had the man. He had come just in time. She remembered the horseman she had seen riding up from the basin. He was doubtless the same rider, she reasoned. It all seemed clear enough—and plausible.

"Now you can have some more," came the agreeable, deep voice. "I guess you can have all you want."

She drank as much as she wished and, with returning strength, smiled up at him. "Thank you," she said in a faint voice.

He rose to his full length, and she looked with wonder at his neat, glove-fitting riding boots, his leather chaparejos, the heavy belt about his slim waist—and then she started. The pearl-handled butt of a huge revolver protruded from a holster strapped about his right thigh over the leather chaps. Then she saw what made the belt heavy. It held a row of cartridges. It was the first time she had seen a man wear a deadly weapon in plain sight, exposed to the view of any who might choose to look, and he wore it naturally, without concern, as a matter of fact. But there was nothing in his bearing to indicate that he wore it as an ornament. Her gaze ranged upward to the soft flannel shirt that covered his broad shoulders, open at the neck, where the scarf was knotted low. Then she looked at him again and found him surveying her coolly while he fashioned a cigarette in his brown, tapering fingers. He was studying her frankly and, she surmised with resentment, curiously. But why should she resent his critical inspection when she had just subjected him to the same examination? She laughed and raised herself on her hands.

The wind still was blowing, but it was less filled with dust. The cattle were nowhere to be seen. The entrance to the opening in the hills, Lost Cañon, was clear. There was a peculiar stillness, save for the drone of the wind in the endless sage and greasewood. High above the towering hulks of the mountains in the west, billowing white clouds rode the sky like vagrant ships. Crimson spangles strewed the blue with the sunset's phosphorescence. Streamers of gold wavered like telltale pennants, flinging their reflections to the eastern horizon to crown the lava hills that swam in a sea of color. Her attention was diverted from the glory of the desert sunset as the man snapped a match into flame and held it to his cigarette.

"You'll be all right now," he told her. "I must look after your man."

"Is he . . . badly hurt?" she called as he moved away.

"He's busted up some, but I reckon he'll make the grade," he said over his shoulder.

As he walked rapidly away, Hope rose unsteadily to her feet. She sat down again promptly, for the pain in her swollen ankle was unbearable. She unlaced and removed her shoe. After this operation, which relieved her to an extent, she saw her rescuer returning, bearing a limp burden in his arms. As he approached, she recognized the white face of Jim Crossley, the little driver. She started to cry out, but the man stopped her with a shake of his head.

He deposited his burden near her and put the coat under Jim's head. It was a hard struggle for Hope to keep back the tears as she saw Jim open his eyes and wince with pain as the man cut the right sleeve of his shirt and felt of the arm. She knew by his look that the arm was broken. With remarkable dispatch the man improvised splints, set the bone, and completed the job of binding it fast with his scarf and the scarf worn by Jim. Then he gave the little driver a drink of water, and she saw Jim whisper to him.

"The horses are all right," said the man. "I'll have them up here after I make camp. We can't start on for the ranch till morning."

Jim sighed with relief, twisted his head, and beckoned to Hope. She crept to his side, and leaned over to him to catch his words.

"There's one of your buckaroos," he said faintly, indicating the stranger.

She looked up at the tall man with a smile, and he motioned her away. But she heard him when he again spoke to Jim.

"Is there anything you want, now, pardner?"

"The devil, yes!" answered the little driver in a stronger voice. "Get that woman out of sight an' give me a chew of terbaccy!"

Chapter Three

Hope could not help laughing softly to herself as she turned away so that Jim could realize his desire. When she looked at the little driver again, she found him regarding her with a quizzical expression in his mild blue eyes. The stranger disappeared on his horse. The desert twilight came swiftly, and as swiftly the shadows of night descended. When the stranger returned, he was driving two burros, heavily laden. The little animals stood quietly while he removed the packs. They wore no halters, and, when he relieved them of their burdens and the pack saddles, they turned away to graze. He unsaddled his horse, hobbled it, and turned it out. Then he built a fire.

His movements were methodic, deliberate, but quickly executed, showing plainly that he knew exactly what he was about. He gave the girl an impression of quiet, cool confidence.

Hope felt thirsty and voiced her want. He brought a canteen, unscrewed the cap, and offered it to her. As she drank, she looked up at him—at his clear-cut profile under the wide brim of his hat, in sharp relief against the ruddy light of the campfire.

"Thank you," she said when she had drunk. "Do you know who I . . . who we are?"

"I know Jimmy, yonder, by sight," he said casually, screwing the cap on the canteen.

"I'm Hope Farman," she volunteered. "I'm going to visit my uncle, Nathan Farman, on Rancho del Encanto."

At this he looked at her sharply with a show of interest. Then his face again became expressionless. He turned back to his tasks without replying.

"Aren't you going to tell me your name?" she called to him.

He came back and stood over her, apparently in indecision. "My name is . . . Channing," he said finally with a light frown.

"I'm sure my uncle will join me in thanking you, Mister Channing," said Hope with a feeling that somehow this man resented having to bother with them.

"Yes, he likely will," said Channing soberly. "Nate Farman ain't a bad sort."

"Oh, you know him?" said the girl eagerly.

"I know him by sight," was the cool rejoinder.

When he left her again, Hope did not feel inclined to call him back. And Jim Crossley had referred to him as one of her buckaroos. Now that she pondered the matter, she realized that in many ways this man Channing did conform to her conception of a genuine Western man. She felt she was sure he would prove interesting. She wanted to ask him questions. But this wasn't easy.

Channing undid the packs and put up a small miner's tent. In this he made a bed and indicated to Hope that she was to occupy it. She demurred, saying that Crossley was hurt and should have the best accommodations.

"You're hurt yourself, I reckon," observed Channing.

"My ankle's twisted, that's all," she returned. "It isn't anything."

"No, it doesn't amount to much, but I guess you're not as used to the outdoors as Jimmy, there," he said. "It gets pretty cool on the desert this time of year."

Hope's chin tilted at this. She had at least expected a show of sympathy for her injury. But instead he had agreed it didn't amount to much.

He had brought a canteen. "Might be a good thing if you bathed that ankle in cold water," he said. "I reckon it hurts some."

She looked up at him gratefully, but he had gone back to the campfire. She bathed the injured ankle, which had swollen considerably. Meanwhile, Channing busied himself at the fire with frying pans and coffee pot and soon the appetizing odors of frying bacon and strong coffee reminded the girl that she was ravenous.

He fed them bacon and beans, biscuits and jelly, and coffee.

Channing made Crossley comfortable with a blanket and the two squares of tarpaulin used as coverings for the packs. Then he again left them, riding his big horse. Hope managed to hobble to Jim's side. There she sat down on the edge of one of the pieces of tarpaulin.

"You can look and act as mad as you want," she said severely to the little driver, "but I'm going to ask you some questions. And don't forget my uncle wrote me he was sending one of his best men to meet me at the station. If that's you, I expect you to be friendly."

"I don't want to be anything else, ma'am," said Jim with a grin.

The girl touched his good left hand lightly. "I'm sorry you were hurt, Jim. You were foolish to try to hold the horses after the buckboard tipped over, but I know why you did it, I believe. You're all man, Jim . . . I think that's a Western saying."

"Shucks, I just didn't have sense enough to let loose," scoffed Jim.

Hope laughed. It was impossible not to like the diminutive driver.

"Jim, who is this man Channing?" she asked, sobering.

Jim shifted on his hard bed. "I reckon that's a hard question, ma'am."

"But . . . he said he knew you and my uncle," said the girl, surprised. "That is, he said he knew you by sight, and surely you must know something about him."

"Nobody knows much about him," was the evasive reply. "He keeps in the desert most the time. Wanders around like . . . no place in particular, I guess."

"But what does he do . . . what is his business, Jim?"

"I dunno. Prospector, maybe. Knows cattle, though. I heard he'd been on a ranch or two on the other side of the mountains. He's a queer sort of duck."

"Is he what they call a desert rat?" the girl persisted. "I've read of such persons somewhere."

"No, ma'am, I don't reckon he is," said Jim slowly. "A desert rat is an old prospector who's been in the desert so long he's forgot how he got there. This Channing ain't so old, an' I can't say as he's a prospector. I do know one thing for sure, though, an' that's that he ain't no man to fool with."

"Hasn't he any home?" asked Hope.

"Well, there's a powerful stretch of this desert, ma'am, an' it's all his home. We're in his back yard this minute, I reckon."

"A desert derelict," murmured the girl absently.

"What was that?" asked Jim.

Before Hope could reply, they heard horses, and Channing emerged from the shadows driving the two grays that had run away ahead of the stampeding cattle. The girl heard Jim grunt with relief and knew he had been worrying about the team. He called to her as she started back toward the tent. "Just wanted you to know, ma'am, I'm right sorry this here all happened!" He raised himself on his good arm. "I didn't figure on anything like this an' . . ."

"That'll do, Jim," said Hope. "I'm from New England, but I'm not altogether stupid. Anyway, it gave me a chance to meet a buckaroo."

She started to hobble back to the tent slowly and painfully when she was suddenly aware of Channing towering at her side.

"I reckon you've just naturally got to be helped," he said in a matter-of-fact tone.

Then he picked her up and carried her to the tent, put her down just within the small opening, and left without further words. Hope, flushed and flustered, sat staring as he replenished the fire. A sudden pound of hoofs brought Channing to his full height. The girl saw him step quickly out of the circle of light into the shadow near her tent. His right hand had darted downward to rest on the butt of the gun on his thigh.

A rider came quickly into view, checked his horse abruptly, and flung himself from the saddle near the fire. He looked about him and spied Channing. In the few moments before he spoke, Hope had an opportunity to scrutinize him. He was a large man, but evidently of a muscular build. His features were swarthy, his eyes dark, and he had a bristly black mustache. He was dressed much after the manner of Channing himself and wore a gun.

"Whose outfit is this?" the newcomer demanded harshly.

Channing stepped toward him. "Who were you looking for?" he inquired.

"I'm lookin' for whoever scared them cattle of mine tonight," snapped out the other. "We've been roundin' 'em up ever since."

"What'd you start 'em runnin' down Lost Cañon for in the first place?" It was the piping voice of Jim Crossley. "It took more'n just dust to stampede that herd, Brood."

The stranger, who Jim had called Brood, strode toward the little driver. "Oh, it's you," he said in a sneering tone.

"Yep, it's me," Jim retorted angrily. "Me with a broken arm, thanks to you. Runnin' cattle that way, Brood, ain't no credit to a foreman."

"Shut up, you little . . ."

"I don't reckon I'd be too strong on the language, friend. The third member of this party happens to be a lady." It was Channing's voice, smooth, almost unctuous, and carrying a peculiar drawl.

Brood turned on him with a smothered curse. Then he appeared to see Hope sitting in the opening of the little tent for the first time. He scowled. "Who's the company?" he asked Channing.

"She hasn't asked for any introduction to you, as I've heard," replied Channing. "You're the Encanto foreman. I take it, from what Jimmy there has said. Seems to me you'd be doing better to be looking after your cattle."

Brood turned his eyes from the girl and surveyed Channing coldly. "If I didn't know that little runt Crossley is workin' for Farman, I'd say it was a put-up job," he said meaningfully. "An' I ain't so sure it ain't."

"Meanin' you want to put the blame on me?" called Jim shrilly.

"Meanin' you're cavortin' with tramps who haven't any business here," snarled out Brood, thoroughly angry.

Channing stepped directly in front of him, so close that the brims of their hats almost touched. "You including the lady when you mention that word tramps?" he asked in a voice that was deceivingly pleasant.

Brood met his gaze with a glare. "Bah!" he exclaimed. "Someday you'll get a receipt for meddlin'."

Channing caught him by the arm as he turned away and whirled him around. The girl caught her breath as she saw the flash in the eyes of the pair.

"You haven't answered my question," said Channing sternly.

"An' you haven't told me who the company is," returned Brood.

"She's Nate Farman's niece come to visit him," said Channing after an ominous pause.

Brood stared at the girl with a frown. "I 'spect that lets her out of the tramp class," he reflected gruffly.

"Good night, Brood," said Channing evenly.

Brood, apparently on the point of making a hot retort, caught himself with an effort, looked at Channing narrowly, and swung on his heel. In another moment he was in the saddle and his horse galloped away, cruelly spurred. Channing's laugh carried after him.

Long after the fire had died and all sounds had ceased, Hope Farman lay in the little tent and puzzled over the quality of that laugh.

Chapter Four

In the morning Hope was awake in time to witness the desert dawn, and saw the sun come up blood red on the far eastern horizon across countless leagues of saffron-colored wastelands, spotted with the never-ending sage and greasewood, presenting a panorama so vast and weirdly beautiful that it caused her to catch her breath in awed wonder.

Channing already was getting breakfast. He paused in his work over the fire and looked at her curiously before he nodded good morning.

He brought her water for her makeshift toilet. "How's the ankle?" he inquired perfunctorily.

Hope displayed the swelling and smiled at him.

"It'll take a few days for it to come around," he said with a shrug. Then he grinned boyishly in a way she liked. "You got quite an introduction to the country," he observed. He sobered as she laughed, and returned to his duties at the fire.

Hope could see no sign of the cattle. Jim Crossley called to her in a cheerful voice, and she asked him about his arm.

"I ain't goin' to have it cut off," he replied laconically as Channing brought their breakfasts.

When they had eaten, Channing broke camp, bringing in the burros and packing his outfit on their backs. He saddled his own horse and strapped blankets on the two grays that had drawn the buckboard.

"Your vehicle's a wreck," he told Jim. "The harness is pretty well broken up and we'll have to leave Miss Farman's trunk here to be sent for. We haven't got any way to pack it, and it's not so far to the ranch."

Jim nodded and looked at Hope, who smiled her consent and approval.

"You and I'll ride the grays," Channing was saying, speaking again to Jim. "There's halters and bridles for both of 'em and we can take it easy. You can make it all right. Miss Farman, you can ride my horse." He turned to Hope and indicated his splendid mount.

The girl looked at the tall animal, champing his bit impatiently, and felt a tremor of doubt. But Channing read her thought and shook his head.

"He wouldn't be any too gentle with a strange man, maybe," he said in a tone of assurance, "but a woman can handle him like he was a kitten. Maybe that's because he sees so few of them," he added as an afterthought. Then he helped Jim mount one of the grays and came toward her. Her right ankle had swollen so that she couldn't put on her shoe. He noticed it at once. "You won't have to put that foot in the stirrup," he told her. "We'll walk the distance an' Major rides like a rocking chair."

"I have a riding habit in my trunk," Hope suggested.

"Sure enough!" he exclaimed. "You ought to have riding clothes on, and that's a fact. We'll go up that way where your trunk is and you can get your outfit."

With that he picked her up and put her side-fashion in the saddle. Hope gathered her skirts about her, picked up the reins in her right hand, grasped the horn of the saddle with her left, and sat looking straight ahead, her face flaming.

Channing mounted the other gray, started the burros out, closed in after them with Jim following, and Hope's horse struck along in the rear of its own accord. Thus they proceeded to where Hope's trunk reposed on the ground. There they halted, and Channing helped her to dismount.

"Jim and I'll ride over that ridge ahead and wait till you call us," he said. "You can slip on your riding outfit and be all set for the trip."

When they were gone, Hope quickly opened the trunk, took out her riding habit, donned it, put her dress in the trunk, and called. Channing and Jim came riding back and soon they were on their way again. Hope rode man-fashion in the deep stock saddle and let her injured right ankle swing freely.

From time to time Channing looked back at Jim and herself. But they had no trouble. They rode for nearly two hours before Channing called a halt for the first rest. He brought out a canteen and they all drank. The sun was mounting, and Hope thought this day was warmer than the day before.

She mentioned this to Channing, and it brought a quick response from the man. For the first time he smiled in genuine mirth, his teeth flashing white against his bronzed skin, his gray eyes laughing. "Ma'am," he said slowly, looking at her with a quizzical expression, "this is downright cold to what's coming. This is winter. Summer, when it comes, will come in a day, and then . . . well, Miss Farman, then it'll be warm."

He concluded rather grimly, she thought. It was as if he was making a promise, rather than stating a fact or prediction. She remembered much of what she had read of the desert, and she looked at him with more respect as she realized that here was a man who knew the desert—the inferno—who laughed in the face of its menace as he braved its perils and fought it. She wondered why? A derelict of that land of desolation, what did he see in it? What was there so acute about the mystery that shrouded him? Was it merely because he was the first of his kind she had met? She accepted the last deduction as the most plausible and resumed the journey, feeling less concerned about him.

They stopped more frequently as the day wore on, and then, in the late afternoon, they turned suddenly up a ridge, and, when they gained the crest, Hope cried out in glad wonder. There was water somewhere ahead, for there were trees—tall, stately trees, from which little fluffs of white were drifting on the breeze.

Jim Crossley was looking back at her with a wide grin.

"Cottonwoods," he called, "an' pines higher up! We're comin' to the ranch!"

They descended the west side of the ridge into a wide cañon up which they rode. Then they came to the water—a thin trickle of stream that gradually widened up the cañon. They now were in the trees, and higher up on the slopes Hope could see the stands of pine—great, green steps that led up the mountains. The cañon widened, and they came out into a great plateau—a mesa. Below the mesa, on the east, separated from it by the ridge they had crossed, lay the desert. On the west the foothills ranged up to the mountains. The great, level space was carpeted with green grass, and irrigating ditches ran through it. Many of the ditches were lined with red, desert willows, and there were clumps of cottonwoods and alders. The road followed the stream that flowed straight across the mesa, and midway the length of the fertile plain stood the ranch house and other buildings, nestling under a magnificent growth of towering cottonwoods.

As they approached it, Hope saw that it was built of stone, and it looked substantial, cool, and inviting with a wide verandah on two sides. Flowers were blooming below the verandah, and there was a tamarack hedge, a brilliant band of pink and green, on either side of the branch of the road leading to the front of the house.

A man came out on the verandah as they drew up. When he saw Hope, he hurried out to greet them, but his look of welcome was tempered by anxiety and perplexity.

"Is this Hope?" he boomed as he hurried toward her horse.

"Yes," said the girl cheerfully, "what's left of me. I would know you anywhere, Uncle Nathan, although I haven't seen you since I was a little girl."

"What happened?" he asked as he helped her from her horse and kissed her. He looked questioningly at Jim Crossley and Channing.

"I guess you'd better tell him," said Channing to Jim. "Do you want to sit on the porch while I put up the horses?" He helped Crossley down.

Nathan Farman stood staring at the little driver's right arm in the sling. The rancher was a large man, gray of hair and mustache, blue-eyed, of medium height and square of chin. He wore gray clothes, a huge, high-crowned hat, and was collarless. As he looked at Crossley, then at Channing and Hope, little lines appeared at the corners of his eyes and he appeared to squint.

In a few words Jim Crossley explained what had happened.

"Sit down on the porch," Nathan Farman commanded. "Missus McCaffy . . . oh, Missus McCaffy!" he called. He gave Hope his arm and helped her toward the steps to the verandah. "My dear child," he said to her, "I wouldn't have had anything like this happen for anything. I'll look into it, you bet, I'll look into it right an' proper. Oh, Missus McCaffy, take my niece here into the house. She's been hurt an' I've got to find out about it. Be careful, Hope . . . there."

A large, florid woman had come out of the house. She came toward Hope, who had gained the verandah, with arms outstretched. "You poor dear," she said in a mannish voice that hinted of a brogue. "I was worrying my brains out. I always said that little shrimp would get himself busted up an' kill somebody else the way he drives." She looked at Jim Crossley in distinct disapproval.

"But it wasn't his fault," said Hope, coming to the little man's rescue. "It really couldn't be helped, Missus McCaffy, and I'm not much hurt."

She had surmised at once that the big Irishwoman was the housekeeper at Rancho del Encanto. As they went inside, she saw her uncle bending over Crossley, who was talking in an undertone. Channing was taking the horses around the house.

"Sit right down here," said Mrs. McCaffy, putting her in a large chair in the cool living room. "I'll get the arnicy an' have the swelling in that ankle down in no time. Just don't you worry. You're home, dearie."

She hurried out of the room, and Hope looked out the door to where the pink of the tamarack hedge showed vividly against the green of the grass in front of the house. Already she felt a sense of comfort. The big room was home-like. Mrs. McCaffy she had liked the moment she had seen her and heard her speak. Rancho del Encanto—the ranch of enchantment. She believed she knew why it was so named.

She saw Channing come up on the porch. He passed out of sight, and the low hum of voices came to her ears, but she could not distinguish what was being said. Then Mrs. McCaffy returned and began to treat the injured ankle, indulging in a vast amount of talk, meanwhile, and adroitly drawing out the story of what had taken place from the girl by clever questioning.

"That Brood!" she exclaimed. "I never did take to him much. I bet he did it on purpose!"

"Why . . . why should he do anything like that?" asked Hope in amazement.

"Oh, he's queer," said the housekeeper. "There's a lot of 'em around here that's queer. They've been queerer than ever this spring." The housekeeper paused in her work of bandaging the sprained ankle. For a few moments she looked out the door. "There, dearie, that'll fix your ankle in no time. It's a wonder an' a blessing that you didn't get killed."

Hope heard her uncle's voice raised on the porch. The tone implied that he was angry. Channing appeared at the top of the steps.

"You're staying to supper, I reckon," she heard her uncle say.

"I hadn't figured on it," Channing replied.

"Then you better start figuring powerful quick, for it'll be ready in half an hour, an' I'm expecting you to stay," said Nathan Farman.

The two of them left the porch with Jim Crossley between them.

"Missus McCaffy," said Hope impulsively, "is there liable to be any trouble because of me . . . because of what happened?"

"Don't you worry about any trouble," said the housekeeper. "How could there be any trouble because of you, dear? As for that, there's liable to be trouble any time in this country. Your Uncle Nate is just naturally mad over this business, what with you coming West for the first time and his wanting you to have a good time. You can't blame him."

"This man Brood, Missus McCaffy . . . he is Uncle's foreman, isn't he?"

"He is that, an' so far's you an' me is concerned he'll be doing well to stick to his cows."

"But last night . . . last night," said the girl in a worried voice, "he came to where we were camped in the desert and had some words with Jim and Mister Channing. He seemed to blame us because the cattle ran away."

"He's got his nerve," responded the housekeeper. "I guess he didn't know who you was, Miss Hope. He'll soon find out for keeps. But Brood's queer. I don't like a man with his kind of eyes."

"Missus McCaffy, if he is Uncle's foreman, why should he want to have trouble with Jim, or anybody else working on the ranch?"

"Child, there's things I know an' things I don't know," said the housekeeper, throwing up her hands. "Usually I can guess at what I don't know an' come pretty close to hitting the nail on the head. But this spring my guesser has been worked overtime, an' I've given up. The best thing for a woman on a ranch to do is take things as they come, especially if she's to have any peace of mind. If you try to figure out what the men are thinking an' doing in this country, an' why, you'll go crazy. Now I'll show you to your room an' you can get ready for supper. If there's one thing Encanto is noted for, it's its table, an' I don't mind saying it a bit."

Hope laughed with her as the housekeeper helped her upstairs.

Chapter Five

If Nathan Farman's welcome to his niece had seemed somewhat perfunctory upon her arrival at Rancho del Encanto, it was due to the fact that he was intensely interested in the accident and its cause. He made up for it in abounding measure when Hope came down to supper. They sat in the living room for a time talking of the East, of John Farman, who had been Hope's father, of Nathan Farman's last trip to New England years before when Hope's mother had died. He had wanted to bring her West then, but she was too young. Only once did Hope's uncle speak of his own misfortune in losing his wife, but the girl could see that he still felt his loss and that he hungered for his own kin.

"I've sent Carlos with a team to get your trunk," he told her, "an' the Mexican will have it back here before morning. It was pure luck you wasn't killed, child." His face darkened.

Hope remembered the shadow over her as she stood before the onrushing cattle, the arm that grasped her, the play of muscles beneath leather chaps, and smiled. "No, I don't think it was all luck, Uncle Nathan. And if there was any luck, it was in Mister Channing's arriving when he did."

Her uncle nodded absently. "I know . . . Crossley told me."

"And Jim was a hero, Uncle," said Hope enthusiastically. "He did the only thing he could do, and he held onto the horses till he was knocked unconscious."

"Jim's a good ranch hand," said Farman dryly. "We've got his arm fixed up best we can. The nearest doctors are in the county seat on the other side of the mountains an' in Bandburg, across the desert. Both places are too far for him to ride for a few days yet. I'll send him to Bandburg soon's he's able to travel, I reckon. We're sort of isolated here. El Encanto is the only ranch in a hundred miles or more. There's the supper bell. Let's go in."

There were four places at the long dining table. Nathan Farman placed Hope at the right of his seat at the head. Mrs. McCaffy stood behind her chair at the foot, so to speak, of the table, and the place at Farman's left was unoccupied.

"Where's Channing?" he asked Mrs. McCaffy.

"Hasn't answered the bell," said the housekeeper.

She had hardly spoken when Channing entered from the kitchen.

"I was shaving," he said soberly, and took his place while Farman regarded him curiously.

Mrs. McCaffy had not understated the facts when she had said that Rancho del Encanto set a good table, as Hope soon discovered. She told the housekeeper so and Mrs. McCaffy beamed.

"We live tolerably well," she said. "I'd've left this god-forsaken spot long ago if it wasn't for your uncle flattering me about the cooking."

"It's one way I keep my men," said Farman to Hope. "When a man on this ranch makes an especial good showing some way, I invite him to eat in the house. Once he eats in here, he's tryin' for another such meal from then on." The rancher laughed loudly and looked quickly at Channing. "If I could get you to settle down here, I might let you eat in the house right along," he said, chuckling.

"It'd be worth considering," Channing commented.

"Then we'll consider it!" exclaimed Farman, striking the table with his palm. "You come on here an' that place is yours as long as you stay."

Channing's white teeth gleamed against his tan. "I'm afraid I can't be so lucky," he said slowly.

Channing's look and tone had been a bit wistful. Nathan Farman appeared provoked. "Don't you figure on settling down sometime, Channing?" the rancher asked.

"I reckon we all have hopes," replied Channing with a faint smile, "but Old Man Time keeps his finger in the pie."

"Yes, an' time's going on right along," Farman observed with a frown. "Channing, you're a waster. You ought to be making a future for yourself. You're a regular desert tramp. I can't see anything in the desert. I never could. I hate it. I want grass an' water an' I've got 'em both. You can make a future for yourself right here on grass an' water if you want to, my boy, an' you're a fool to go on like you are."

Channing raised his eyes slowly to look into Farman's. "Your future is built on cattle, Nate, so far's you know. Isn't that so?"

Farman nodded. "You can build yours on the same thing," he said.

"Where would your cattle be if it wasn't for the bunch grass and the white sage?" Channing drawled out. "The desert supplies that."

Farman put down his knife and fork, looked at him searchingly, and shook his head. "You're hopeless," he said. "The desert's got you."

"I'm not complaining," said Channing with a swift smile at Hope. The girl was puzzled by the look in his eyes, by something his tone implied but did not reveal, by the adroitness of his replies and his apparent tolerant disdain of Nathan Farman's offer and opinions. Her uncle had called him a waster. Did he then lack ambition? Was he content to be a derelict?

She remembered what Jim Crossley had said about Mendicott, the outlaw. For a fleeting moment she considered Channing in a new light—a most unfavorable light. But that flashing smile and the look in the gray-brown eyes reassured her. Still, she couldn't forget the laugh she had heard the night before.

After supper they moved to the sitting room, but Channing soon excused himself. Hope was very tired, her ankle pained, and her shoulder hurt where she had fallen when thrown from the buckboard. She told her uncle she believed she would go to bed, and he hurried for a lamp to show her up the stairs. Mrs. McCaffy accompanied them, anxious that Hope should have everything she needed to make her comfortable. Her solicitude for the girl's welfare nearly moved the visitor to tears.

When she was in her robe, ready to retire, Hope blew out the light in the lamp and sat before the open window. Her room was a large corner room with windows on the north and east. It was by the north window that she sat. The space between the ranch house and the bunkhouse was below. Farther back, she could glimpse the barns and other outbuildings. She marveled at the quiet beauty of the night. The shoulders of the mountains were lined against a sea of stars. A breath of wind was stirring, and it brought the scent of pine and fir from the timbered slopes. She could see the dim outline of the ridge to eastward, and her imagination pictured the silent, brooding desert that lay beyond.

Her reverie was interrupted by the sound of galloping hoofs. She looked down and saw a rider come swiftly up the road toward the house and swing around in the direction of the barns. Then she heard her uncle's voice calling from the porch.

The rider brought his horse to a stop almost directly beneath her window. As he turned in the saddle, she recognized him. It was Brood, the foreman.

Nathan Farman came around the house from the porch as Brood dismounted. There was another with Farman; it proved to be Channing.

"You're a long time getting up here," said Farman crossly.

"Had trouble with the cattle," answered Brood shortly. "Stampede in a dust storm. I guess it was the dust. Had to gather 'em up. They're in the south flat."

Brood stood before the rancher while Channing leaned against the side of the house, smoking a cigarette. The bunkhouse door opened and Jim Crossley came out. He hobbled toward the trio as rapidly as he could.

"How'd those cattle happen to come out of Lost Cañon so fast?" demanded Farman.

"I guess the wind started 'em," replied Brood easily. "It blew strong up there. Lots of dust. They were away from us before they could be stopped."

"That's an excuse," said Jim Crossley as he reached them. "I was in front of 'em, but I got a glimpse of what was behind 'em. Them cattle was driven!"

"An' you busted into them, like a fool!" Brood exclaimed. "Busted into 'em an' split 'em an' made it all the worse."

"You mean I ran from 'em," said Crossley hotly. "It's just luck that Miss Hope wasn't killed."

"By your breakneck drivin'," Brood broke in viciously.

"Just a minute," said Farman sharply. "This is serious business, Brood. My niece was in that buckboard with Crossley, an' she might have been killed, like he says. I'm not satisfied with your explanation of how the cattle came to be running out of the cañon like that. An' I know that just wind won't start any stampede."

"Well, it started this one," said Brood with a hint of insolence.

"You tried to blame it on me, last night," Crossley jeered.

Brood turned on him with an oath. "You an' that tramp with you made it all the worse, didn't you? You could have took things easy. I didn't know you was comin' down that road or who was with you, did I?"

"That's just it, Brood," said Nathan Farman in a cold voice. "I think you did know. You've been acting strange of late, an' I've laid it to spring orneriness, but if I thought you deliberately stampeded that herd, I'd . . . I might kill you."

Brood laughed harshly. "I take it the tramp's been puttin' some sort of bug in your ear," he said scornfully. "Maybe he don't like me any too well."

Channing joined the group. "The tramp can talk on his own hook, Brood. If I had had anything to say about how this stampede started, I'd have said it to your face last night. But I reckon Jimmy knows what he's talking about."

"You goin' to butt in here on something you don't know anything about an' that's none of your business?" snarled out Brood.

"Oh, I'm not butting in," said Channing, waving his lighted cigarette nonchalantly. "You sort of dragged me in by hinting around about putting bugs in people's ears. You talk, Brood, like you had a bug in your brain."

"You're a meddler, you desert loafer!" cried Brood. "You ain't even as good as a desert rat . . . he'll work!"

"That's enough," said Farman sternly. "You haven't given me a satisfactory explanation of how the stampede started yet, Brood."

"I'm layin' it to the wind an' ain't goin' any further," retorted Brood.

"In that case I know it isn't spring orneriness," said the rancher coldly. "You're too anxious to shove the blame for this thing where I know it doesn't belong. I guess your usefulness as foreman on this ranch is gone. You can quit any time an' it'll be all right with me."

"Quit?" Brood blurted out the question in an incredulous tone. "Me quit?"

"That's what I said," Farman replied evenly. "Any time you want to, an' right now is just as good a time as any."

"After all I've done on this ranch?" cried Brood in a white heat of anger.

"You've been well paid for all you've done," said Farman, "an' you've done some things you wasn't paid to do."

"I suppose you're goin' to hire the tramp," said Brood sneeringly. He turned on Channing. "Been back-talkin' yourself into a job, eh?"

"I hadn't been thinking of going to work here," drawled Channing.

"But you've been thinkin' mighty hard since this talk started, I'll lay to that!" shouted Brood. "You butted in yesterday an' you're Johnny-on-the-spot tonight! Looks all regular, don't it? Pawin' around the boss an' his niece! Funny you stayed away from this place so long till the girl . . ."

"Leave her out of it," commanded Channing. "You know how I met Miss Farman. Nate, here, will tell you I refused to go to work here before he ever thought of letting you go. You're feeling mean tonight, that's all."

"An' you're tryin' to pull off something under cover," shot Brood through his teeth. "You think you can get by wearin' a gun an' floatin' a tough reputation. Here's one that ain't side-steppin', an' you can take that any way you want to."

Brood stepped back and assumed a half crouch. Both men were looking steadily into each other's eyes, their narrowed gazes locked.

"How do you want me to take it?" asked Channing in a low voice.

"You're yellow!" snarled out Brood.

"No gun play!" cried Nathan Farman hoarsely, leaping between them just as it seemed the draws would come. "You've lied tonight, Brood, an' I order you off the ranch. Get out, d'you hear?"

Brood hesitated, his breath coming fast, his eyes narrowed to slits, his lower lip thrust out. Then he straightened and stepped back. "Farman, you're a fool," he said with a sneer. "You don't know why yet, but you are. When you wake up, you'll wake up with a bang!"

"You won't gain anything by threatening me," said Farman in a voice that trembled with the force of his feeling. "Are you going?"

"I'm going," said Brood, his lips curling, "but that ain't sayin' I'll never come back. Listen!" His voice became a hiss. "You've been lucky, understand? Till now!" He swung on his horse and galloped swiftly out of sight in the direction of the road leading around the barns toward the foothills.

Hope Farman drew back from the window. She sat and stared straight ahead into the shadows of the darkened room. It was all incomprehensible, but appallingly real. Tragedy had stalked under her window. She realized dully that in some way her uncle was menaced, and that her coming had hastened a climax. And, although she was new in this country of man-made laws, she sensed that Brood and Channing had been on the point of drawing their weapons against each other—that her uncle's life, too, had been in danger. It was an awakening. She thrilled, and then she caught herself. These men were not at play!

Chapter Six

Channing was at the breakfast table. He was silent and thoughtful. Nathan Farman, too, was in a thoughtful mood, although he strove to conceal the fact from Hope. It was Mrs. McCaffy who was the life of the meal. She chatted with Hope on sundry topics and asked many questions about what was going on in the world beyond the desert.

Farman and Channing left the table before the women had finished eating, and this gave Hope the opportunity she was awaiting. "Missus McCaffy, do you know what took place last night?"

The housekeeper looked startled. "What do you mean, child?"

"Didn't you hear? My uncle, Brood, and Jim, and Mister Channing?"

"Was you listening?" countered Mrs. McCaffy. "Dearie, you shouldn't pay any attention to the men's doings on the ranch."

"But it was over the accident we had coming here," said Hope. "And it sounded to me as though my uncle and Jim suspected Brood of deliberately trying to run the cattle on us. Why should he want to do that?"

"He didn't want to do that, child, of course he didn't. I'll tell you this much, Miss Hope, an' then you forget it. There's been some trouble around here before and your uncle was waiting his chance to get rid of Brood, I think. I always figured that man was treacherous."

"There's just one more thing, Missus McCaffy, and I . . . I don't want you to think it strange of me to ask. You see, Mister Channing saved my life and I can't help but feel an . . . a mild interest in him. Is it true that he is just a desert tramp . . . a waster, as my uncle says, and depends on his gun and his reputation, as Brood intimated last night? What do you know about him?"

It was some time before the housekeeper replied. Then she said: "I don't know a thing about him except that he's good to look at, polite in his way, and, I believe, dangerous."

"I was wondering if . . . if maybe he had an occupation . . . oh, Missus McCaffy, after what Jim told me about this outlaw, Mendicottt . . ."

The girl stopped speaking suddenly when she saw the frightened look in the housekeeper's eyes as the latter put a finger to her lips in silent admonition.

"Come out an' I'll show you my flowers," said Mrs. McCaffy, rising.

They went out on the porch and walked slowly along the flower bed, the housekeeper pointing to the roses that she had nursed so carefully. As they rounded the corner of the porch toward the bunkhouse, a team and wagon came up the road. A small, swarthy-faced man was driving.

"It's Mendez bringing your trunk," said Mrs. McCaffy.

Mendez stopped the team in the space between the ranch house and the bunkhouse where Channing was just in the act of mounting his horse, preparatory to leaving. Hope saw Mrs. McCaffy's house girl, Juanita, standing near the kitchen door. She saw, too, the look that Mendez threw at Channing—a look that was brimming with hatred and malice. It seemed to her that emotion of some kind was continually asserting itself in the looks and actions of the people about her in this new land. Then Channing came riding toward her.

Hope looked up at him as he swung his hat low in his free hand. Her look expressed cool surprise. Then she remembered that she probably owed her life to this man, and she smiled. He leaned from the saddle so that his words carried to her ears alone. "If you should get into a mess, and you probably will, and need a friend, remember my name."

With that he was gone, galloping toward the barn where his burros, packed and ready for the trail, were waiting patiently. Hope remained standing in the same spot where she had received his message, staring after him as he urged the burros into the foothill trail and disappeared from sight among the first growths of pine. If she should get into a mess—what a way of putting it. And he had intimated that she would. Why should she get into a mess—into trouble? She tossed her head in resentment.

A cavalcade of horsemen came riding up the road to the ranch house. In the lead was a tall, blond, blue-eyed, boyish-looking individual, dressed in regulation cowpuncher regalia. Nathan Farman met them and called to the leader.

"What's the matter, McDonald?"

The cowpuncher indicated the men behind him with a jerk of his thumb over his shoulder. "Quitting," he said laconically. "You'll have to ask 'em what's wrong. I don't know."

He rode on toward the barn and dismounted while Farman confronted the half dozen men sitting their horses.

"What's the matter?" he demanded, addressing them as a whole.

"We want our time," said one of them, a burly man with bristling red whiskers.

Nathan Farman's face darkened. "You mean you're quitting me right at the start of the spring roundup?" he asked sternly.

"That's about the size of it," replied the other, while the men with him nodded their heads. "We're plumb through an' ready to go."

"It ain't done!" cried Farman. "Men don't quit at the start of a roundup on this range or anywhere else. You'll have to stick till we get the calves branded, anyway."

The spokesman for the men shook his head. "Can't do it. You didn't give our foreman any notice, an' we don't have to give you none. We're quitting an' we're quitting here an' now."

"So that's it!" roared the rancher. "This is Brood's work, eh? Goin' to cripple me by leaving me short-handed. I've got the right to fire a foreman on a second's notice, but that's no sign you men have the right to quit the same way. You go back an' brand those calves. McDonald . . . McDonald!" He turned to the tall young cowpuncher as the latter came striding toward him. "I make you foreman. See that these men go back to work."

The men muttered among themselves and turned dark looks on both Farman and McDonald.

"You heard what he said," McDonald told them. His eyes seemed to have changed a bit in color, and he pressed his lips together tightly.

"Don't make no difference," said the spokesman for the men. "You can't make us work. We're quitting an' we want our pay."

"You'll get no pay from me till you've branded those calves!" shouted Farman. He seemed to notice Hope and Mrs. McCaffy for the first time. "You women go into the house," he ordered peremptorily. Nathan Farman's face was white with rage as he again confronted the men. "You heard what I said about the pay," he said grimly. "When you've branded the calves, you can have your pay, an' what's more . . ."—he bit his lip and frowned deeply—"I'll give each man a bonus of twenty dollars. It's highway robbery, but I've got to have the calves branded, for I'm taking a big bunch of stock into the forest reserve this summer, an' some might stray an' get mixed with other cattle. Now go to it. McDonald's the boss."

But the men sat their horses stolidly, looking at their spokesman. The latter sneered openly at the rancher and McDonald. "We don't want your bonus," he said. "All we want is what's coming to us now. We're here to get it. Then we'll leave."

"If you leave me this way, you'll leave without it," was Farman's retort. The rancher was shaking with suppressed passion.

A jeering laugh came from one of the men. He hurled a curse at Farman. McDonald sprang toward the man's horse, evidently intending to pull him from his saddle, but, as he did so, the spokesman for the belligerent party drew his gun. McDonald whirled and dropped to his left knee as a bullet sang past his head. His gun barked from his hip, and the spokesman lurched forward in the saddle.

Farman, unarmed, ran to the rear door of the ranch house as Jim Crossley appeared in the bunkhouse door with a pistol in his good hand. McDonald had covered the others. They put spurs to their horses and galloped for the north trail. McDonald ran for shelter as a fusillade of shots came from the five departing horsemen.

Nathan Farman confronted the two women in the kitchen.

"I'm afraid things are coming to a showdown," he said in a thick voice. Then he dropped into a chair.

Chapter Seven

While the women, stunned and frightened with the sudden tragic turn of events, stood looking at Nathan Farman, who had buried his face in his hands, McDonald appeared in the doorway leading to the yard. Farman looked up quickly and his eyes put the question.

"Done for," said McDonald, his face white under its tan. "Had to do it or he'd've got you or me, or both of us."

The rancher nodded dully. "Wasn't your fault, McDonald." He rose. "It's Brood's work," he said savagely. "I've seen it coming all along. He's been acting queer all spring. I believe he stampeded that herd intending to hurt my niece or Crossley, thinking it would get me off the ranch for a time while I took them to the doctor's or something like that. I don't know just what he's after, but he's pretty near out in the open right now. How many men have we left?"

"There's seven of us, not counting Crossley or the Mexican," McDonald replied.

"An' all the spring work to do with not another hand to be got for love or money," said Farman.

"We'll do our best," said McDonald in a more cheerful voice. "May take us a little longer, that's all."

"All right," said the rancher, showing his old spirit. "Go to it, McDonald. You're foreman. But watch out, for that crowd has you marked after what happened today."

"I'm going to drive all the cattle to the mesa an' work close to the ranch," said McDonald. "When we've got the calves branded,

41

we can run the stock up Lost Cañon into the hills. We can get more hands from across the range before fall an' be sitting pretty. Are there any more orders?"

"No," said Farman. Then, as McDonald turned to go, he stopped him. "Tell the men I want to have a talk with them tonight," he said. "Bring them in here after supper."

McDonald nodded and, seeing that the rancher had nothing further to say, left to take up his new duties as foreman of Rancho del Encanto with a sadly depleted crew.

Nathan Farman turned to Hope. The smile was again on his face, although it was grim and lacking in its customary humor. "I guess you landed at Encanto at a poor time," he said in genuine chagrin. "This thing had to come sooner or later, but I didn't expect it would come until you had had your visit. I'm sorry, Hope, an' I guess I'll send you to the county seat for a spell till things get all settled again."

"But, Uncle, I'm not going to the county seat, or anywhere else," Hope protested. "I'm going to stay right here. I . . . I can't help but feel that my coming started . . . started all this trouble." There was a catch in her voice as she finished.

Her uncle stepped to her and put an arm about her. "Child, you have nothing to do with it. Maybe Brood used your arrival as a means to start things, but I see now it wouldn't have made any difference whether you an' Crossley had that accident or not. He had half a dozen of my men with him, all ready to back him up. Maybe he's got more of 'em for all I know. That's what I'm going to try to find out tonight. I guess it won't be necessary for you to go to the county seat, at that. I don't reckon it would be healthy for anyone to make war on women in this country."

Hope remembered Channing's last message. Here was trouble already—a mess, as he had called it. Had he foreseen it? Had he known it was coming? If so, he had deliberately ridden away from it, declining to help her uncle. And that remark about remembering his name if she needed a friend. What did it amount to?

Suppose she were to need him, where could she find him? How could she get word to him?

Her uncle patted her on the shoulder and went outside.

"Missus McCaffy, you were right," she said spiritedly. "It isn't for us women to worry about what the men are doing. We can help my uncle by making the house as cheerful as possible for him. That will be something and more than that man Channing, who deserted, would do. I'll help you with the work."

She had the satisfaction of seeing Juanita's eyes flash in quick anger, but paid no more attention to the house girl. She helped the housekeeper the rest of the morning. Her uncle seemed his old self at dinner, and he joked about the loss of Brood and the men, saying it was a good riddance. He had Jim Crossley in to dinner, informing him that he could eat in the house while his arm was mending.

"It's lucky I didn't break both of 'em," said the little driver, waving his fork in his left hand and boldly winking at Hope.

But Hope hadn't forgotten her glimpse of Jim in the doorway of the bunkhouse holding a revolver in that same left hand, and she surmised that he was being kept close to the house for other reasons than the one so subtly given by Nathan Farman.

Mrs. McCaffy was strangely taciturn during the afternoon. She insisted upon treating Hope's ankle again, although the girl was able to get about very well with the aid of a cane that had been found in the bunkhouse.

They had an early supper and were all sitting on the porch in the gathering twilight when they heard the pound of a horse's hoofs coming along the trail from the foothills. Nathan Farman had hardly time to rise from his chair when the horseman came around the corner of the house and brought his mount to a stop near the steps. They were dumbfounded to see Brood in the saddle, grinning at them insolently.

"¡Buenos días!" he called, doffing his hat with an exaggerated gesture.

"What are you doing here?" demanded Farman angrily.

"I'm keepin' a promise," said Brood, his teeth flashing again. "I told you I'd come back."

"An' I told you to stay away," was the rancher's swift retort. "You're not welcome here, Brood."

For answer, the ex-foreman swung quickly from the saddle. "Maybe I will be when you hear what I've got to say, Farman," he said, his smile vanishing. "I'm here with a proposition that'll interest you."

"If you're aiming to hand me back those men you took away, you're wasting your time an' mine," said the rancher stoutly. "You've made your play, Brood, an' what you've started I'm going to finish."

There was a short laugh from the former foreman. "The finishin' ain't in your hands, Farman," he said in a mean voice. "But if you want the men back, you can have 'em . . . on certain conditions."

"I'm just curious enough to ask the conditions," said Farman, "but I'm not promising to take 'em back."

"You can have 'em," said Brood with a wave of his hand. "Only . . . I come back with 'em. How's that? We all come back an' brand the calves. The boys ain't particular about the bonus you offered 'em. They're just foolish enough to be loyal to me, see?"

"Yes, I see. They lit straight for you after you'd got word to 'em to quit. Now you want to use 'em as a club to get your job back. You couldn't work on this ranch again, Brood, if you was the only man within a million miles of here."

"That's the way I figured it," said Brood coolly. "Didn't expect you to take us back. No, I didn't think you'd be interested in that proposition, Farman, but I reckon you'll be interested in this one. I'm ready to buy the ranch."

Nathan Farman stared in amazement at the man he had discharged yesterday. Crossley, Mrs. McCaffy, and Hope stared, too.

It was an astonishing statement from one who had been working for wages, and not very high wages, at that. Yet, there was a calm air of confidence about Brood that showed he was in deadly earnest. Farman recognized this attitude in Brood.

"You know Encanto isn't for sale, Brood," he said with a puzzled frown. "An' if it was on the market, it would command a big price, more than you think."

Brood swaggered to the bottom step, placed a booted foot upon it, took tobacco and papers from his shirt pocket, and proceeded to roll a cigarette while he looked up into Farman's face narrowly. "It's up to you to name the price," he said, when he had lit his smoke. "An' it's up to me to pay it. All right . . . that's fair enough. Name it."

"I told you it wasn't for sale," flared the rancher. "I'm not going to let loose of the only home I've got. It won't do you no good to argue or make any offers, Brood, for Rancho del Encanto is not on the market at any price."

"You ain't had time to think it over," said Brood with a crafty grin. "You've just heard the proposition. There ain't many comin' up here offering to buy this place, stuck off from everywhere like it is, an' you know it."

"An' I know you're not offering to buy it, Brood," said Farman harshly. "It's some kind of a trick, an', if it isn't a trick, then somebody else is behind this thing an' making a bid for the place through you."

Brood laughed coarsely. "It ain't a trick," he said coldly.

"Then my other guess is right," said Farman with conviction. "In that case I'd have to know the name of the real buyer before I'd consider any offer."

Brood laughed again. He seemed to be enjoying himself. There was something in his manner that worried the others. He was too confident. His attitude was too much that of a man who holds the whip hand and knows it. "I have a backer," he confessed shortly, flecking the ash from his cigarette.

"That's what I thought," said Farman. He was thoroughly interested now. "I knew you didn't have money enough to buy this place, Brood."

"I'm figurin' on borrowin' some," said Brood, lifting his black brows. "I ain't ashamed none to borrow from one who has lots of it, an' can spare it."

Farman's face froze into grim lines. He went down the steps and looked Brood squarely in the eyes. "Did this person give you license to tell me his name?"

"Oh, I don't think he'd care," said Brood with the trace of a sneer.

"Who is he?" demanded Farman.

"Mendicott!" said Brood in a hissing voice that carried a chill.

Nathan Farman stood still, with clenched palms, his face deathly white in the half light of the first faint stars. His breathing became labored.

Brood had dropped his cigarette as he breathed the dreaded name of the outlaw. The heavy lids had narrowed over his gleaming, black eyes. His hand rested lightly on the butt of his gun.

Crossley had leaned forward in his chair, and Hope saw Mrs. McCaffy stiffen. The girl's uneasiness increased as she realized it must be something grave and menacing that the mention of that name portended.

"He sent you here?" Nathan Farman asked hoarsely.

"I've answered enough questions," said Brood insolently. "Now you can answer one for me. What do you want for this place?"

Nathan Farman leaped up the steps. "I told you once to get out of here, an' now I'm telling you again!" he cried, turning as he gained the porch and pointing a shaking forefinger at Brood.

As in answer, Brood drew his gun with lightning like rapidity and fired in the air. Farman ran into the house. Crossley hurried toward the end of the porch, but Brood stopped him with a sharp command. Then a number of riders broke through the trees and shrubbery north of the house. They raced toward the porch, and Mrs. McCaffy stepped beside Hope, who had risen.

Brood shouted something in Spanish to the horsemen, and they gathered in front of the house, two of them flinging themselves from their mounts and running for the porch. Hope screamed as Nathan Farman came out with a gun leveled at Brood. The ex-foreman leaped aside, and red flame darted from his right hip. The rancher stopped, wavered, and fell in a heap as two of the men came up the steps.

The housekeeper rushed toward them and one, with a laugh, rudely flung her aside. Then Hope felt herself grasped in strong hands, and a cloth was flung over her head; she was picked up, fighting as best she could, and carried down the steps. In another moment she was held in a saddle and felt a horse move under her.

From somewhere below the house came shouts, and she thought she recognized McDonald's voice. He was bringing the men to the house for the conference, she reflected with a choking sob. There was more firing, guns roared to either side of her. She managed to tear the cloth from about her face. It was dark, but she saw they had passed the barns and were in the trail that she knew led into the foothills and the vastnesses of the higher mountains.

She screamed, and the man who held her in the saddle chuckled evilly. The shooting ceased. They were galloping madly, and the girl realized that they were mounted on an excellent horse. She tried to strike the man behind her, and a laugh was the only result. She saw Brood dash past them to take the lead. Undoubtedly McDonald and the others were rapidly being outdistanced. She screamed, and a hand closed roughly over her mouth. Then came darkness.

Chapter Eight

When Hope recovered consciousness, she found herself on the bank of a small stream. Her blouse had been opened at the throat and someone was laving her temples with cold water. The moon had risen and she saw horses and men about the pines in a natural clearing in the hills. She sat up and pushed away the hands of the man who was ministering to her.

"Oh, you've come out of it," he said shortly.

"She'll be all right," came a voice she recognized as Brood's. "Just give her a little time an' we'll be on our way."

To Hope's own surprise, she laughed. In the reaction from her extraordinary experience upon arriving in the desert country, she felt suddenly cool and collected, and thought of her captors, and possible murderers of her uncle, with infinite contempt. "Will one of you . . . tell me where we are supposed to be going?" she asked coldly.

"That's the way you feel about it, eh?" She recognized Brood in the moonlight, standing before her, looking down upon her with a half grin. "Well, Miss Farman, if you just keep calm and don't fly off the handle, you'll be all right. We don't attempt to predict what's goin' to happen, but we don't intend to harm you."

"I don't suppose a brute who would shoot a man down in cold blood would harm a defenseless girl," she said sarcastically.

"Your uncle wasn't defenseless," replied Brood with growl. "He came out there with a gun an' wished what happened on himself. It ain't good policy to try an' swap words with a man after he pulls his gun."

"You had no business there," flared out Hope. "You came there to start trouble in the first place. You are the one who is responsible."

"Well, now, young lady, there ain't a bit of use in our arguing. All I've got to say is that if your uncle hadn't flew off at the head, things would have been different, or might have been different even so far as you're concerned. I'm actin' under orders, maybe, an', if I am, you can bet I'm goin' to carry 'em out. You can have a horse by yourself to ride, if you'll promise to keep in line an' not try any funny business. But you're sure goin' with us, an', if you don't want to come peaceable, we'll have to use force. That's all I've got to say. I'm through talkin' about it."

Hope caught his tone of absolute decision and reflected that it would be better to have as much liberty as possible than to try to circumvent the men under the circumstances. "Bring my horse," she said coolly, rising in a way to favor her injured ankle.

"Now that's showin' some sense," Brood approved.

He gave an order and a man led up a horse. Hope was compelled to accept Brood's assistance in mounting, and, when she was in the saddle, he handed up her reins and told her to fall into line behind him.

In a few moments they were again on the trail, climbing higher and higher into the foothills, Brood leading, with Hope riding behind him and the several others bringing up the rear. It was weird, almost uncanny, this experience, thought the girl. She had to struggle to keep back the tears when she thought of her uncle, and she wondered if he were dead. She was cheered somewhat because of the fact that Mrs. McCaffy and others were at the ranch to nurse him, if he had merely been wounded, and to rush him, perhaps, to a doctor, or to send a messenger for one. As for her own plight, she failed to realize that it was serious. She could not conceive of such a melodramatic move as carrying a woman away into the hills except for a ransom. But Hope was struck by another thought, a thought that was more disconcerting. She had known for some time, through letters, that her uncle really thought a great deal of her. He had intimated on more than one occasion that someday she would likely inherit Rancho del Encanto. And this night Brood had offered to buy the ranch and had met with immediate refusal from Nathan Farman. If her uncle had been killed—she caught her breath with a sob at the thought—it was possible that she owned the ranch. In such event, this might be a most serious business, an effort on the part of Brood and the dreaded outlaw he had mentioned to compel her to dispose of Rancho del Encanto. And in her heart she felt that if her uncle were dead, she would not want to live on the ranch. Indirectly this fact might be a potent weapon in the hands of her enemies. She thought more and more of this as the night wore on, with the moon silvering the stands of pine, and a scented wind sighing in the branches that overhung the dim trail they were following. She shuddered instinctively as she recalled Brood's mention of the name of Mendicott, and the startling effect it had produced. In the dark hour preceding the dawn she came to the disturbing conclusion that she was being taken to the rumored rendezvous of the outlaw. And for the first time she had a real feeling of fear.

They had proceeded over many ridges, each higher than the one before, and they had long since left the worn trails they had first encountered. With the first graying of the eastern sky, Hope saw that they were hardly following any trail at all. They were on a thin ribbon of path that might have been made by wild game; in fact, she had caught a glimpse of an animal she surmised was a deer in a patch of moonlight in a meadow. They had been in water at intervals, too, and she suspected this was to cover their horses' tracks. She doubted if the men from the ranch would be able to follow them with any degree of certainty, and, if they were headed for Mendicott's hidden retreat, the force from the ranch would most likely prove inadequate to cope with the outlaws. It might be days, even weeks before a successful attempt could be made to rescue her. This added to her growing sense of misgiving and apprehension.

When the sun came up, she was treated to a wonderful sight. They were riding along the rocky spine of a high ridge. Below them lay the hills, green with their stands of timber, and far to eastward was the shimmering haze of the desert. Above were the towering peaks, crowned with the silver remnants of the winter's snows. The ridge they were on appeared to be a divide between the lower hills and the sheer cliffs and spires of rock leading up to the summits of the highest mountains.

Brood turned in his saddle and grinned at her. She tossed her head in disdain, although something in his manner convinced her that he meant her no harm. He was probably Mendicott's agent, had likely been associated with him for some time, and her uncle might have been suspicious of this.

The other men rode stolidly behind. They were mostly unshaven and roughly dressed. They all were armed. Hope could recognize none of the men from the ranch. She decided they looked like outlaws; certainly they fulfilled her conception of what bandits looked like, and their furtive glances served to convince her.

The sight of the far-off desert reminded her of the mysterious Channing. Had he been in earnest when he told her to remember his name if trouble befell her? She doubted it, for he had left no way of communicating with him. But his eyes were far different from Brood's.

She was startled to hear Brood calling to her. He had stopped just ahead, and she reined in her horse.

"We're goin' down a tricky piece of trail here," he said, nodding soberly. "Keep lookin' at the rocks on the left . . . on the left, understand? An' let your horse pick his own way." He waved a signal to the others, and they started on.

Hope was puzzled, but her perplexity lasted only until they turned down the west side of the ridge. The descent was so steep that at times the horses actually slipped along, their shoes striking fire from the smooth rock. On the left was an almost sheer wall of rock; on the right was a yawning gulf, seemingly hundreds of feet deep. The girl held her breath and followed Brood's advice by looking to the left. She felt that, if she looked down the precipice on the right, she would grow so dizzy she would topple from the saddle. It seemed hours, although it was only minutes that their horses carefully picked their way along that narrow, rocky trail of peril.

Eventually it widened, and the girl breathed deeply in relief. They came down into a basin or cup in the high hills. There was a stream in the basin, and through the pines and firs that studded its steep sides Hope could see the silver flash of a waterfall. The basin was carpeted with rich grass, and horses were grazing there among the cottonwoods, alders, and small firs. She glimpsed a number of small buildings that proved to be log cabins and realized that they had arrived at their destination. It was a natural rendezvous. She suspected that the steep, treacherous trail down which they had come was the only means of entrance to the place. It would not be difficult to defend the retreat against invasion if such were the case.

When they reached the group of buildings among the cottonwoods on the banks of the little stream, Brood signaled them to stop.

"Wait here till I come back," he said sharply, and rode to a larger cabin up the stream from the others.

He was gone but a few minutes when he galloped back. Hope had seen men near some of the cabins and among the horses, and there was no longer any doubt in her mind but that she was in the mountain hiding place of the outlaw Mendicott. Well, she said to herself with a measure of relief, I'll soon know what he wishes to see me about.

Brood rode up to her and indicated that she was to follow him. They proceeded to one of the cabins, and there she was asked to dismount. Again she had to accept Brood's assistance, and, when she was on the ground, he bowed to her and made an exaggerated gesture toward the cabin.

"There's your quarters," he said with a grin. "Make yourself right at home."

She left him, her chin in the air, and entered the cabin. She had resolved to accept the situation with as good grace as possible. Certainly it would do her no good to exhibit fear. Even an outlaw would be likely to admire spirit in a prisoner. She would face every new move calmly.

She was surprised to find the cabin well furnished. The bunk had a clean white spread on it; the table was covered by a runner, hand woven, and on it was a lamp with an ornamental shade. There were white muslin curtains on the single window, a good rug on the floor, a homemade bureau with a mirror, an armchair, and two other chairs. There was a fireplace, too, and closet space. The white chinking between the logs seemed to give it an added air of cheerfulness. It was altogether such a cabin as Hope would never have expected to find in such a place, and she surmised that it was furnished and well kept purposely for guests. There were even comb and brush and other toilet articles on the bureau. The few pictures on the walls were magazine covers, but they were attractively arranged. There was a white stone outside the door. Neither window nor door was barred, and there was nothing to indicate that it was intended as a place for imprisonment.

Hope frowned in fresh perplexity. Did they intend to let her have the run of the place? Then she remembered the narrow, dangerous trail by which they had entered the basin. It was probably the only entrance and constantly guarded. Therefore the whole basin was a prison in itself. It didn't add any to her peace of mind to reflect that Mendicott was more than apt to be clever. The fact that he was reputed to be inexorable in his depredations did not necessarily mean that he lacked cunning, or wisdom.

She took off her hat and jacket and made a fresh discovery. On one side of the closet was a washstand with wash basin, soap, a mirror, and a pail of water that was cool, evidently freshly drawn. There were clean towels, also. She bathed her face and hands, drank a glass of water, and felt greatly refreshed, although she was stiff and sore from the many hours in the saddle.

There came a knock at the door, and, when she answered it, she found a man with a tray of food over which was a snowy napkin. He placed it on the table, looked at her for a moment, and went out. The girl was surprised by his appearance, for he looked not unlike an Eastern waiter. He had red jowls, his eyes were mild and blue, he was clean-shaven, and his hair slicked back. But her greatest surprise came when she inspected her breakfast. There were two fried eggs, some sausages and bacon, a plate of hot cakes, syrup, plenty of butter, a pot of steaming coffee, and a little pitcher of pure cream. The china was good, and so was the silver. She couldn't resist a smile as she sat down to eat. The china and silver undoubtedly had been stolen on a raid, and the food, too, for that matter, or purchased with the proceeds of a robbery. But this did not affect her appetite.

She ate with relish and found the food of excellent quality, splendidly prepared and served. Her respect for Mendicott increased. He was clever enough to feed his men the best, evidently. It was one way of keeping them satisfied and loyal.

After breakfast she went out in the shade of the trees by the little stream. The sun was shining brightly, the pines on the steep slopes were a vivid green, the big meadow was splashed with wild-flowers, there were birds and bees, and she saw a herd of cows that looked like thoroughbreds. It was a wondrously peaceful scene. It might have been such a spot as the monks of Switzerland would select for a retreat. It was altogether too peaceful, for its quiet was disturbing. The girl was obsessed by the sense of waiting— waiting for what?

Men passed, looked at her curiously, went on about their business. They were rough-appearing, roughly dressed. None seemed to hurry. She found herself conjecturing what Mendicott would look like. She pictured him as big of body, cruel-eyed, domineering. Wouldn't he have to be some such person to rule these men with an iron hand?

She saw a rider trotting his horse up the other bank of the stream. Something about his posture in the saddle and his horse appeared familiar. She stepped behind a small fir tree and watched him. As he rode across the stream, she recognized him with an incoherent cry. She gazed after him till he disappeared among the trees in the direction of the large cabin up the creek. Then she hurried back to her quarters and sat on the bunk, staring straight ahead with a baffled expression in her eyes. The rider had been Channing!

When the man came for the breakfast dishes, she roused herself and started to ask a question.

"I am not supposed to talk to you," he said politely, with a short bow. And he left at once, carrying the tray above his head in best approved style.

Hope Farman sat on the bunk and laughed. But her laughter soon changed to tears, and later she slept.

While she slept, a man strolled to the door, looked in while he rolled a cigarette, then walked away up the stream, smoking idly. Men he met nodded and stepped aside, but he gave no sign of recognition.

Chapter Nine

It was sunset when Hope Farman awoke. She was amazed to find she had slept for a good eight hours. But she felt rested and refreshed, and, after she had bathed her face and hands with cool, fresh water she brought from the creek, she found herself looking forward to the evening meal with real anticipation.

The basin was aglow with the reflected color of the sunset, and banners of crimson and gold hung over the western rim of rock high above the floor of the cup in the mountaintops. She saw some riders go down on the farther bank of the stream, and surmised it was the change of guard proceeding to the trail from the ridge.

The long twilight had descended when the man came with her supper. It proved to be another excellent meal, even to a salad, with a pitcher of fresh milk.

She lighted the lamp, closed the door, and ate in quiet seclusion.

After supper her spirits had revived to a point where she was much less worried about her own situation than she was anxious as to her uncle's fate, and acutely interested in the presence of Channing in the rendezvous. She tried to put thoughts of her uncle from her mind, realizing that under the circumstances nothing could be accomplished by worrying. She speculated at length on Channing. If she were in the retreat of the outlaw, Mendicott, then Channing's presence could mean but one thing—he was connected with the band.

She remembered he had taken a trail toward the hills when he left the ranch. There was a possibility that he had been taken prisoner by the bandit, perhaps because of his altercation with Brood. She hoped this would prove to be the case, for she did not like to think of him as an outlaw himself, although it would explain the mystery surrounding him. But, if he was not a prisoner like herself, she had only her first deduction as an alternative. And if she were indeed in Mendicott's camp, why didn't the outlaw appear and make known the reason for her abduction? Her thoughts were interrupted by a light knock at the door. She rose with quickened pulse and answered it. It proved to be the man for the supper dishes. When he had taken up the tray and was prepared to depart, he turned suddenly. "Is there anything you want?" he asked in the same polite voice he had spoken in that morning.

"Yes, I'd like to ask a question," she said pleasantly, smiling.

"I don't think I can answer it unless it has something to do with your quarters or something you want," said the man uneasily.

"Whose place is this?" she asked.

"Yours for the time being," he answered, bowing.

"But I mean . . . who has charge here?"

The man merely shook his head and smiled faintly.

"Is it Mendicott's place?" she persisted. "If you don't answer, I'll assume that it is."

"I'll answer by saying that I can't answer such questions and you can assume what you want to," replied the man with a slight frown. "Now, is there anything you want here?"

"Yes," said the girl in a tone of resignation. "I'd like to have something to read."

The man bowed and was gone.

She went outside to find the twilight had deepened into night and the bowl of the sky over the basin was filled with stars. She noticed a man standing nearby, looked at him as closely as she could, and decided she would go back in her cabin. She had a peculiar feeling of confidence that she would not be harmed, but she also suspected she was being watched now that night had come. It was an uncomfortable sensation.

Inside the cabin she made sure the window was fastened and pulled down the shade. The door had a latch, and she found the latch could be secured. This gave her a sense of security, for one to enter would have to make his presence known either by knocking or forcing the door or window. She sat at the table in the soft glow of the shaded lamp. She was restive and not at all sleepy. The table and the lamp reminded her of her home in New England. Then the whole affair seemed incredible—a dream. But the illusion was immediately dispelled by a knock at the door, and, when she opened it cautiously, she found the man with some reading matter.

She thanked him and he departed with a curt: "Good night."

There were three magazines of recent dates. Hope glanced casually at the covers; she wasn't sure that she wanted to read. Then she started and stared at a name written on one of the covers. Channing. The name was lettered in a bold hand; it seemed to stand out more forcibly than the flaming illustration and the magazine's title. She remembered his last message—to think of his name if she were in trouble. She realized with a thrill that she was, indeed, in trouble, and here was his name staring at her, doubtless put there by his hand and intended, perhaps, to convey a message. Had the man who brought the magazines gathered them at random, and chanced upon one belonging to Channing, or had Channing learned of her wish and sent one with his name purposely lettered upon it? It might contain a further message.

She searched the magazine carefully, page by page, several times, but it contained no other written word. Just the name on the cover. But she felt that it had got there by more than mere chance—that he was reassuring her. And it caused her to feel easier, and after a time she did read for an hour. Then she unlatched the door softly, turned down the light in the lamp, and peered outside. She glimpsed the moving shadow before the door and quickly withdrew into the cabin. She had ascertained to her complete satisfaction that she was being watched.

She sat up for two hours more, and then went to bed. Reaction from the worry that had been visited upon her, the continual thinking and puzzling, the loneliness and uncertainty of it all soon asserted itself and she fell into troubled slumber. But she slept until dawn.

It was another wonderfully beautiful morning in the secluded basin. Hope was out in time to see the sun's first, early rays strike the slopes and cliffs. There had been a heavy dew, and grass blades and leaves gleamed with diamonds. She picked some wild roses that grew in profusion in the big meadow and put them in a glass of water in the cabin.

Her ankle was so far near well that she walked a way down the bank of the stream. The guard who had watched the cabin during the night was not in sight. There were cabins below the one she occupied, and, as she neared one of these, she came suddenly upon Brood. He had been to the stream for water and was carrying a pail filled.

He stared at her a minute and grinned broadly. She started back, then turned suddenly. "Have you heard anything from the ranch?" she asked with a note of pleading in her voice.

"The telegraph ain't workin', I reckon," he replied with a smirk.

"But you must know something," she said, trying to be pleasant, but unable to keep the loathing out of her eyes.

"I'm not givin' out any information," he said, scowling.

"It seems to me you all might be decent enough to tell me who is in charge of this place," she said, stamping her left foot in irritation. "You have me captive here, and it surely cannot do any harm to tell me who is responsible for it. I'm certain to know sooner or later and . . . if you'll tell me, I won't let on as if I knew."

Brood shook his head. "Can't be done. Just take it easy. You've got things pretty nice, isn't that so?"

She turned from him impatiently just as a horseman rode across the stream and stopped near them. She saw it was Channing and halted abruptly.

Brood had started back as if he had been struck. He looked at Channing in amazement—astonishment so genuine that it left him open-mouthed, appearing ludicrous. It was all too plain that he had seen Channing there for the first time. And it was doubly mystifying to the girl.

"Go to your cabin," Channing ordered, speaking to Brood.

Brood's surprise still held him rooted to the spot.

"Did you hear me? Go to your cabin," Channing commanded.

His look and tone caused Brood to obey, muttering to himself in wonder.

Then Channing rode back across the stream without so much as a look at Hope, whose spirits had risen only to fall again when he failed to recognize her. It appeared that he was merely ordering Brood to remember the admonition of someone not to talk with her. Anyway, it was now apparent that he wasn't a prisoner. He was there as a member of the band, perhaps a lieutenant of Mendicott's.

She walked slowly back to her cabin convinced that she could expect no help from him. She did not relish her breakfast so much this morning. The worry had returned when Channing deliberately ignored her. And how she hated Brood! She never knew she could feel so toward a human being. But he was probably her uncle's murderer.

Hope walked again that morning, returned for lunch, dozed and read by spells during the quiet, lazy afternoon. No one visited her. It was nearly maddening—this futile waiting. She tried without avail to get the man who brought her supper to talk to her. She wanted to talk to him about anything, even if he wouldn't answer her questions. But he was obdurate, and she was left alone, conscious only of the guard pacing outside.

The third day passed the same way, and the girl finally resolved to bring something about by walking to the trail leading out of the basin. She tried this in the afternoon, but was turned back by horsemen before she had reached the lower end of the big meadow. She gave it up and returned to the cabin.

Then she had another idea. She would skirt the trees and get to the large cabin up the stream. In this, too, she was detected and escorted back to her quarters by two men who gave her to understand by their looks that she had been on dangerous ground.

One of the men remained near her cabin, and she realized that her two ventures had resulted only in a guard being stationed over her during the day as well as at night.

After supper she sat, disconsolate and discouraged, by the table. The inaction, loneliness, isolation, doubt, and uncertainty were telling on her. Her spirits were low and she was on the verge of tears when she heard a sharp rap on the door.

She knew it was not the man who served her meals, for he had taken away the tray and bade her good night. It was a different rap, too—a rap that rang of authority. It was repeated before she could reach the door. When she opened it, a man stepped in.

She retreated to her chair by the table as he closed the door, removed his hat, and stood looking at her keenly. He was a small man, sunburned rather than tanned, his face showing the scars left by smallpox. His eyes held her gaze. They gave her a chill. They were cruel eyes, piercing—penetrating. He was dressed in worn riding clothes such as affected by men of the cities, and he wore military boots, a cartridge belt, and a gun.

For some reason she could not have explained, he reminded her of a wasp. "Will you sit down?" he asked. "I want to talk to you."

The voice was reinforced by the eyes, the cruel look, the brisk manner.

"Who are you?" she asked, although she felt she knew.

"I'm Mendicott," he said curtly.

She sank into her chair. "I'm glad you've finally come," she said.

He pulled a chair to the table and seated himself with a short laugh.

Then the still night air was suddenly rent with the reports of guns. The girl half rose, startled.

The outlaw motioned her back to her seat. "It's a man we caught stealing from the commissary," he said, baring his teeth in a queer smile. "He tried to get away. He was unpopular, and I ordered him shot."

Chapter Ten

Hope Farman stared fixedly at the outlaw in undisguised horror while he coolly fashioned a cigarette of brown paper and loose tobacco. Her gaze was drawn to his fingers, moving so deftly, and she saw that his hands were slim, his fingers tapering, his nails well kept. In spite of his eyes and the look in them, which betrayed the real man, he had a certain debonair manner. His movements were graceful. He held his head at an aristocratic angle; he radiated confidence and deliberation. There was no doubt he was as clever as he was dangerous. But she wondered about the shots. Had he ordered them fired with an idea of impressing her—of frightening her?

"You don't believe it?" he asked quietly.

She started. He had read her mind. "I guess you would do it," she confessed, convinced he had spoken the truth.

"No man can steal from me," he said coldly. "And no person can leave this place without my permission." His tone was significant, and Hope knew he had made the statement for her benefit. He held up the finished cigarette. "Do you object to smoking?"

The girl shook her head. She had a desire to see him smoke, to note his movements. Already she had lost much of her fear of him because he interested her—fascinated her, perhaps.

He did not snap a match into flame with a thumbnail as she had seen most of the men do. Instead, he drew a silver matchbox from a pocket and made something of a ceremony of lighting his cigarette. He inhaled deeply, and looked at her closely as the smoke drifted out his small mouth between the tight, cold lips. "Are you comfortable here?" he asked.

"Oh . . . yes . . . but I'm lonely," replied Hope with a catch in her voice. "Oh, why did you bring me here?" she added earnestly.

"It was necessary," he answered calmly. "In fact, we looked for you before you arrived. I think you'll be able to save your uncle a heap of trouble."

"Oh . . . then he isn't dead?" Hope asked eagerly.

The outlaw shook his head impatiently. "Brood didn't shoot to kill," he said shortly. "Your uncle is a fool . . . a big fool. He's known for some time that he's not wanted in this country."

Hope's eyes dimmed as she breathed deeply in relief at the welcome news. But she remembered quickly that Mendicott had said they anticipated her coming. They wished to use her in some way. Then the stampede had been part of a plan to frighten her and harass her uncle, and her uncle had suspected as much, which explained his being so angry with Brood. "Why isn't my uncle wanted in this country?" she demanded boldly.

"Because I say so," replied Mendicott sharply. "I've adopted this range. There are plenty of ranches in better spots than the one he's in that'll be good enough for him. This is scrub cattle country, anyway. But there's no need for our talking about that end of it." He looked at her shrewdly. "I don't suppose you want to stay here any great length of time?"

"No . . . no!" exclaimed the girl. "It isn't . . . right."

"Right and wrong is according to the way you look at it," he retorted.

She saw the hard look in his eyes, and it instantly recalled all the formidable things she had heard about this man who respected no law except his own will, and who depended upon his weapon and his hold over his followers to enforce it.

"It might be necessary for you to stay here some time," he went on in modulated tones. "But there's a way you might go free in an exceedingly short time."

"What . . . what is it?" she asked in a low voice.

"I suggest that you write a letter to your uncle."

"Oh, and have him come for me?"

Mendicott laughed mirthlessly. "I wasn't thinking of inviting him. If I'd wanted him here, I'd have had him here long ago. No, you don't have to tell him to come for you. We'd have to guide him up, anyway." He chuckled at this.

"Then what do you wish me to write to him?" asked the girl, puzzled.

"Suppose I dictate it," he suggested.

"And I'm . . . to write it?"

"Exactly. I dictate and you write it and sign it. I have a fountain pen here and paper. I will see that the letter is delivered tomorrow."

"And then I am to go free?" she asked suspiciously.

"That will depend upon the effect the letter has on your uncle," was the cool reply. "I promise nothing. But it's your one best bet, Miss Farman, and you can believe me when I say that."

He took out his fountain pen, produced a piece of writing paper, drew back the table cover, and placed them on the bare table top before her.

She took up the pen with a feeling of misgiving and prepared to write as directed.

"Just take this all down," he said. "Then, if you wish to ask any sensible questions, we can talk about it a minute. But I haven't much time."

She nodded in compliance.

He proceeded to dictate:

Dear Uncle Nathan:

I am held a prisoner by Mendicott in a place I do not know where. I am in a dangerous position, and he has no intention of letting me go until you have agreed to sell the ranch. He hasn't harmed me in any way, but I am losing my health through my fears and worry. Why don't you sell the ranch at a good price and we go to a better place and buy a new ranch and be happy? If you will make a deed according to his orders, he will let me go. He says he can make the deed good, and he won't let me go until it is done. Please do this, Uncle, and let's go away from here. I am very much afraid.

"That's all," said Mendicott after a brief pause. "Just sign it and I will see it is delivered. When the deal is made, you can go, and I will see that you get out without being molested."

The girl put down the pen and looked straight into the cruel, black eyes of the outlaw. "But Uncle doesn't want to sell his ranch," she said seriously. "He told that man Brood that before he was shot."

Mendicott shrugged. "He may change his mind when he gets your letter," he said significantly.

"Why do you want Rancho del Encanto?" asked the girl.

This caused the outlaw to frown. The scars on his face took on a white hue. "That is a point we won't talk about," he said coldly. "It's enough that I want it. I have my reasons, and . . . my reasons are good enough for me . . . and for him. He knew this was coming up, if he isn't too much of a fool."

"But a deed obtained in this way would hardly be legal, would it?" Hope asked shrewdly. "When they found out the facts, the authorities could cancel it, couldn't they?"

"They could," he agreed with a short laugh. "But I said that I could make the deed good. I mean it. And that note will have to be returned to me. If he made a yelp about the deed, he would find it hard living there again. He knows that, I guess."

Hope's face was pale. She wanted to spar for time, but could not see that it would do her any good. She was completely in his power, and she knew he could enforce the deed, hunt her uncle to earth if he made a complaint. She knew, too, that her uncle would consent to sell the ranch in order to remove her from Mendicott's power. And she knew how Nathan Farman loved Rancho del Encanto. "My uncle thinks a lot of that ranch," she said slowly, in a low voice. "He loved his wife and she died there, and it has associations that mean everything to him. If he was to lose it because of me, I could never forgive myself. I can't sign that paper. I just . . . can't."

Mendicott rose swiftly from his chair by the table. His face had darkened and his teeth were bared in a sneering smile. "You may change your mind," he said in an ominous tone.

"Oh, you have me completely at your mercy," said Hope, rising and throwing back her head. "You can be a half man or a thorough beast. But I won't sacrifice the . . . the thing I believe my uncle holds most dear."

He looked at her narrowly. "Don't get me wrong," he said, stepping to the door. "I want that ranch. I'm going to have it, and . . . I hate women!"

"And what do you think women think about you?" asked the girl scornfully.

"I don't care!" he flung back at her. "Think that over with the rest of it . . . tonight."

The door closed after him and Hope was alone. She took up the paper, tore it fiercely into shreds, and flung them into the cold, blackened fireplace.

Chapter Eleven

Long into the night Hope sat on the bunk and thought. She strove to evolve a plan by which she could get out of the basin. Once out, she would take her chances on getting back to Rancho del Encanto. She could at least go down the mountains, by whatever trails she came across, and once in the foothills she believed she could find her way to the ranch. But to get out! She knew there was now a guard over her by day. She looked out twice during the night and saw the guard outside—the night guard. She had a wild idea of getting out the window and trying to find her way in the darkness. It would be all right in the vicinity of the stream, where she could see its silver ribbon in the starlight, but once away from it she would be lost. And she did not know just where the trail led out of the lower end of the basin. It seemed hopeless—the idea of escape.

She next considered a way to trick the master outlaw. If she signed the letter—which Mendicott would doubtless be glad to dictate again—she knew her uncle would give up the ranch rather than risk her being in the bandit's hands any longer. Then she would be released. She believed Mendicott would keep his word. After that it might be possible to find a way to circumvent the outlaw. A large posse might capture him, or he might be killed. In any event, her uncle could expose the fraud, and, when the time was right, they might be able to corner Mendicott, even if he had had possession of the ranch a year, or two, or more. She thought long over this and finally decided it would be her best move. She speculated on the offer being a ruse, but could not determine how such a trick would aid the outlaw in any plan he might have other than acquiring the ranch. She believed she knew why he wanted Rancho del Encanto. It was isolated, and it was fairly convenient to the mountain rendezvous. He might not want to live there himself, but he could keep some of his men there, and it might aid him in his cattle-stealing operation. Anyway, the plan seemed more sensible than remaining Mendicott's prisoner. And her uncle might need her. She went to bed fully decided to put it in effect the next day.

She was cheerful in the morning and up early. She took a long walk before breakfast, followed at a distance by the guard, who evidently had instructions not to molest her unless she entered forbidden territory. As she walked down the little stream, she was puzzled as to what became of it. It seemed to widen down the basin, and yet there was no opening in the sheer walls below where it could go out. The trail, as she remembered it, was cut in solid rock just before the final descent into the basin. She was minded to ask, out of pure curiosity, what became of the stream, but doubted that she would get an answer. She turned back, still puzzling over the stream's disappearance.

Shortly after she reached the cabin, her breakfast arrived. It consisted of six thick slices of bread. She looked at the bread in surprise, then gazed at the man in dawning comprehension. The man avoided her eyes. But he looked at her in astonishment when she dropped into a chair and laughed heartily.

"He's going to starve me out?" she asked, sobering with an effort. Then she jumped out of the chair and faced the man angrily. "Take that back to your master and throw it in his face!" she cried. "But tell him I had changed my mind long before the breakfast arrived. Bring me some more to read and tell him I want to see him when he's ready. You know who I mean. Go and do as I say!"

The man hurried out with the small tray. Although the incident amused Hope, she realized that the outlaw could make it so miserable for her that she would have to yield to his wishes in the end. She did not underrate his cunning ability or fail to give him credit for a certain misguided ingenuity. In a remarkably short time the messenger returned, bringing an excellent warm breakfast and an armful of magazines. He wore a broad smile and served the meal on the table with elaborate pomp and obsequiousness.

"Did you tell him I had changed my mind before I saw the breakfast you first brought me?" Hope demanded.

"Yes," was the polite reply, accompanied by a bow.

"What did he say?" asked the girl curiously.

"He grinned," was the answer as the servitor withdrew.

After breakfast Hope took another walk. Her ankle was well again; she was happy that her uncle had been merely wounded; the air was cool and exhilarating and scented with the subtle perfume of wild blooms; the sun was bright, the sky as blue as deep water, and birds were singing joyously. For a time she forgot her troubles and reveled in the beauty of the sheltered spot. Then she descried Mendicott sauntering toward her cabin. She returned at her leisure and found him waiting for her, lounging against the log wall where she knew he had been watching her between the trees. He gave her a strange look in which she imagined she detected a glimmer of admiration. She returned his gaze coldly.

"You will have to dictate that letter over," she said, entering the cabin. "I destroyed the one I wrote last night."

"I thought you would," he said. "I'll make a change in this one and instead of mentioning my name make it 'a man you know.' Farman will understand all right, and, if he has any doubts, my man will tell him."

"I wouldn't think a man of your reputation and nefarious accomplishments would have to use much caution," Hope scoffed.

"I don't and I do," he snapped out. "Are you ready to write?"

"When you're ready to dictate," she answered with a look of contempt.

He didn't appear to mind her manner or her words, but produced the pen and paper, and she again wrote the letter, which was practically the same as the one he had composed the night before.

"I want you to know that I had changed my mind before I saw that miserable breakfast you sent," she said, holding the pen poised for her signature. "You couldn't have starved me into signing this."

"I didn't intend to starve you," he said, frowning. "That was to last today only."

"You thought a day would do it, or that you'd feed me well tomorrow and convince me by showing me what you could do if you wanted to?"

"You wasn't to get anything tomorrow," he said dryly with a flash of the cruel black eyes.

"Oh, then you did intend to starve me!" she accused in disgust.

"Next day you were to have good food again," he said. "But there were to be a number of these . . . these examples."

She caught her breath at his look and tone. In that instant she knew that he would have tortured her if necessary. She signed the letter, pushed it toward him, and rose. "Now let me out of here as soon as you can," she said. "I am doing you honor by believing you will keep your word."

"It isn't the first time I've been honored like that," he said grimly, as he put away the letter and pen. "I never forget my . . . promises. There's a promise in this letter, only maybe you don't know it."

With that he was gone, leaving Hope to ponder over his words. The statement seemed to possess a sinister significance. She wondered if it wouldn't be better, after all, if her uncle left the country. But she pressed her lips tightly, and her eyes flashed with defiance when she considered the fact that it would break his heart to leave Rancho del Encanto.

It was not long before she saw three riders galloping down the basin. Mendicott had lost no time in sending the message on its way. Possibly he would have an answer back that night. How soon, she wondered, would she be free? And how soon before Mendicott's power could be broken and her uncle live in peace in the home he loved?

She took one of the chairs out under the cottonwoods near the stream and went back for the magazines. There were nine of them, many of them old, all of them showing signs of wear in the hands of many readers. She looked at the covers first, remembering the name she had found written on one of those she had first received. Her lips curled in scorn as she thought of Channing. If he had been her friend and had meant to help her, he could have given her a signal and she would not have signed the letter Mendicott dictated. But he had ignored her. Moreover, he had given Brood an order, and Brood had obeyed. There was no doubt in her mind that Channing was a lieutenant of the outlaw's. Why not? He was skilled in the use of a revolver. Mendicott was a notorious gunman, as Jim Crossley had hinted. Didn't birds of a feather flock together? She knew nothing, of course, of the customary rivalry and jealousy between men of the lightning draw. Appearances and events were all against him. These deductions passed rapidly through her mind as she looked at the magazine covers. And now her gaze froze on the cover of a particular magazine. A figure had been inscribed upon it—the figure 12. She puzzled over this. Then, grasping the significance of the figure, and at the same time considering it foolish, she turned the pages of the magazine to page twelve. There, written in bold letters at the bottom of the page was a single word—tonight.

Hope's eyes widened and her breath came fast. She recognized the handwriting. It was the same as that in which Channing's name had been written on the other magazine. Was it Channing's own writing? If so, he had indicated a page and left a message. Tonight! Did it mean that he intended to attempt to see her that night and wanted her to be expecting some signal from him—to be alert? What time would he attempt to come? She became excited and hurriedly began the examination of the other magazines so that if anyone were watching he would not become suspicions. Then she let the magazines slip to the ground and smiled. The message had been written on page twelve. What could it mean save that he intended to come at 12:00 that night. It was reasonable, cleverly done. The writing of the name the first time had paved the way for the next message. He expected her to ask for more reading matter. He had access in some way to the magazines the messenger secured. He had avoided her to prevent exciting suspicion. But hadn't Brood told Mendicott of their first meeting, of the time Channing probably saved her life? Possibly Channing had more influence with Mendicott than had Brood. It might be Brood could not talk to Mendicott when he wished. Hope gave it up, but resolved to remain awake that night—all night, if necessary—to await results.

And the letter had been sent! If she had known this, had even anticipated anything of the sort, she would not have signed the letter. But it was now too late, she realized with dismay. Too late—unless she could reach the ranch before her uncle acted.

She took the magazines into the cabin, destroyed the evidences of the message, and sat down to think it over. But she had to keep moving because of her excitement. She walked idly about under the trees the rest of the day. Again she found herself wondering about the outlet of the stream at the lower end of the basin. But she quickly forgot it.

She did not see Mendicott again that day, nor did she see Channing. At supper the messenger again asked if there was anything she wanted.

"I'd like to ask a question, and I don't care whether you answer it or not," she replied with a yawn. "It's just curiosity, but if this place is a sort of bowl in the mountains, where does that stream out in front go to, how does it get out?"

The man considered a few moments. "It disappears in a hole in the rock wall at the lower end," he replied finally. "An' it's never seen again," he added as he gathered the dishes.

She nodded and yawned again, to give the impression she was sleepy. "I don't want any callers tonight," she said as he departed.

It was to allay suspicion and prevent another visit by Mendicott, as she suspected her conversation would be reported to the outlaw chief. She looked out but once and saw that she had not lost her night guard. Then she put out her light and waited in the semidarkness with the window shade up and the muslin curtains pulled aside so she could see the stars.

It seemed hours and hours that she lay on the bunk, her heart beating fast, and sleep luckily out of the question. She had no watch or clock and was unable to tell the time. She had given up hope, thinking midnight long since past, when there was a shadow at the window and a light tapping on the glass. It startled her. She rose hurriedly and, looking out, recognized the form of Channing. She thrilled at the thought that he had come to her aid.

He was motioning to her to open the window. She unfastened the catch noiselessly and pulled the window upward.

"Climb out ready to go," he whispered swiftly, and dropped into the shadow near the ground.

She put on her coat and hat, placed a chair before the window, and climbed through. He helped her from outside. But, as she wriggled across the sill, the window came down with a crash.

Channing pushed her down to the ground in the shadow and stood with his back closely against the wall of the cabin. Almost in that instant a shadow appeared at the corner of the cabin nearest him, and he leaped. Hope heard a muffled cry and saw Channing strike out. The other man reeled back, his right hand came up, and the girl caught the glint of the starlight on dull metal. Her heart was in her throat as Channing darted in and caught the wrist that held the gun. There was a flash of flame, and a sharp report shattered the stillness in the basin. The two men went to the ground, and rolled over and over in a mighty struggle. They were so close that Hope could hear their labored breathing. She heard something hit the ground at her feet. She reached down and felt cold metal. She hurriedly picked up the gun.

Then the struggle ceased as quickly as it had begun. Channing was groping about on the ground while the form of his opponent lay still. In a few moments Channing straightened, stepped to her side, and took her arm.

They hurried back from the cabin into the shelter of a grove of poplars. Shouts came from upstream and once, looking back, Hope saw the gleam of a light. She had no chance to think of anything but her footing, for Channing almost ran with her through the trees. They got through the poplars and he guided her down the basin to a stand of firs. They skirted these, keeping on the side toward the wall of the basin, and hastened on.

When they reached an open space, Channing whispered: "Can you run?" For answer, Hope ran as fast as she could toward the next grove of trees. She stumbled and nearly fell once, but her companion caught her and steadied her. The mishap caused her to lose the gun she had been carrying.

More shouts rode down the basin on the light breeze, then came the barking of guns in a general alarm. They had discovered she had gone. It seemed to her that they reached the rock wall at the lower end of the basin in remarkably short time. Here Channing directed her to the right, which was south. She knew the trail out of the basin was on that side in the direction they were following. They were screened now by the trees to westward. They heard another sound—a sound that caused the girl to shiver with excitement and fear. She was nearly out of breath. Louder and nearer came the sound, off to the southwest of them. It was the pounding of flying hoofs. The horsemen would surely beat them to the trail, and even if they didn't, there were the guards on the trail.

Channing halted suddenly. They were at the stream. Hope could see a yawning cavity in the rock wall through which the water rushed. "We're going in here," said Channing in a low voice. "Trust me, I know. It's the only chance. We'll only be in the water a minute . . . less than that, I guess. Get down with me, put your arms around my neck, and hold on. Choke me to death but hold on!" He knelt down at the edge of the stream. After an instant of hesitation she clasped him tightly about the neck and closed her eyes. He moved forward and they were in the swift-running stream. The inky blackness of the hole in the wall of rock swallowed them. They plunged downward, the roar of the rushing stream in their ears, and then Hope felt the water close over her with tremendous force. She was thrown away from Channing, and her hold loosened, but he caught her by the arm, struck out to the left with his own free arm, and as she started to strangle they came out of the water and were swept upon a bar of sand.

Chapter Twelve

Channing drew Hope up on the sand where it was dry. They were soaking wet. The place was pitch dark and filled with the sound of rushing water. Hope marveled that she had had the courage to follow her rescuer's instructions and brave the torrent in the dark. But now she trusted him.

A match flared into flame, and she saw Channing reach above his head. He brought down something that looked like a stick, and the match went out. He lighted a second one and applied it to the wood. There was a little tongue of flame that rapidly swelled into a torch of fire, and she saw he had lighted a piece of pitch pine. The pine torch illuminated the place and disclosed a subterranean passage. Its ceiling was low, and directly above them was a ledge where Hope made out the ends of several more pine knots. Evidently Channing knew the place well and perhaps had gone out of the rendezvous that way before. The sand they were on stretched along the side of the stream. It was a strip about three feet wide that narrowed at a point below them.

She finished her inspection of their location and looked up to find Channing inspecting his gun, which had gotten wet. She remembered having seen him use a small, metal matchbox and so knew that it was waterproof and had prevented the matches from getting wet. She remembered another matchbox—the one used by Mendicott. It gave her a start. Surely the outlaw must know of this means of exit from the basin, if it was an exit. In that event they could surely expect pursuit.

"I reckon we better be moving, Miss Farman," said Channing. He helped her to her feet. She was wet and shivering, for it was cold in the passage. "We'll walk fast to keep warm till we get out of here," he told her. "Just follow me and keep close behind."

They started off at a brisk pace. Hope was thrilled to know they were to leave by another way than the basin outside. That meant they were leaving the rendezvous of the outlaw. She walked close behind Channing, who led the way along the narrow strip of hard sand, holding the pine torch over his head.

Weird shadows played in grotesque shapes upon the walls and ceiling of the long, narrow cavern. The cavern twisted and turned to left and right. It seemed to the girl that it was miles long. She was on the point of breathlessly calling a halt to rest when they rounded a turn to the left and came into a cave leading off from the stream. It was a big cave and the ceiling was high. Channing paused to rest and looked at Hope keenly to see how she was standing the ordeal. She smiled at him and wondered to herself how he had managed to keep his hat in the wild torrent of water. She had lost her own, and her hair was about her shoulders. He pointed ahead and above them. She looked and saw a small square of starlit sky. It was the means of egress from the cave.

"Will they follow us here?" she asked anxiously. "They must know of this way out, don't you think?"

"Yes, I reckon they do, ma'am," Channing replied. "But I don't think they'll try to make it in the night. There's none of 'em very good in the water. They used ropes when they explored this place. I guess we've got about four hours' start of them. Now we'll get out of here."

He led her up a long slope, taking her arm and helping her over the boulders that strewed the path. Thus they climbed to the ceiling of the cave, and there he lifted her through a narrow opening and she climbed out on a slab of granite to find herself on a ridge with the forest about her and the moon and stars overhead.

"We've got to keep exercising while you're wet," said Channing as he pulled himself up through the aperture.

He had thrown the pine torch back into the cave and now he led the way across a rocky plateau and down the east side of the ridge by a thin, hard, steep trail leading through the timber. Several times Hope fell against him. He stopped and asked if she was too tired to go on and wanted to rest. She denied her weariness. Her joy and excitement at having escaped from the basin kept up her spirits and lent her strength. They could get to the ranch in time to stop proceedings for its sale. Even though the messengers had started back to the rendezvous to report to Mendicott, they could still reach Rancho del Encanto before the next important move was made. That thought gave her courage. She kept her eyes on the tall, broad-shouldered man ahead—the man of the desert. She upbraided herself, mentally, for having mistrusted him. He had kept his word with her even if he was an outlaw. And wouldn't Mendicott hunt him to earth for this? Wasn't he risking his life for her? How well he had planned it! The others might never have known they had left the basin had it not been for the slamming of the window of the cabin that attracted the attention of the guard. She wondered if Channing had killed him. She was surprised at herself because of the fact that she didn't care whether the guard had been killed or not!

The trail widened on a level and came out into a small meadow. Hope saw horses standing in the center and breathed a sigh of relief. The rapid travel had kept up her circulation. She did not feel the cold. Her clothes did not feel so wet.

"Wait here a minute," Channing ordered.

She stood near the horses while he hurried to the edge of the timber. He returned with a saddle and quickly saddled one of the horses. He went back for the other saddle and soon both horses were ready for the trail. From the rear of one of the saddles he untied a Mackinaw coat. He took a cap from the coat pocket and insisted that she put on both coat and cap. Then he assisted her to mount, swung on his own horse, and they were again on their way.

Hope was becoming accustomed to riding for long distances, and she liked the stock saddles of the West. She liked the horses, too, and she was pleased to find herself once again on Channing's own splendid mount. She thought how fortunate it was that she had been wearing her riding habit. They wound down into the foothills. She saw that they were not taking the trails by which the outlaws had escorted her to the rendezvous. Channing was making no attempt to conceal their tracks, but was proceeding by the most direct way.

When dawn broke, they were in the lower foothills. From the top of a ridge Hope saw the desert stretching below them, swimming in color. They rode down into a little valley and stopped at a cabin. The girl was astonished when Channing dismounted, opened the cabin door, and a burro came out. He entered the cabin, brought out pack saddle, pack sacks, and a roll of bedding. These he secured on the burro. He again swung into his saddle, and they went on.

Hope was puzzled, but assumed that Channing would be entering the desert after he had taken her to the ranch and was taking the packed burro because of that fact. There was no sound of pursuit; the morning was wonderful; birds were singing; a grouse whirred into the trees. Hope's spirits were high. Soon she would be back at Rancho del Encanto again.

They stopped at a small stream, and Channing filled two water bags. Hope had no chance to question him.

On the trail again, they dropped over a high ridge and suddenly left the green of the hills behind. Cottonwoods, alders, willows vanished as if by some subtle magic. Ahead was the vista of endless wasteland, of sage and greasewood, of bare stretches of ground, of shimmering heat waves—the desert. Channing put his horse to a sharp trot and Hope's mount followed. They turned to the left, where the floor of the desert was rolling, and after a time

Hope saw a pool of water from which trickled a small stream. They stopped there. She stared at the pool of water in wonder. It was white, or the rocks that formed its bed were white—a ghastly white like so many bleached and polished skulls.

"Arsenic Spring," said Channing, noting her look of bewilderment. "A cup of that water would kill a man . . . if it took that much. We'll stop here for breakfast."

He helped her dismount and she gazed at him curiously. Then she looked around. She had lost her sense of direction and could remember no such place as this near Rancho del Encanto.

"When will we reach the ranch?" she asked.

Channing shrugged and began to unpack the burro. "That'll depend on how things look," he replied enigmatically.

She threw off the heavy coat and hurried to him.

"But the letter!" she cried. "Mendicott made me sign a letter to my uncle stating I was in peril and he would have to sell the ranch before I could be released. The messengers took it to the ranch yesterday. We must get there before my uncle can act. We must hurry!"

"You signed that?" he asked slowly. His look caused her to flush.

"I signed it because it was the only way I thought I could get out of that place!" she exclaimed somewhat haughtily. "You had made no effort to help me. You had ignored me, and I was desperate. I . . . I thought there might be a way to beat Mendicott afterward, for a ranch obtained in such a way would . . . well, it all wouldn't be legal."

"Mendicott could make it legal, or the next thing to legal," said Channing with a grim smile.

"I know that, but now that we're out, we can get to the ranch in time to prevent my uncle from signing a deed."

Channing proceeded to roll a cigarette. "That would be the first place they would look for you," he drawled.

"But what of it?" cried Hope. "We can get there and get away before the messengers or Mendicott can get back."

"I reckon not," said Channing, lighting his cigarette nonchalantly. "We're some piece of hard riding from the ranch, Miss Farman."

"We can try," Hope pleaded.

She saw in his eyes that he did not intend to try. "Oh, then it was a trick!" she exclaimed. "And you're taking me somewhere else at Mendicott's command. I thought you were a common outlaw and against me . . . against all of us. Now I know it!" Her voice rang with contempt.

Channing looked at her calmly, although his lips compressed and a shade of gray showed through his tan.

"Where are we going?" Hope demanded.

"We are going into the desert, ma'am," replied Channing.

The girl turned away from him in despair and looked down into the ghastly waters of Arsenic Spring.

Chapter Thirteen

Hope Farman imagined her disappointment and despair reflected in the death waters of the spring. Her trust had been betrayed. She had virtually risked her life with Channing to escape from the retreat of the outlaws only to find that he was not returning her to Rancho del Encanto. Nathan Farman would sell his home. She turned and looked fiercely at Channing, who was getting breakfast. Her Puritan training and the attendant conventions were momentarily overshadowed by her mortification, grief, and anger. She wished she had not lost the gun the guard had dropped in the struggle by the cabin. If she had the gun—her brows drew together with a new and puzzling thought. If Channing had taken her out at Mendicott's order, why should he have had to fight the guard and to take her through the dangerous water passage? For the sake of appearances, she told herself, scorn flashing in her eyes. To make her think she had been rescued. But this deduction did not seem plausible, for it could have been accomplished so much easier and she would not have known the difference. Hope gazed at Channing with a new light in her eyes. Had he really rescued her—for a purpose of his own? Did he intend to take her into the desert, to some secret retreat to force a bargain with his outlaw chief? Or was it another blow aimed at her uncle from another angle?

She started to walk thoughtfully along the bank of Arsenic Spring. A shrill sound stopped her. Instinctively she jumped back, her face blanching. Channing came bounding from the fire he had made. His gun barked twice on the still air. A thin curl of smoke drifted upward from the long barrel of his weapon as he turned to her.

"You must be careful when walking on the desert, ma'am," he said gravely. He thrust his gun into its holster and strode back to the fire.

Hope looked down at the fat coils of the dying rattler and shuddered. She turned away, faint and sick, and retraced her steps to the camp, keeping her eyes on the ground and avoiding the clumps of sage. More than ever she was a prisoner. With a canteen she might have braved the trackless desert in an effort to escape back to the foothills that she could follow to the ranch road, but she knew she would not dare walk out alone after what had just happened. She sat down on the pile of bedding.

Channing went quietly about his work and soon had a palatable meal prepared. The girl accepted her plate without looking at him.

"Better drink a hot cup of coffee first," he suggested. "It's warm here already an' your clothes are dry, but you look a little peaked. All women do after they meet up with their first rattler."

She accepted his advice. Then she ate almost greedily, for she was ravenous. She watched Channing, who ate more slowly, and who looked off into the desert frequently the way they had come. "Did you kill that guard at the cabin?" she asked suddenly.

"No. Just laid him out for a spell till we could get a start."

"I don't suppose Mendicott knew we were going," she said rather sarcastically.

"I forgot to tell him, if that's what you mean."

"Did he really have a man shot last night for stealing from his commissary and trying to get away?"

"Yes."

Hope saw that she had not been mistaken as to the look in the outlaw leader's eyes. After all it was perhaps better to be away from there. "Where are we going?" she asked in a more amiable voice.

He pointed toward what she thought was the east.

"How far?" she inquired.

"Quite a ways," he answered. "To Ghost Wash, and then we turn south."

The look of worry and despair returned. She gazed off across the desert, burning hot now, for so early in the season. Where and how was it all to end? "You wrote your name on the cover of a magazine that man brought me," she accused.

"I did that thing," he agreed.

"You remember you told me if I should get into trouble to remember your name?"

"Yes, I remember that." He did not meet her eyes.

"And you have betrayed me!" she exclaimed bitterly. "You fooled my uncle, his men, and . . . me. And I trusted you. Do you think you have achieved anything? Haven't you any sense of manhood?"

He looked at her, biting his under lip until it was white. Then he proceeded to clear the camp and pack the burro. While he worked, he sang, and Hope, who had walked to her horse, listened in surprise. He had an excellent tenor voice, and he was singing an air from *The Tales of Hoffmann*.

"Where did you learn that?" she asked, unable to conceal her curiosity.

"From a girl who sings in a dance hall in Bandburg," he replied coldly.

Hope tilted her chin. He frequented with dance-hall girls. Well, it was to be expected. His occupation should have led her to expect it. This caused her to look at her own plight in a new light. Her eyes widened.

At that moment he finished packing the burro and turned toward her. His look was the same he had given her shortly before. Was it—could it be malice, or just resentment because of what she had said about him? Or—was it something else? "We're ready to go!" He had never used such a curt tone in speaking to her before.

Hope again looked across the burning waste where the heat waves shimmered above sage and greasewood and an occasional cactus. To Ghost Wash and then south! Away from Rancho del Encanto. And she had trusted him—relied on him. Into the desert with an outlaw, a man who sang songs taught him by girls who sang in dance halls. A man whose eyes appeared to be those of an honest, self-respecting man, but that burned with a light that caused her uneasiness. Hope put her hands to her face and sank down upon the hard, sun-baked earth. Then came the tears. When she finally looked up, Channing was standing before her with his hat in his hand. The sun turned his hair a brilliant bronze, his lips were pressed tightly together, and the peculiar look in his eyes was gone.

"I'm sorry, Miss Farman," he said in a softened voice. "I ain't often seen a good woman cry. I ought to have told you before, but you sort of riled me with what you said. You have no cause to worry, none whatever."

"Then . . . we're going back . . . back to the ranch?" she asked, her lips quivering.

"No, Miss Farman. I reckon you've just got to take my word for it that it isn't safe for you to go there. We're going to Ghost Wash, camp there tonight, and then push south to Bandburg."

"But . . . my uncle . . . ?" The girl's voice choked in a sob.

"If he gives in, and he will on your account, that's sure, they'll have to have a notary to put his seal on that deed. The nearest notary's in Bandburg. Your uncle's hit in the side, I hear, not bad, but bad enough so he can't be moved pronto. So they'll send to Bandburg for a notary. We'll be in Bandburg before they can cover the ground and get their messenger there."

"But suppose we are," said the girl, although she was beginning to understand.

"They won't get the notary, and we'll get word to your uncle Nate in the bargain."

Hope saw with joy that he was speaking truthfully and contritely. "Was this your plan all the time, Mister Channing?" she asked.

"It sure was. I'm sorry I failed to tell you a bit back."

"Then you're . . . you're not connected with that awful Mendicott?"

"In a way, I am," he confessed to her amazement, looking her in the eyes.

This gave her pause. How could he be taking both sides at once? Was it because of her? She didn't wish to ask him this. And another question occurred to her. "Mister Channing, why does Mendicott want my uncle's ranch so badly?"

"I reckon I can't answer that," he replied, stiffening. "Not now."

"Well, I guess I can forgive you under the circumstances," she said.

He favored her with his flashing smile and put on his hat. "If you're ready to go, ma'am, we'll just naturally slope."

Hope turned to her horse. He stepped to her quickly and helped her up. He attached a canteen of water to the horn of her saddle. She watched him swing into his own saddle and start the burro. Then they were again on their way.

Ahead of them the heat waves shimmered. The sun beat down upon them and Hope took off her jacket and put it across the saddle in front. Far to northward a range of bare, black hills rose against the horizon. Behind them the purple mountains retreated, veiling their lower slopes in a haze of blue. Elsewhere was desolation—dreary, complete, no sign of water, sage and greasewood, a cholla cactus spreading its thin arms in ridiculous gestures—sage and greasewood, and heat and glare. Hope Farman stroked her horse on his glossy neck. She was alone in the desert wastes with a man she had every reason in the world to believe was a member of a ruthless band of outlaws—robbers, rustlers, killers—and she was not afraid.

Chapter Fourteen

As the sun mounted toward the zenith, the heat increased. There was no shade, not a vestige of tree growth large enough to screen them from the burning rays that beat down upon them. The horizon was bathed in a thin, blue haze, but the world close at hand was dazzling. It was a yellow world, with gray and dull green spots where the clumps of sage and greasewood grew. Occasionally they would cross a rise strewn with round, smooth boulders that looked as if they had been smoke-stained. Then would come a wash, white with alkali drawn by the water that filled the wash during the infrequent storms when the rain fell out of the sky in a short but violent downpour. Lizards scurried across their path. They rode side-by-side. Major, Channing's horse, continually nosed toward his master. The burro plodded on ahead, waving an ear at times, otherwise proceeding as if walking in his sleep. Their progress was slow.

Channing brought out a pair of sunglasses and handed them to Hope. She thanked him. The extraordinary brightness of the sun's rays thrown back from the yellow earth was telling on her eyes. It was particularly bad, in another way, when they crossed the patches of alkali. Here the white glare was similar to the sun shining on a field covered with snow, but more intensified. Fortunately these patches were not very wide.

They rode in silence. Hope was busy with her thoughts, for surely she had much to think about—least of which was the wonder of it all. Channing was not disposed to talk. He apparently was at home in this environment. Hope studied him furtively. He had an excellent profile, a strong face, and he was handsome. He was such a man as women like. She wondered if he sang in the desert when he was alone. She decided he did. He didn't seem to mind the heat at all; of course he was accustomed to it. He was rugged enough, quiet, almost always serious. He appeared to be of the very desert itself.

"Summer must have come today!" she called to him. "It's hot enough."

She wanted to catch his smile again and she was immediately rewarded.

"This is just a sample, ma'am, of what it'll be right soon now," he said with a laugh.

"How hot is it?" she asked, genuinely interested.

"Around ninety, I 'spect."

"Well, how hot does it get?"

"A hundred and thirty . . . or more." She looked at him incredulously, decided he was beguiling her, and didn't ask any more questions.

An hour passed without a word being spoken. Then Hope began to wonder how Channing kept to his course. She could not tell by the sun in which direction they were traveling; she only knew they were going east because he had said they were to go that way. She thought the knowledge of how it was done might prove useful sometime.

"How do you keep sure of your directions?" she asked loudly.

"Landmarks," was the laconic reply.

She looked about with fresh interest. The black hills seemed to have disappeared. The mountains were still behind them, but they were mistier with haze, and they seemed to have shifted somewhat. There was nothing else she could seize upon as a landmark except a pink cone to the right of them, a long distance away.

"Where do you find your landmarks?" she asked, knowing that the query sounded silly.

"I pick 'em up as I go along," he answered with a grin. "But I usually have one that's a long way off," he continued, sobering. "When we get on top of the next little ridge, you look away ahead and you'll see a button sticking up on the horizon. That's what it's called . . . Button Butte. Ghost Wash is between here and there. But I know these local marks, like the flats and washes and monuments . . . those funny-shaped rock pillars and chimneys sticking up . . . and I go by them, too. Sometimes I have a mark behind me and one in front and keep on a line between 'em, and sometimes I have a triangle of marks, and sometimes, ma'am, I don't have a dog-goned thing 'cept a sense of direction the devil must have given me to make me like the desert."

The finish of his speech seemed appropriate to Hope. It was such a country as the devil must favor. But this desert lore was interesting, and it made Channing more interesting.

Channing did ask her twice if she wanted to make a dry camp and eat, or push on to their destination, and she decided on the latter. She drank frequently from the canteen of water suspended from her saddle horn.

It was cooler, and the sun was slanting well to westward when they rode up a long rise and she saw a great wash, or dry lakebed, ahead. There was another rise on the opposite side, and then, to her astonishment, she saw a cabin nestling among some green trees larger than any she had seen on the trip from the foothills. It evidently was a verdant spot.

"We're here!" Channing called to her, pointing to the white bed of the wash.

Hope decided the place was well named in being called Ghost Wash, for ghosts were proverbially white. She didn't know it hadn't been named for the reason she thought. She suspected there was water on the other side where the green trees grew. She asked the name of the trees.

"Paloverdes," replied Channing. "There's water there. We'll camp there tonight and make Bandburg tomorrow."

They rode around the wash to the cabin. There was a patch of green grass in front of the cabin and Hope smiled as she realized, for the first time in her life, the real beauty of plain green grass. It savored of living things and of water. Then, remaining in the saddle, she looked for the water and saw what appeared to be a small well, filled and slightly overflowing. She dismounted and went for a drink. The water was surprisingly cool, but had a flat taste.

"Little alkali in it," said Channing, noting her look, "but it won't hurt you."

She walked around, exploring, while Channing unsaddled the horses, hobbled them, and unpacked the burro. When Hope returned, he was busy building a fire.

"Why don't you use the cabin?" she asked.

"No stove in there, and I'd rather do it this way. The cabin is for your use, Miss Farman," he concluded, looking at her and smiling.

The door was open and Hope looked in. There was a bunk on which he had spread two blankets, a rude table, a bench, some shelves with some canned goods and other scanty provisions on them, and a few cooking utensils. It was plain this was one of his stopping places, for she did not doubt but that the things there belonged to him. Probably he had many such retreats in the desert. There were two windows, both open, but she noted they could be closed and fastened. There was a bar on the inside of the door that could be slid into place.

He had said the cabin was for her use. She turned back to him, smiling. "It's very nice, Mister Channing. And I'm as hungry as a bear. Shall I set the table?"

He indicated a pack sack that reposed on the ground with its straps unbuckled.

"You'll find the things in there. I reckon they're cleaner than the things inside."

She set the table and pulled up the bench. He brought the food and coffee, and then took down a can from one of the shelves.

"I never carry canned stuff with me in my packs," he explained, "'cept maybe on a short trip. I packed this stuff in here for an emergency." He looked at her quickly. "And I always knew I brought this can of peaches in for something or other, but I never knew just what till now."

Hope's laugh was good to hear. He grinned with her and opened the can with his knife.

"Let's eat," he invited, taking off his hat and throwing it on the bunk. "I wish you'd tell me everything that happened on the ranch after I left, if you'd just as soon."

So Hope recited the details of the quitting of the men after Brood left and concluded with short pursuit of Brood and the gang by McDonald and the other ranch hands who had remained loyal.

"McDonald likely quit because he saw it was no use," Channing mused. "Never could follow that outfit without getting shot to pieces, never could find where they'd gone."

"Do you think Brood stampeded the cattle on purpose?" asked Hope.

"Dunno. Maybe so, maybe no. I wouldn't put it past him."

Then Hope remembered the day she had seen Channing and Brood meet in the rendezvous, when Channing had ordered the ex-foreman of the ranch to his cabin.

"Did you go straight to Mendicott's place the time you left the ranch?" she asked.

"Almost," he answered after a spell of hesitation. "First I went over where we got the jack out of the cabin last night."

"Oh, by the way, how did you come to have everything ready there for us?" she demanded.

"I went out and made things ready," he said with a light frown.

"Well, to get back to what I had in mind. That day you met Brood near me on the edge of the stream there and he seemed so surprised, was that the first time he ever saw you in there?"

Channing looked at her and considered the question for a time. "What makes you ask that?" he countered.

"Because his face showed it," Hope answered readily.

"Well, it was," he confessed, scowling.

"Was it the first time you'd ever been there?" Hope asked eagerly.

"Miss Farman, you're powerful curious. Tell me now isn't that an honest fact?"

"Yes, I am," Hope conceded. "But I don't see why Brood obeyed your order so promptly when you told him to go to his cabin."

"If you try to figure out everything you don't understand in this country, ma'am, you'll just naturally go plumb crazy," he remarked, rising.

It was Mrs. McCaffy's admonition all over, but it provided Channing with a loophole to avoid further questioning. Hope saw this and desisted. But she had learned something. Brood evidently hadn't known Channing was acquainted with Mendicott, or an associate of his, until that day. Therefore Channing had no connection with the staging of the accident—if it had deliberately been planned. His action in saving her life and aiding Jim Crossley had resulted from an honest, courageous motive. The knowledge increased her sense of security with him.

"I'll wash the dishes," she volunteered, following him out of the cabin. "You look after the horses and that other animal."

"That other animal," he said testily, "learned to look after himself a long time ago."

Hope smiled to herself. There was little to fear from this man, whatever he might be. She told herself she was beginning to like him. Then she caught herself up with a prim tightening of the lips. There was a well-defined gulf between their stations—a vast difference in their positions.

He went off somewhere and left her to take care of the dishes. After this she walked from the cabin to a point on the ridge behind it. Below, the great white bed of the wash stretched for more than a mile. Beyond, on all sides of the ridge, in every direction lay the desert. She watched the great gold ball of the sun drop steadily in the west. The air was cooling rapidly. To her astonishment some birds flew over her. Birds in that inferno? It seemed impossible, but she had seen them and heard them and she knew to a certainty they were there.

The cloth of gold above the purple hulks of the mountains, where the sun had disappeared, silvered. The sky blushed a faint pink that deepened into crimson till the peaks ran with the red blood of the dying day. Higher and higher into the great arch above flared the vermilion fires. Then they wavered, pennons of gold broke through, appearing like spangles on a carnival robe, lengthening into streamers, drifting on a sea of fading red. The desert was pink, and blue, and amethyst—spotted with tints of orange. Then the skies grew lighter, admitting the faint violet tones that betray the twilight.

Hope drew a long breath and looked about her. To northward she saw what appeared to be a lake of silver in the waste of sage and greasewood. She looked along the ridge and saw Channing standing, his hat pulled low over his eyes, staring into the west. He had been watching the sunset, and he appeared to the girl to be symbolic of the silent majesty of the desert. He approached her and she greeted him cheerily.

"I've got two more questions, Mister Channing. Will you please answer them?"

He frowned at the challenge in her eyes. "You seem to be made of questions, Miss Farman. What are they? I won't promise to answer 'em."

"Some birds flew over my head," said the girl. "I was wondering what they were."

"Desert doves, ma'am. They breed here and then go away. They're about due to leave now."

"And that sheet of silver up there in the north, Mister Channing?"

"That's a deposit," he said, gazing toward it.

"A deposit? A deposit of what?"

"Potash . . . borax . . . some salt," he said casually.

"Is there any gold around here, Mister Channing?" asked the girl with interest.

"Gold!" he said with a snort. "That's all most folks who come to the desert think of . . . just gold, gold, gold. Why, there's more silver than gold. And hundreds of other things. There's a man down below the line in Arizona who has a soap mine. He sends that soap clear to India because the Hindus, or whatever they are, won't use soap with grease in it. You'll see plenty of gold in Bandburg from the Yellow Daisy glory hole, but that isn't all they find in this country."

He appeared so vindictive about it that she forbore questioning him further. They walked back to the cabin in the twilight. He took the tarpaulin and a blanket and spread them for himself behind some trees.

"If there should be . . . anything bother you in the night, call me," he told her. "I'm a light sleeper. You better get all the sleep you can for we've got another hard ride tomorrow," he added almost gruffly.

Hope retired to the cabin after bidding him good night. She was tired, but sleep did not come readily. It was still rather warm in the cabin and she left the door open.

She slept fitfully. Once when she woke and looked through the door at a patch of sky alive with stars, she saw the unmistakable form of Channing on the ridge, and knew he was keeping vigil.

Chapter Fifteen

When Hope woke in the morning, she heard Channing singing. He was not singing opera this time, but humming homely ditties of the cow camps and other native airs. She was not so much interested in the quaint wording of the songs as in his voice, which was undoubtedly an excellent tenor.

The sun was rising when Hope came out of the cabin and greeted him. He barely nodded to her in response, and she felt piqued, but she tossed her head and went to the overflowing spring for water. On her way back she stopped near him. He was bending over the little fire where he was getting breakfast. His hat was off and she noted that the luxuriant, copper-colored hair was combed. Finally he looked up inquiringly.

"I see your hair is combed," she remarked, pushing back her own tousled strands.

His face broke into an amiable grin. "You wouldn't think of using my comb, would you, ma'am?"

"I might, if it were offered to me."

He went to his coat and took the comb from an inside pocket, handing it to her gravely. "I haven't got a looking glass, ma'am."

"I'll try to make out without one," said Hope, and retreated into the cabin.

I must be a sight, she thought. Well, what difference does it make? Nobody around but him, and he doesn't care, and I wouldn't care if he did. But she took a great deal of care with her hair, just the same. At breakfast she asked him why the place was called Ghost Wash.

"Man died of thirst within twenty feet of that water hole," he explained. "The old desert rats think his ghost walks here."

"The rats here must be quite smart, if they can think about such things," said Hope.

"We call an old prospector a desert rat," Channing replied smoothly.

"I believe I saw the ghost walking on the ridge last night," Hope observed quietly.

He looked at her quickly. "Didn't you sleep, ma'am?"

"Did you?" she parried.

He shrugged and went on eating.

"I bet you stayed up all night," she accused. "Do you think they will come after us here?"

"Dunno. That outfit doesn't know the desert any too well . . . that is, this part right in here. They're better acquainted with the southern part where the towns are."

"But . . . Mendicott knows it all, does he not?"

Channing scowled. "Miss Farman, you'd make a good lady lawyer if there is any such thing."

Hope's laugh echoed in the cabin. "Mister Channing, you have a way of ignoring questions that answers them," she said lightly. "But I certainly have learned lots about the desert from you. How long have you been in this country?"

"I was born here," he said simply.

Something in his tone caused her to look at him quickly. Was he proud or ashamed of the fact? Or was he reproving her in some way? There were many times when he was too deep for her, and that made him all the more interesting.

After breakfast Hope attended to the dishes while he packed the sacks. When everything was packed away, he stood up. The sunlight grew fainter and he looked quickly at the sky.

"Dog gone!" he exclaimed. "We're in for a storm."

Hope looked up and saw a large black cloud riding down from the north. Elsewhere the sky was clear.

"I guess it'll only be a shower," she remarked.

"That's all," he said. "Just a shower, ma'am. I'll have to tie the jack."

He left and came back shortly leading the burro. He tied the little animal behind the cabin where there was a shelter roof.

"I thought you said that animal could take care of itself," said Hope.

He looked at her curiously, started to reply, changed his mind, and hurriedly carried the packs, saddles, bedroll, and bridles into the cabin.

"Any burro's liable to stray in a storm," he said when he had finished. "I don't want to have to go out and hunt him up. It's natural with 'em."

The huge, black cloud raced down upon them, obscuring the sun. The desert took on a weird, saffron-tinted haze, and then darkened. They stood in the little green plot before the cabin watching. Hope looked at the sides of the ridge that formed a crescent about the dry lakebed and saw that they were corrugated. There were deep gullies leading into the wash. The storm signals reminded her of the fact that there was water in the draws and dry riverbeds of the desert at times.

It grew darker rapidly as the cloud came overhead. Then the storm broke. There were no preliminaries—only a very short period of sprinkling. As they stepped back into the cabin, the heavens opened and the world was suddenly gray and filled with water. The rain came in a deluge. In a very short interval the water was rushing down the sides of the ridge and into the gullies leading to the lakebed. Another interval and these gullies were roaring torrents, pouring into the lake that began slowly, almost imperceptibly to rise.

Hope had heard of the wild ferocity of the sudden storms occurring in the desert. She was seeing one for the first time. Its violence amazed and appalled her. It was a veritable cloudburst. She looked at Channing, who grinned at her. "Nice little shower!"

he shouted above the uproar of rushing water and pound of the deluge on the roof.

"How long will it last?" she called.

He threw up a hand in a gesture signifying that he didn't know.

The flood now came racing down past the cabin. The horses were plunging about, restricted by their hobbles. Channing watched them through the doorway. Hope went to one of the windows and looked down into the wash. She estimated there was a foot or more of water in the lakebed. She could hardly believe what she saw with her own eyes; it was an extraordinary contrast to the heat and customary aridity. In a remarkably short time the downpour began to slacken, the rain fell with less force. And then, as if by magic, it ceased.

They went out on the sodden grass plot. The cloud rolled on and the sun shone again on the desert. The air was cool, stimulating—amazingly clear. The mountains to westward seemed miles nearer and were sharply outlined against a cloudless sky. There was a haze in the south where the storm was sweeping on. Water still poured into the wash from the gullies, but this stopped by the time they were ready to start. It was a lake of white.

They rode around the wash below the ridge and were nearly at its lower end when Channing, looking back, cried out in surprise. Hope looked back and saw three horsemen on the other side of the wash. They were making gestures that she took to be hostile. She looked askance at Channing. He was frowning, urging the burro to a faster pace. She knew by his look and manner that the three riders were pursuing them. That could mean but one thing. Some of the outlaws had discovered their means of escape and had taken the trail.

She looked again across the wash and saw an interesting sight. One of the men had pushed into the lake. His horse slipped and fell, sending its rider headlong into the water with its white surface of alkali. He got to his feet and made his way back out of the wash, the horse following him. Hope could see him gesticulating to the others who were pointing around the wash.

She heard Channing indulge in a short laugh. "They want to go around and he wants to cut across," said Channing. "I hope he does. Lot he knows about that stuff. It's slippery as greased ice in there."

The two mounted men continued to argue with the man on foot, and the latter finally stepped into the wash and slowly started across. The water was about up to his knees. He made slow progress but would be in range of the fugitives before the others, if he intended to shoot. The others proceeded to gallop around the wash.

Channing turned toward the ridge, driving the burro as fast as he could, which was at a fast walk. Major swung in behind his master with Hope. When they had climbed a gully a short distance up the slope of the ridge, they found a projection of the hard, baked earth. Channing drove the burro in behind this. He got down and swiftly removed the packs and pack saddle. Then he mounted and led the way back down the ridge.

"We may have to run for it!" he called to Hope. "If we do, just hold on as tight as you can and Major'll carry you."

The two riders coming around the draw were almost in range. The man who was crossing through the water was about a third of the way across. The fugitives had to make the lower end of the ridge ahead of the two horsemen to gain the open desert, for the sides of the ridge here were too steep for their horses to scale. Channing put the spurs to his mount and the horse broke into a gallop. Hope's horse did likewise, and she clung to the saddle horn as they dashed for the end of the ridge. Then they heard the sharp reports of guns and lead whistled over their heads. The shots came from the man in the wash. Hope's heart was in her throat as she saw Channing look across at the man and draw his gun. There was something about the man in the wash that struck her as familiar. She looked fixedly at the big form outlined against the white surface of the lake and started with surprise. It was Brood, or else she was very much mistaken.

If it was Brood, why wasn't he at the ranch trying to close the deal for its sale? The man in the wash stopped shooting and put a hand across his eyes as if dazed. She heard Channing laugh again.

"He's going snow-blind!" he cried.

Hope saw that this might be the case. The sun was dazzling white on the surface of the lake, whiter and more brilliant than it could be shining on snow. She saw the man stop and start to grope about. There was no further danger to be expected from him then. But the other two horsemen were coming around the lower end of the wash at a furious pace. Channing looked back at Hope.

"Hold him in!" he shouted, checking his horse until the girl could get a tight rein on Major. "Hold him back all you can."

Then while Hope held the horse she was riding with all her strength, Channing spurred his mount and dashed ahead. She saw flecks of white float back from the oncoming riders and the dull echoes of shots came to her. Then she saw Channing veer to the left. His right hand and arm went out and his gun spoke—once, twice, three times. Hope gasped as one of the approaching riders lurched in his saddle, then fell forward on his horse's neck and was thrown to the ground. He lay motionlessly while the horse fled with reins flying. The other rider checked his pace quickly, turned, firing as he did so, and started to retreat. Channing shot three times more and the fleeing rider forced his horse to a mad gallop, running around the wash.

Hope had brought Major almost to a stop. She could see the man in the wash standing helplessly, trying to shade his eyes from the terrific glare of the sun on the white surface of the water. She heard Channing calling to her and saw him beckoning. She rode swiftly toward him.

"We'll leave the burro and hit for Bandburg," he told her, setting a stiff pace.

When they reached the end of the ridge, she looked back and caught a glimpse of the hostile rider dismounting at the edge of the wash on the farther side. Evidently he was going into the wash to bring out Brood, or whoever it might be, who was helpless.

They rode around the end of the ridge and Channing headed east toward a low range of black hills. They reached these in an hour and took a path that led across them. On the east side of the hills they again turned south, preceding at a sharp trot.

"We'll get to Bandburg quicker without having to bother with the jack," Channing told her.

Hope nodded in reply. She was sore from the ride of the day before, and the swift riding had been a hardship. Again she sweltered and gasped in the intense heat of the desert. Channing continually twisted in his saddle to look back. His face was grim, his eyes narrowed. The girl wondered if he had killed the man who had been shot from his horse. She shuddered at the recollection of Channing's merciless marksmanship. This, then, was the way of these wild spirits. It did little good to take into consideration the fact that he had shot while protecting her escape. She suspected that the time required to get the man out of the wash, and for the two to ascertain how badly their companion had been hurt, would give Channing and herself sufficient of a start to enable them to reach Bandburg before they could be overtaken. She did not want to see another gun battle.

Shortly after noon they came to an oasis in the desert. There was little shade, and very little green about the spring, but there was water. Channing stopped here.

"We'll water the horses and eat a cold bite," he said. Then he laughed. "I mean we'll water the horses," he amended. "We won't eat no cold bite because it's in the pack sacks, and they're a piece behind."

"Will you get them back?" she asked. "And how about the burro?"

"Maybe I'll pick 'em up later. The jack'll mosey along into Bandburg. He knows enough for that."

When they were ready to resume the journey, he turned to her. "I ain't asking you to promise anything, Miss Farman," he said seriously, "but you don't need to say any more about all this than you want to. I mean about our getting away up there and what's happened afterward."

"You mean you don't want me to tell Uncle when I see him?"

"No, I don't mean that. I don't care what you tell your uncle. I mean . . . when we get to Bandburg. You don't have to promise not to say anything, and I don't know as if it'd make much difference. Well, we'll let it go at that."

"I'll say nothing to anyone except my uncle," she promised.

She thought he favored her with a look of admiration as he helped her into the saddle, but she wasn't sure.

Late in the afternoon they crossed a granite ridge and dropped down into the desert mining town of Bandburg.

Chapter Sixteen

Bandburg was a typical boom camp, although it had one very well-established mine, the Yellow Daisy. It was built on the side of a barren hill and its one main street was steep and short, but studded with buildings on either side. Cabins and shacks and tents perched upon the side of the hill above the street, and also below it. The street was thronged and a strange medley of sound came from the numerous resorts that lined the thoroughfare. Channing led the way along the side of the hill below the street until he reached its upper end. He pointed out the famous Yellow Daisy, above town, where the sun struck saffron gleams from the sides of a great hole in the hill.

"They're taking out ten million in gold up there," he told her.

At the upper end of the street they rode up to it, crossed it, and picked their way between cabins and shacks till they reached one lone cabin that was higher on the hillside than any of the others. Here he reined in his horse and spoke to her in a low, earnest voice.

"I'm bringing you to the one place in Bandburg where I'm sure you'll be safe, Miss Farman. You can depend upon being safe here till I come back for you." He dismounted and started for the door of the cabin. "I reckon Lillian's still asleep, but we'll sure have to wake her up."

Before he had a chance to rap on the door, however, it was opened and a flaxen-haired girl appeared. Hope saw that she looked at her at once. The girl was pretty, and had baby-blue eyes. She was larger than Hope and wore a blue gingham dress with a blue ribbon band around her head.

"Hello, Lillian," Channing greeted. "I've brought you a guest."

"Where did you pick her up?" the girl demanded in a tone that Hope thought carried a note of resentment.

"She's Hope Farman, Nate Farman's niece," said Channing. "She got lost on the desert and I happened along. I'm going to take her home an' I'd like to leave her here for a little spell while I look around because I know she'll be safe here."

"Oh, she'll be safe enough," said Lillian, looking at Hope suspiciously.

Channing helped Hope dismount and walked with her to the cabin door. Lillian retreated, and they entered.

"This is Miss Lillian Bell, Miss Farman," Channing introduced.

Hope held out her hand and smiled. Lillian took it, looking at her keenly, then dropped the hand and closed the door. "I was just getting breakfast," she said. "I suppose you folks want to eat. Take off your hat an' make yourself at home, Channing . . . you're no stranger here."

Channing laughed easily. "No, I reckon not, Lillian. But I can't stay to hang on the feedbag. I've got to take care of the horses and then I've got some important business to tend to that won't wait. But I take it Miss Farman is starved, so you better feed her."

"I'll fix her up if she can stand ham and eggs and my biscuits," said the girl, staring again at Hope. "You look as if you'd been lost on the desert about a month."

"Well now, wait a bit, Lillian," Channing put in as Hope was about to reply. "I just told you that to ease the thing along plausible-like at the start. Miss Farman's had quite an experience. She's been in the mountains as well as the desert. Rode all day yesterday and today. She can tell you what she wants to about it. But I got to get going. I'll be back later." He stepped to the door and turned with his hand on the knob. "Lillian's all right," he said to Hope. "You wait here till I get back." With that and a word of leave-taking to Lillian, he departed.

Lillian surveyed Hope for several moments and noted the coat she was holding in her hand.

"Guess it was pretty warm on the desert," she said. "And from the looks of your face and hands, you're not used to it. Put your coat in my bedroom, there," she said, pointing to an open door at one end of the cabin. "And come out to the kitchen and wash up. Then you better put on some cold cream and cocoa butter. You'll find everything on my dresser." She smiled, showing white even teeth, and from that moment Hope liked her, but there was a peculiar, tired look in Lillian's eyes.

She did as Lillian told her, after thanking her and explaining that she was new in the country.

"Well, you've had some initiation, I'll say," Lillian vouchsafed, going into the kitchen at the other end of the cabin.

The odor of cooking food was delicious in Hope's nostrils. She washed and laved her face, hands, and arms, which were terribly sunburned, with the cocoa butter, after Lillian had had her bathe them in witch hazel. By the time she was through, the meal was ready.

They sat down to table in the commodious main room of the cabin. It was richly furnished, Hope noted. There was a large divan, overstuffed chairs, a player piano, a phonograph, a magnificent sideboard, littered with cut glass, and a china cabinet with every shelf full. There were original oil paintings on the walls, too, and a thick, expensive rug on the floor.

"You have a very nice place here, Miss Bell," Hope volunteered.

"It's about all I have got," she said, "and don't call me anything but Lillian. How far'd you come today?"

Hope told her and she opened her eyes wide. Then she poured the coffee. "That's a funny place to come from," she observed. "Nothing out that way. And the day before?"

"From Arsenic Spring," replied Hope

Lillian put down the coffee pot. "You and Channing had some ride."

Hope flushed. "He was very kind to me," she said with spirit.

"Oh, that's all right," said the girl. "I know Channing. He's a good sort. He's been good to me many a time. Where'd he find you . . . where'd you folks start from, anyway?"

Hope hesitated. She did not know whether to tell or not. She had given her promise to Channing not to talk to anyone except her uncle, but he had said she could tell Lillian what she wished.

"That's all right, dearie," said Lillian. "You don't have to spill anything to me. You're welcome here as a friend of Channing's, and I'll look after you. Eat a good breakfast and then maybe you'll want to get a wink of sleep. He may want to take you back to the ranch tonight."

"It isn't that I don't want to tell you anything," said Hope quickly, "but I don't know what to tell and what not to tell. He might . . . "

"Then keep mum," said Lillian with a wise look that made Hope flush again. "You can trust me, and the whole camp knows that." The tone and the look that caused Hope to flush prompted her to speak.

"Mister Channing rescued me from an outlaw who took me from my uncle's ranch," she said quickly. "That's how we came to be riding so . . . so far."

Lillian put down her knife and fork. "From an outlaw? Took you from your uncle's ranch? It wasn't . . . it couldn't be . . . ?"

But Hope anticipated her question and nodded.

Lillian indulged in a low whistle and stared at her. "Did he have you up at his place in the mountains?" she asked in a tone of disbelief.

Again Hope nodded, and the other girl saw she was truthful in the matter.

"Well, Channing's the boy who could do it," she said with conviction. "Took you out of there, huh? You know what?" She leaned toward Hope and tapped the table with her fingertips. "Channing's the only man in these parts that Mendicott's got any respect for, and that's a statement."

"Why . . . why does he respect him so?" Hope asked.

"Because he's got just about as many friends as Mendicott has, that's why," answered Lillian forcefully. "And because Mendicott don't know but what he's just as fast and accurate with a six-gun as he is himself, that's why."

"Would Mendicott have a man shot down in cold blood because he found him stealing food and trying to get away?" Hope asked. She was still doubtful on this point, despite what Channing had told her.

"Would he? I'll say he would. He'd have him drawn and quartered, if he felt like it. Listen, girlie, Mendicott's bad . . . he's bad! And he's a fiend for cleverness. He's slick as Old Nick himself. Did he treat you all right?"

"Yes," Hope replied, "except that he was going to put me on bread and water once."

"What for?" asked Lillian.

"Well, Lillian, to explain that, I'd have to tell just what all the trouble is about, and something . . . well, I . . . "

"Don't tell it," Lillian broke in. "But is that what Channing's working on now?"

"Yes, I am quite sure that it is."

"Then don't tell it," warned Lillian. "Channing wouldn't want even me to know what he was up to. Channing's smart, too."

"Is Mister Channing an . . . an outlaw, too?" asked Hope breathlessly.

Lillian looked at her speculatively. "That's a hard word, child. Channing says words are what you make 'em, and I guess he's right so far's that word's concerned. There's so many ways you can be an outlaw. Why, I guess we're all outlaws. Oh, I'm not talking about you, but the rest of us would have a hard squeeze getting by that word. Let me tell you this. Channing's all right. He's square if he does pack a fast gun and a slippery rep."

"My uncle thinks . . . thought he was just a derelict or a . . . a tramp."

"A tramp? Ha, ha, ha. Channing a tramp? Say, if Channing's a tramp, then I'm a great singer."

"Mister Channing has a very good voice," she told the other with a smile.

Lillian frowned. "Was he singing for you?" she asked.

"Oh, not for me. But he was singing a little, and I couldn't help but hear him. He was singing opera once, too."

Lillian leaned back in her chair and looked down at her plate. "I'm the one that taught him," she said. "I sing in the Bluebird dance hall, and I know a little opera and have lots more of it on that phonograph. I make my money singing songs for a lot of roughnecks, and in a dance hall, at that, but here I have . . . music." She rose from her chair quickly. "We'll do the dishes and then I'm going to fix you a bath and get you out some clean clothes. Oh, yes, I am, so don't shake your head. I have lots of water up here. It's in a barrel outside with a pipe that runs right into the tub. And you can wear my clothes in a pinch."

Hope did as directed, and with the arrival of the twilight she was bathed and dressed in a fresh, clean frock, and felt much better. Lillian, too, had dressed and put on her hat.

"Listen, girlie, I'm going downtown for a while. I don't have to go to work till nine, if I don't want to, and I won't want to tonight. You stick around, and if Channing comes before I get back, tell him I dropped in at the Bluebird to tell 'em I'd be late. Don't worry. There won't nobody come snooping around here. They know better."

When Lillian had gone, Hope sat before the open door of the cabin and looked down on the town. She could see the main street plainly and the crowds of roughly dressed men fascinated her. She was seeing a gold camp in the raw, she thought to herself with a thrill.

The twilight was drawing its blue veil over the desert when she saw two men ride into the upper end of the street. One of them she recognized instantly. It was Brood. Whether they were two of the three men who had been pursuing Channing and herself, or not, didn't matter so much as the fact that Brood was in town. If he saw Channing—if he saw Channing before Channing saw him . . .

Hope rose and paced the room. She knew Channing should be warned. Very likely he wouldn't want Brood to see him. And— what was more probable—it might be that Channing's life was in danger from Brood. She knew Brood hated Channing. She believed he was the man who had entered the wash. He had been shooting at them, then. He might shoot on sight.

The more she thought of it, the more nervous Hope became. She wished Lillian would return. The twilight was gathering fast. Brood was in town and Channing had to be warned. She repeated this over and over again.

Finally she slipped on a coat and hat of Lillian's, closed the cabin door, and stole down toward the street.

Chapter Seventeen

It was nearly dark when Hope gained the street. The thoroughfare was thronged with a motley crew of miners, prospectors, promoters, gamblers, teamsters, engineers, and other men in the rough that go to make up the population of a successful gold camp in its early stages of development. It was lighted only by the beams that shone from the windows of stores, cafés, assay offices, and resorts. The mixture of sound was indescribable—a babble of voices, bursts of loud laughter, shouts and yells and jeers; the rumble of heavy ore wagons, cracking of drivers' whips, curses and cries; the jangling of pianos and screeching of phonographs, and the barking of dogs. There was movement everywhere. Dust from the street clouded the air. Men swore and spat and talked of gold. Everywhere one could hear it—this talk of gold.

"My assay shows fifteen hun'erd to the ton to start."

"Rich as the Yellow Daisy or I'm a lizard."

Men stood in groups listening to accounts of fresh finds, with the narrator always keeping the exact location veiled. Burros wandered into the street, scurrying before the horses of the ore wagons. There were frequent commotions when men fought and others crowded around to cheer and shout profane advice. It was all a reversion to the primitive.

Hope, swallowed and jostled by the milling, moving throngs, had not the slightest idea where to find Channing. The street, comparatively quiet in the late afternoon when they had arrived, now was a veritable maëlstrom of perspiring, swearing masculinity. She was tempted to turn back. Her mission seemed so futile. But her conviction that Brood's presence in the town portended trouble for her champion spurred her on and bolstered up her failing courage. Wasn't Channing there on her account? Wasn't he, even then, engaged on a mission that had to do with the interests of her uncle and herself? She suspected he had gone to see the notary to learn if he had been summoned to Rancho del Encanto. He might be in the notary's office at that minute. But where was she to find the notary? Channing and Brood might meet any minute. Her imagination—made more vivid by the events of the past few days—pictured all sorts of dire consequences if this meeting came about. She saw a man attired in corduroy and high boots who looked reliable. He was standing at the edge of one of the short stretches of sidewalk. She approached him as bravely as possible.

"Could you tell me where I can find the notary?"

He looked at her in surprise, then touched his hat. "Right down the street in the little white office this side of the hotel," he answered politely.

She thanked him and moved away. As she proceeded down the street, she kept a strict look-out for either Channing or Brood. She wanted to see the former, but she did not want Brood to see her. She suddenly realized that she herself was in danger. What could she expect if Brood were to see her? Recapture and return to the rendezvous of the outlaws? Very probable. She became more wary.

She saw the hotel ahead. It was one of the few buildings two stories high. And she had no trouble finding the little white office. But it was dark and locked! Hope turned away at a loss as to what to do next. It was next to impossible to continue on the street, and she could only hope to meet Channing there by the merest chance. Her chance of meeting Brood was equally as good. She looked into a resort or two, through the windows and doors, and realized it would be rank folly to go inside any of them and ask for him. Then she bethought herself of Lillian Bell and the things she had told her. The girl had said she sang at the Bluebird dance hall. She looked around. It shouldn't be difficult to find the place; it must be large if it had singers. She decided to walk up the other side of the street and look for it.

Curiously enough, Hope did not stop to consider that there was anything unusual in her search, or in being the guest of the girl, Lillian. Her gentle sensibilities had been somewhat numbed by her experiences. The little white house in Connecticut, with its green shutters, its flowers and trees and stone fence, seemed far away. Her life there seemed some subtle dream of a vague past. The change in environment was working a change in her trend of reasoning. She felt like a different girl—an individual with whom she was none too well acquainted. These things ran in her mind at random as she proceeded to cross the street and walk up the other side. She had not gone half the way back when she saw a big sign over a wide sidewalk bearing the word composing the name of the dance hall for which she was looking. But when she reached it she found it was not only a dance hall but a drinking and gambling resort as well. The bar and tables where games of chance were in progress were in the front of the building, which was packed with male patrons, and the dance floor evidently was in the rear. She couldn't see it, but she could hear strains of music coming from beyond where the crowd was congregated.

She hesitated before the wide open door. Should she go in and ask for Lillian? What if Lillian were not there? It was even probable that the girl had attended to her business and gone back to the cabin on the hill. It was possible Channing had gone back, too. As Hope stood at one side of the door, hesitating about going in and considering the other angles of the matter, a fight suddenly started inside. She stared breathlessly as she saw two men strike out, others push back and quickly form a ring about the combatants, shutting off her view. The place was in an uproar, and she started away. To go in there after what she had seen was impossible. She would return to the cabin, and, if she found no one there. she would wait. It was all she could do. She did not understand the ways of this wild camp, or how to act with men she might meet.

She felt a hand on her left arm and in another instant was whirled about. "I thought so," came a thick voice she recognized instantly with a sinking of the heart. It was Brood. "Takin' in the sights?" he demanded with a leer. "Just lookin' around?"

"Get away from me!" she commanded, desperate with fear and the desire to get back to the cabin on the hill. "Let go of my arm, do you hear me? I'll appeal to these men on the street if you don't."

"Lot of good that would do you," said Brood with an evil smile. "Where's your man? Run away an' left you? That wasn't very nice."

Hope's eyes blazed with anger. She sensed in that moment of rage how men could sometimes kill in the wink of an eye, without premeditation. "You are a vile beast!" she cried. "You are worse than a beast. Are you going to let me go? If you don't, I'll not try to conceal who you are or what you are."

"You're not goin' till we have a little talk," he said, his face darkening. "An' it won't do you any good to get frisky here. There are friends of our bunch right here close. You might as well take it easy, or I'll hustle you back where you came from without waiting to talk." He did not release his hold on her arm.

Hope was thinking fast, her face set and white. "Can't we talk without you pinching my arm?" she asked in as steady a voice as she could muster.

"Oh, that's all right . . . but don't try to get away," he said, releasing his hold. "We'll just walk around behind the Bluebird where we can talk in private."

He motioned to a narrow, dark space between the big resort and the building next to it. Hope looked and knew instantly that everything would be lost if she went with him. He would surely overpower her, take her somewhere, and hide her until he figured he could safely return her to Mendicott. She took two steps toward the opening between the buildings, then she turned in a flash and ran up the street. But it was too crowded for running. She hadn't gone five yards before the grip was on her arm again and her progress halted. She heard Brood laugh and tried to cry out. The lights from the windows and the forms about her swam. Her free hand went to her throat. Then Brood's grasp was loosened.

"What's going on?"

Her senses returned to normal as she heard the voice. She saw the tall form of Channing confronting Brood, who was swearing in inarticulate gutturals.

"What were you doing with that girl?" Channing asked sternly.

"Oh, you came back for her, eh?" sneered Brood. "You'll get yours for this, you double-crosser!"

Channing pushed him away with his left hand, then his right shot out, caught Brood fully on the jaw, and sent him sprawling into the dust of the street. The crowd yelled, and Hope was pushed into the front of a ring of excited spectators that quickly formed. Brood twisted on his left side in the street. Hope could see his features contorted in a fierce snarl of rage. Channing stepped back and looked around. In that instant Brood's right hand darted to his gun. Hope cried out, but Channing had moved like a flash. There was a spurt of red at his right hip and Brood fell back. Then Channing stepped to her, took her arm, and led her hurriedly through the crowd.

They hurried up the street without speaking, although many people nodded or spoke to Channing. He directed their course to the cabin on the hill. Hope saw a light in the cabin and realized that Lillian had returned and found her absent. Channing threw open the door and pushed her inside. He came in after her and shut the door. Lillian was standing by the table with her hat on. She evidently had just put down the lamp, as she held a cloth in her hand and the nickel base of the lamp shone as if it had been polished.

"How'd she get out?" Channing asked angrily, addressing Lillian.

"I don't know, unless she walked out by her lonesome," replied Lillian. "I left her here because I had to tell the boss I might be down late."

"I thought I told you to stay here," Channing said sternly to Hope.

"I saw Brood and another man ride into town . . ." Hope began.

"Don't you know it's dangerous for you to be running around this town?" he interrupted harshly. "What do you suppose my idea was in bringing you up here?"

"I suppose you thought I would be safe here," Hope replied coolly, raising her head high. "When I saw Brood come into town, I thought it might mean danger to you and I . . . I went to . . . to warn you."

Channing's jaw dropped. He looked at her steadily for several moments. "You . . . went out in that mob to warn me?" he stammered, incredulous.

Hope nodded. "I knew there'd be trouble if you and Brood met, and I thought there might he a chance of his seeing you first."

Channing looked around with a vacant expression on his face. Then he recovered himself and frowned. "See that she doesn't get out again," he said to Lillian. Then he took his departure.

Hope saw the door close after him. She stepped to the divan, dropped upon it, and burst into tears.

Lillian stared at her, holding the cloth in her hands foolishly. "My heavens," she muttered, as if in wonder. "Do they still make 'em that way?" She put down the cloth, went over to the divan, and gathered Hope into her arms.

Chapter Eighteen

Outside the cabin on the steep slope of the hill, Channing stood looking out over the lights of the town to the shadowy desert. His legs were braced well apart and his hands rested on his hips. His face was set and serious and a reminiscent light played in his eyes, clouded for a moment, then shot forth in a gleam. He turned and looked at the cabin, then he strode off down the hill. He walked down the street, keeping an eye to the left and right, and watching the other side of the street. Thus he saw the glitter of a nickeled shield before the wearer saw him. He stopped the deputy with a touch on the arm.

"Looking for me?" he asked in an affected drawl.

"Not right now," was the answer. "I see you've been at it again."

The deputy, a short, thick-set man with a red face, sandy mustache, and brown eyes, moved back a pace

"What of it?" Channing flared. "He drew first. Plenty of people saw him. He can be thankful I didn't bore him for keeps."

"Oh, he'll get out of it all right," said the deputy with a wry smile. "I heard he drew first. But you hit him, I understand. Well, you fellows can fight it out among yourselves. I got a hard enough job as it is. Who was the skirt?"

"That don't matter," answered Channing. "There's more to this than a skirt, Adams. Have you been called out of town anywhere lately?"

"Not lately . . . no," replied Adams. "Not in a month. There's no place around here to be called to. Why . . . where would I be called?"

"I dunno," Channing returned. "But you might be called somewhere. How long will it be before Brood can get around to his devilment again?"

"Two, three weeks . . . maybe a month," replied Adams. "Going to be waiting for him?"

"I'm not going to be hot-footing it out of the country because I'm scared of him," said Channing with a light laugh. "See you again."

"I wouldn't be a bit surprised if you did," the deputy muttered in an undertone as Channing moved away. He stared after him until he was lost in the crowd.

Channing kept on down the street, continuing to be just as alert as when he had started out. At the lower end of the street he stopped before a small building and peered in through the window. There was no one in the front room, but he could see a light in a rear room. He knocked sharply at the door.

A man came out, holding a lamp over his head. He made sure of the identity of his visitor before he unlocked the door and opened it.

"What you got now, Channing?" he queried in a squeaky voice as he stepped back. He was an old man, white of hair and mustache, with watery blue eyes.

"Haven't got a thing, Pap," said Channing cheerily. "Fact is, I want something."

"Well, I haven't got much," the other quavered as he shut the door. "You been hittin' the stud too hard?"

"You never saw me hard up yet, Pap," Channing answered laughingly. "And you never heard of me going clean broke at stud . . . not clean broke, Pap. I don't want to borrow any money. Maybe we better slip in the back room to talk, eh, Pap?"

"If you want to . . . yes. I guess it'll be all right."

They moved into the rear room that was an assay workshop. Channing shut the door leading to the front room and dropped into a chair. The old assayer sat down at a table where he was eating his supper.

"Well, what is it, boy?" he asked, looking at Channing shrewdly.

Channing leaned forward. "Say, Pap, do I look like a danged fool?"

The old man did not appear surprised. He seemed to ponder the question in all seriousness, studying his visitor the while. "Not right offhand, you don't," he said finally, "but you never can tell. What you been up to now? You still in with that hell hound . . . ?"

Channing interrupted him by holding up a hand. "That wasn't a fair question, nohow, Pap. It doesn't give you a lead as to what I'm driving at and it wouldn't do you any good if it did. Pap, I want some information."

"I've been in these hills a long time, young man."

"These ain't hills," Channing scoffed. "They're just humus in the desert. Say, Pap, is the Yellow Daisy petering out?"

The old man put down his knife and fork and wiped his hands on a bandanna handkerchief he had in his lap. He looked at Channing intently. "Whatever give you that idear?" he asked.

"A question doesn't answer a question 'cept on rare occasions, Pap. Is the glory hole losing her glory?"

"I thought you wanted to consult me professionally," said the assayer with a scowl.

"I do," said Channing with a nod.

"I can't discuss properties except with their owners or officials connected with them," said the assayer. "You ought to know that."

"I do. I own two shares of stock in the Yellow Daisy. Won 'em in a game with Turner. You know I know the big guns, Turner and Wescott, pretty well. Two shares aren't worth so much, but they ought to get this information for me. Aren't I entitled to know, Pap?"

"Two shares is pretty thin ice to stand on in a case like this," was the reply. "You know what it would start to have the news that the Yellow Daisy was giving in get around?"

"I know, Pap," said Channing with a smile, "but it isn't going to get around. Not from me, anyway. Listen, Pap, I want this here information for my own sweet self and nobody else. I won't tell a soul. You know me, Pap, and you know there's one thing I don't do. I don't lie."

"It's not ethics," grumbled the assayer. "You shouldn't put me up against it like this just because I'm assaying the samples from up there. I like you, all right, but . . . what do you want this information for?"

"May never have the least use for it," said Channing. "I know pretty well how things stand . . . Turner and Wescott hinted some to me . . . but I've got to be sure. And when I'm sure, I'm going to ask you to do me another big favor, Pap. I'll have to keep my word to make sure you'll do me this other favor, don't you see? And I've done you a turn or two in the past."

"You saved my life on the desert, dang you!" the old man blurted out. "An' there's where you've got me."

"Is she petering out, Pap?"

"She's getting a little thin," the old man confessed, lowering his voice.

"She's gutted!" exclaimed Channing as the assayer held up a hand. "How long will she last, Pap?"

"Two, three months, maybe. An' they might run into something new."

"Not on the record of all glory holes, Pap," said Channing. "When a glory hole loses her glory, she's gone. Now, Pap, when she's gone for certain, you send word to me. Remember that. They'll be no harm in sending word to me because everybody else is going to know it. Only I want to know it as soon as anybody else, understand?"

The assayer nodded with a twinkle in his eye. "Little before wouldn't hurt, I take it. Where'll you be?"

"At Nate Farman's Rancho del Encanto across the desert west of here," replied Channing. "Don't forget the place and don't forget to send word. I'll pay the man that brings it. You won't forget?"

"I can still remember occasionally," grunted the old man. "You'll be there sure? What you doing over there?"

"Pap," said Channing, rising with a short laugh, "it's a big country . . . all full of cactus."

The assayer followed him into the other room and let him out with another admonition not to let a word of what he had learned about the Yellow Daisy leak out. Channing promised faithfully and shook the old man's hand.

Channing walked back up the street thoughtfully. He looked into the various resorts as he proceeded, and entered some. In this way he came finally to the Bluebird and here he entered, also. He moved casually about among the tables where patrons were gambling, and then scanned the faces of the men at the bar, reflected in the mirror. He caught a glimpse of a man at the lower end and strolled over to him.

"Hello, Morton."

The man he addressed swung around with a startled look. He was lean, unshaven, dressed in cowpuncher garb.

"I was wondering if I could have a word with you," said Channing easily. "Out back here where it's quiet, say."

"I know why," answered the other in a surly tone. "I ain't lookin' for you."

"But you were," drawled out Channing. "You were looking for me this morning out at Ghost Wash. I reckon we better have that little talk, Morton."

The other's face paled. "What do you want to talk to me about?" he asked suspiciously.

"Does it make any difference?" demanded Channing coldly.

"It might. I don't aim to take any chances after you plugging Brood."

"It was his own fault, Morton. You aren't likely to get hurt if you keep hold of your ball of yarn and don't try to play with the cat. Are you coming?"

The man hesitated, but after a long look at Channing he put down his glass and walked with him across the dance floor to a rear door that led out on a little porch with a railing around it and steps leading to the ground.

Channing sat on the railing, swinging a leg. "Morton, how did you three happen along out there at Ghost Wash?"

"Brood knew how you got out," was the sullen reply. "We went around by the trail and picked up your tracks. All we did was foller 'em. Brood's a good trailer."

"So I've heard," Channing admitted. "Was that man I shot badly hurt?"

"He's dead."

"Too bad. He didn't leave me any way out whatsoever. You can't shoot a man in the arm or some other soft spot when he's bobbing around on a horse. You're lucky to hit him at all. I knew that was Brood in the wash. When you figure on going back?"

"Dunno. Never, maybe. Mendicott'll be pretty sore."

"You better start back tonight," said Channing slowly.

"Eh? I will not."

Channing's right hand moved with incredible swiftness, and the starlight glinted on the dull metal of his gun. "I want to send a message to Mendicott," he said in the same low voice. "I want you to get it to him as fast as you can. I want you to light out for up there tonight. Understand?"

"You . . . you got the message wrote?" asked the other nervously.

"No. I'm going to tell it to you. You just tell Mendicott that I was in Bandburg, that I took Miss Farman out, and that I'm going to the Farman Ranch to stay. Understand? I'll repeat it." He repeated the message carefully several times and had the other repeat it after him. "Now," he said, getting off the railing, "you know what to do. You can tell Mendicott I shot that man and Brood. You can tell him anything you please. But you get there and you deliver that message. Understand? Do as I say and hurry up about it."

The man hastily went down the steps and faded into the shadows.

Channing walked back through the Bluebird and out to the street. He turned down the street and walked nearly to its lower end where there was a livery barn. He went in and gave an order to the barn man. As he came out, a rider galloped into the space before the barn. Channing whistled softly as he caught sight of the man's face in the starlight. It was the little driver from Rancho del Encanto—Jim Crossley.

Chapter Nineteen

Hope's torrent of tears gradually subsided as Lillian Bell held her and stared at the shaded lamp on the table. The older girl no longer seemed puzzled; there was a knowing look in her eyes, a dawning wonder and a hint of bitter resentment. But she patted Hope on the shoulder and spoke to her soothingly.

"You've got a good cry coming to you, girlie, so have it out. I wish I could do the same. But it wouldn't do me any good. It'll do you good, though, so don't you care."

Hope raised her head finally and dried her eyes. She smiled at the other girl. "I couldn't help it," she said slowly. "He seemed so . . . so angry. And he's really done a lot for me . . . for us. I should have known he could take care of himself and stayed here."

Lillian rose and went into her bedroom. When she returned, she was without her hat. She sat down in a chair opposite Hope and coolly lighted a cigarette.

"You don't know much about men, do you, honey?"

Hope flushed and looked at her dubiously.

"I mean men like the kind we've got out here," Lillian explained. "They're a queer bunch . . . the best of 'em. Some of 'em are plain scum and ain't worth considering. But the good ones have to be handled. Tell me what happened tonight."

Bit by bit Hope recounted her experience, omitting nothing, from the time she had left the cabin until she returned.

"Channing just naturally bored Brood to keep him out of the way," said Lillian. "Don't worry; he hasn't killed him. Channing would have to have it in for a man pretty bad to shoot him for keeps. But Brood's been meddling, I can see that. It don't pay to meddle in Channing's affairs."

"You know him very well?" asked Hope.

"Tolerably well. I got a funny job here, girlie. I sing at the Bluebird and I've got a pretty fair voice, if I do say it. It draws trade and packs the joint every night. I dance with the men, too, and get a percentage on what they buy. I make good money. That's why I'm here. But sometimes they get a little bold. Channing's sort of been my friend. He's sent several of those hombres on their way to new diggings to protect me. We're sort of . . . sort of . . . friends."

Hope saw a wistful look in the older girl's eyes. It was impossible not to understand that look. It betrayed Lillian's secret as much as so many words would have disclosed it. She loved Channing.

"I can't understand him," Hope said to relieve the silence, although she spoke the truth.

"You couldn't be expected to," said Lillian in something of a superior tone. "Channing's desert, that's what he is. He's as mum as a niggerhead cactus, usually. You can't tell what's going on in his mind. There's usually something up, though, when he starts to sing. Shows he's thinkin' hard about something, and he's liable to be mad. I'd hate to be a man and have Channing come after me with a gun . . . singing!"

"He trusts you absolutely," Hope observed.

"Why not?" said Lillian with a flash of her eyes. "I'm like a bank. I know lots and say nothing. I've done Channing a turn or two myself." She nodded as if in triumph.

Then Hope wondered if this girl resented the fact that Channing was helping her? Did she feel a subtle pang of jealousy? It was all absurd. But was it all so absurd? Hope could readily see how Lillian would certainly fall in love with Channing. This would be the case not alone because of Channing's personal appeal, his good looks and splendid physique, his air of mystery, and his quiet ways, but because he had befriended her where others had sought to annoy her. And it seemed to Hope that Lillian was the kind of girl that should naturally attract Channing, who had lived so long in the raw. She didn't want Lillian to think that she was in any way interested in Channing other than as her benefactor. "I guess Channing appreciates what you've done for him, Lillian," she said. "I know he likes you."

But as she spoke she remembered Channing's casual tone when he had mentioned the fact that the song had been taught him by a girl who sang in a dance hall.

"Oh, he likes me," said Lillian, waving her cigarette in a gesture that could mean anything. "But that's all."

"Maybe he loves you," Hope advanced.

Lillian blinked. "Say, girlie, I'm not kiddin' myself. I know a thing or two about men and a whole lot about Channing. He might fall for something like you, but for me . . . never. Channing hates the tinsel, and I live in it."

Hope was stunned. "Why, Lillian, there's no reason in the world that Mister Channing should fall for me, as you put it. I've never . . . why, I'm not his kind of people. I don't understand him or his . . . his viewpoint. And it's certain he doesn't understand me. It's ridiculous . . . unthinkable."

"You'd be surprised," said Lillian knowingly. "You'd be surprised what that fellow knows. I'll bet he's out right now slipping a word into the ears of his friends as to what he's doin'. That means he's on your side. Do you think that devil of a Mendicott will run a chance of a ruckus with Channing by botherin' you again? It'd tear this country wide open. What Channing starts, he finishes. Why's he on your side? Tell me that."

Hope could only flush and stare. It was too preposterous. And she detected a note of bitterness in the other girl's tone—a poignant sense of the difference in their positions. Suddenly she felt sorry for the girl of tinsel. "I don't know what he's doing," she said slowly. "I can't say that I know exactly why he is on my . . .

on our side. But it's the right side, Lillian." She looked at the older girl hopefully.

Lillian lifted her brows ever so slightly. "Yes, that's right," she conceded. "You're sure right. Listen, girlie, you look tired. You'd better get a wink of sleep. I'll put you in my room. I told 'em down to the joint that I wouldn't be around till late and I might not come at all. So I'll stay right here with you. You do that . . . go in and snatch a few winks. Channing may want to leave tonight."

Hope yielded to the other girl's entreaties and lay down on her bed. She tried to think, to reason matters out, but her mind refused to obey her will and soon she was sound asleep.

She woke suddenly, in the midst of a dream, and found Lillian standing by the bed, shaking her gently and holding a lamp.

"Channing's here, and another . . . a man from your ranch. You're goin' to start now. It's about two in the morning so you've had a nice rest. You better put your riding things on. They're waiting for you."

Hope rose hurriedly. Her spirits were high. At last she was going back to Rancho del Encanto—back to her uncle, and Mrs. McCaffy, who she had come to love through remembrance of her many little favors. She put on her riding habit, shoes, and cap, and went out into the large room.

Channing was standing by the table and the other man was sitting on the divan. She cried out joyfully when she saw Jim Crossley.

"How is my uncle?" she asked breathlessly.

"He's flat on his back, Miss Hope, but he's doin' fine," replied Jim, beaming. "He'll be up in a week. I came in to town to get some medicine for him tonight."

"And the others . . . Missus McCaffy?"

"Havin' the time of her life nursing your uncle an' worryin' about you. She'll be glad to see you. McDonald an' the bunch took after that crowd when they took you away, but they couldn't do anything. We lost one man an' had two hit an' had to quit.

McDonald sent here for the doctor an' he came out. I rode in for medicine an' met Channing down at the barn."

"And your arm?"

"Doctor wouldn't reset it," said Jim, moving the arm in splints. "Said Channing did too good a job."

"I reckon we better be moving," Channing put in. "We're going to the ranch, Miss Farman. Two men came in to see the notary," he added with a grim smile. "But I think they'll still be looking for him tomorrow an' we'll have plenty of time to beat 'em back to the ranch. Are you ready to go?"

"Yes," said Hope, turning to Lillian. "After I've thanked Lillian. I can't tell you how . . ."

"Don't try to," said the older girl with a flourish of a hand. "I can guess just what you want to say. It's all right. Any friend of Channing is welcome here." She looked at Channing, who nodded unsmilingly.

Hope thought she saw a ray of disappointment in the girl's eyes as she turned away. "We wouldn't have inconvenienced you, and kept you up this way . . ."

"Kept me up? Girlie, my day's just starting."

To Hope's surprise, Lillian threw her arms about her and kissed her. Then she led her to the door with Channing and Jim Crossley following.

"Remember, Channing says words are what you make 'em," Lillian whispered in Hope's ear as she bid her good bye. "And men are what you make 'em, too."

Channing led the way to the horses.

Chapter Twenty

They rode along the hill to the upper end of town. There was no moon and the side of the hill was mostly in shadow. They turned north above the town and proceeded for some time in that direction. Then they swung down into the granite hills and soon gained the desert at a point some distance northwest of town, where they put their horses to a trot and rode westward.

It was plain to Hope that Channing wished to screen their movements, and she suspected that Mendicott had many friends in Bandburg as well as Channing. Then he had mentioned that two men had ridden in for the notary. They might be followed by them. Channing evidently had seen to it that they hadn't got to the notary, but it was evident that Nathan Farman had received the letter and was ready and willing to dispose of the ranch in order to secure her release. The knowledge caused a lump to swell in the girl's throat. It did appear as though her arrival had been the signal for the start of trouble. She again found herself on Channing's horse. He was riding on her right and Jim Crossley was riding on her left. Both men maintained an absolute silence.

The desert was a great field of shadows. The horses picked their way around clumps of greasewood and cantered across the short open spaces where their hoofs echoed sharply against the hard earth. Hope, becoming more and more used to the saddle, found herself enjoying the ride. The air was cool and exhilarating, and a light, scented breeze blew gently from the north. It was comforting to know her uncle was recovering rapidly from his wound. Comforting, too, to know that Brood would not be able to bother them for some time. She did not blame Channing in the least for shooting Brood; she only marveled at the memory of the speed with which he did it. Brood had given her uncle far less chance.

In less than two hours came the desert dawn. Hope turned in her saddle time after time to look at the glory of the eastern skies. She saw Channing look, also, and began to understand something about his love for the desert—something of which he never spoke but which was always discernible in his looks and actions. She saw Jim Crossley look across at him many times. The little driver appeared puzzled. It was plain he couldn't make Channing out. But it also was plain that he admired him and entertained great respect for him. Hope could understand why Channing was a man's man as well as one who would naturally appeal to women. He appealed to her, she confessed to herself. But she flushed as she remembered the veiled hints of Lillian. Surely Lillian had a vivid imagination.

They halted late in the morning at a place Channing called Dick's Wells. It was a typical desert water hole, the spring having been built up until it was in reality a small well. The greasewood was high here, affording a wee bit of shade if one had a good imagination, as Jim Crossley put it, and there was some green grass where the water seeped through. Channing prepared a light meal from the scanty supply of provisions he carried on the back of his saddle. While they ate, Hope asked numerous questions of Jim Crossley. She learned that the letter she had written and signed at the insistence of the outlaw leader had been duly delivered to Nathan Farman. Her uncle had considered her safety only, and had readily agreed to sign away his ranch, knowing full well that Mendicott had it in his power to enforce the deed. He had sent a reply to that effect to Mendicott, and a message of good cheer to her by the messengers. This had been two days before, for the messengers had remained at the ranch overnight—the night Channing had aided Hope to escape. The next evening two other messengers appeared. They had expressed surprise that Brood was not there. He had started, they had said. Evidently they had not known that Brood had taken the trail of Channing and Hope. These messengers had remained at the ranch that night, and then, anticipating that Brood would arrive during the day, they had pushed on to Bandburg to get the notary. They had arrived the evening before. The ranch was to be deeded to Brood, Jim understood. Thus, as matters were, the messengers were in Bandburg looking for the notary—an individual who Channing said, with a grin, they would have a hard time finding and a harder time doing anything with when they did find him. Now, on the third day after the escape, they were on their way back to Rancho del Encanto.

Hope was so happy she threw her arms about Jim Crossley and hugged him. "Jim," she said, laughing, "you needn't be afraid to chew tobacco when I'm around."

"Miss Hope," said Jim, rather red in the face, "I reckon you're larnin'."

Channing's beautiful tenor burst forth in song as he tightened the saddle cinches. Hope looked at him quickly. He seemed in good spirits. Apparently her mood was contagious. And during the long, hot afternoon, when the sun blazed down upon them, and it seemed as though they never would reach the blue foothills in the west, Channing sang more than once.

It was sunset when they rode over the ridge that separated the mesa of Rancho del Encanto from the desert. They cantered down the west side and up the road lined with hedges and brought up at the front door. Mrs. McCaffy had heard them coming and looked out the door. When she saw who it was, she came out on the porch and down the steps as fast as her feet would carry her.

"Bless my stars!" she panted. "Bless my stars, dearie, is it you? Come down here this minute an' let me give you a bear hug. Why, you poor dear! Jim Crossley, stop grinning like an ape. Here, dearie, let me help you down."

Hope literally fell into the housekeeper's arms, and Mrs. McCaffy hugged her and kissed her. Then she stood off and wiped her eyes with a corner of her apron.

"My eyes, but it's good to see you again, girlie," she said with a catch in her voice. "What you've been through! How did you ever come to get back?"

Hope pointed to Channing, who was looking on soberly.

"Oh, it's him again, is it?" said Mrs. McCaffy. "Well, I'm glad there was a man on the job." She scowled at Jim Crossley and Hope surmised that there was good-natured discord between them. "Well, we'll be going in the house, dearie," Mrs. McCaffy went on. "It'll do your uncle a world of good to see you again. He's worried his heart out. You menfolks put up them horses and get ready for supper," she added, addressing Channing and Crossley.

Hope walked up the steps ahead of her and hurried into the house. She found her uncle on a bed in the big cool living room and dropped on her knees beside it. The tears came, but they were happy tears. Nathan Farman stroked her hair and told her in endearing terms how glad he was to have her back.

"But . . . you were not hurt badly . . . Uncle?" she asked anxiously.

"I'll be around in no time, now that you're safe again, Hope," he said cheerfully. "I saw this thing coming for a long time. I ought to have known better than to go out on the porch with that gun. I should have shot Brood from inside the door an' I'd do it if I had it to do over again."

"He won't bother us for a while, Uncle," said Hope. "He . . . he molested me in Bandburg, and . . . Mister Channing shot him."

"Channing?" said her uncle quickly. "Did Channing bring you back?"

"Yes, Uncle. He got me out of that place up there and brought me home."

She rose as Mrs. McCaffy passed through the room.

"You just sit right there with your uncle a piece," the house-keeper said to her. "Supper'll be ready in a few minutes, but you'll have time to put yourself to rights. Why, Nathan looks lots better already."

Hope rearranged the pillows under her uncle's head and drew up a chair.

"Now do you think you can tell me about it?" he asked, taking one of her hands in both of his. "Or, if you're too tired . . . but you must be."

"No, Uncle Nathan," Hope said with a smile, "I guess I've passed the stage of getting tired any more. Now that it's all over, I look upon it as an interesting adventure. If it hadn't been for my uncertainty as to how you were, and about that . . . that letter about selling the ranch . . ."

"I sent word right back that he could have it," Nathan Farman interrupted.

"But I didn't want him to have it," said Hope quickly. "Oh, Uncle! I signed the letter because it was the only way I could see to get out of there at the time, and I wanted to get to you. I thought we would find a way somehow to get the ranch back, because getting it that way would be illegal."

"Mendicott usually gets what he goes after," said her uncle in a troubled tone. "When he starts working to an end, he keeps goin' till he succeeds. How did he treat you, Hope? Did he mis-treat you in any way?" Nathan Farman's voice was fierce as he put the questions.

Hope shook her head. "He was going to put me on bread and water," she said, "but he told me afterward that he only intended to do so for a day or two. But . . . I wouldn't have liked to stay up there long. He has a terrible pair of eyes, Uncle. I've never seen anything like them. I shiver when I think of them."

"Men shiver, too, Hope," said Nathan Farman seriously. "Mendicott has terrorized this part of the country till even the authorities are afraid to move a hand against him. That's why I didn't bother sending for the deputy at Bandburg or the sheriff at the county seat. It wouldn't do any good. It would just make him all the more vicious. It's a shame that a man like that should practically rule a district as big as two or three of the states in New England, but he does . . . an' that's all there is to it."

"Someone will break his power, Uncle," said Hope with conviction.

"There's only one way to do that," said Nathan Farman slowly, "by killing him. An' I don't reckon, there's a man on this whole California desert, or in the valley across the mountains that could stand up against him."

Hope wondered. She thought steadily for several moments. Slowly her viewpoint was changing. She was considering the chances of Mendicott's power being taken from him in the way her uncle had suggested.

"Do you want to tell me about it?" he asked. It was plain he was anxious to hear the details of Hope's experience.

Hope started slowly and told him the story of what had happened from the time she had been taken from the ranch. She told her experience at Ghost Wash and in Bandburg. She omitted nothing except the meeting of Brood and Channing in the rendezvous. She didn't include that because she passed lightly over Channing's presence in the retreat of the outlaws. She said nothing to indicate that he was one of them. She did not tell her own views and surmises and conjectures. But it made a thrilling story as it was.

When she had finished her uncle was silent for some time. Then he cleared his throat and looked at her in the fast-fading light. "How did Channing come to be in that place?" he asked quietly.

"Why . . . I . . . I don't know," Hope faltered. "I'm only glad he was there."

"Did you see him with Mendicott at any time?" her uncle inquired.

"No. I only saw Mendicott the two times he visited me at the cabin."

"Was Channing a captive, also?" Nathan Farman persisted.

"No . . . that is . . . oh, I don't know, Uncle!" Hope exclaimed.

"Supper's ready!" called Mrs. McCaffy from the doorway of the dining room. "Do you want to eat in there with your uncle, dearie?"

"No, she'll preside at the table," said the rancher, speaking for Hope. "We have a guest."

Hope understood and went hurriedly upstairs to wash her face and hands, change into a dress, and arrange her hair. When she came down, she kissed her uncle before she went into the dining room. Channing was there with Jim Crossley, McDonald, and Mrs. McCaffy.

The men were mostly silent, except for a light discussion of range affairs. Mrs. McCaffy rose again after they were seated and took Nathan Farman's supper to him herself.

Hope's brain was in a turmoil. She had anticipated her uncle's questions about Channing, but had no idea how she was going to answer them until it came to the actual test. She knew Channing was connected in some way with Mendicott, yet she had sought to protect him. Why was she protecting him? In doing so, wasn't she condoning his association with the outlaw? True, he had saved her life, but she had practically lied for him. She recalled Lillian Bell's final message: Words are what you make 'em, and men are what you make 'em. too. That was the gist of it. She looked up at Channing. A last feeble ray of the gorgeous sunset stained his copper hair a deep auburn. His gray-green eyes, shot with flecks of brown, were turned on her frankly for an instant. She flushed deeply.

Chapter Twenty-One

Hope hardly spoke during the meal. Mrs. McCaffy and Jim Crossley kept up a continual fire of banter that brought many a laugh from the others. Channing and McDonald talked ranch matters. But Hope saw that McDonald was not as free with Channing in his conversation as he was in his occasional remarks to Crossley. This, she assumed, was because Channing was not employed on the ranch.

After supper Hope and Channing went into the living room. Nathan Farman was sitting propped up in bed with a shaded lamp on a small table near his head. He looked keenly at Channing when the latter asked how he was getting along.

"How long will Brood be laid up?" he asked.

"Three, four weeks," replied Channing, taking the chair Hope drew up for him. "He'll be out too soon, as it is, I reckon."

Farman brooded over this. "Funny Mendicott is so anxious to have the ranch deeded over to Brood. Must be Brood stands pretty close to him, or else he's got him where he wants him."

Channing vouchsafed no comment.

"I cannot understand why he wants the ranch," Hope put in.

"I know why he wants the ranch!" exclaimed her uncle. "He wants it because of how it's situated. It's away from everywhere an' everybody. He wants it to house some of his gang in and for a place to keep stolen stock. With Brood running the place as his own, under his own brand, they'd have a fine chance to fatten up the cattle they could steal on the forest reserve range and over on

136

the other side of the range. He wants it bad, that's certain," the rancher concluded gloomily.

"Well, he'll never get it," Hope declared.

"I don't know," said Nathan Farman dubiously. "He's dead set on it, it looks like, and, when he gets dead set on a thing, he keeps his mind on it."

"I believe his kidnapping of me was an attempt to bluff you, Uncle," said Hope. "It seemed serious enough when I was up there, but those things aren't done these days . . . are they, Mister Channing?"

"It was done in your case," said Channing quietly.

"You don't know that devil," said Farman to his niece. "I tell you he won't stop at anything. He's got me guessing right now as to what his next move will be. He isn't fooling."

"Why don't you report the matter to the sheriff at least?" Hope asked.

Nathan Farman laughed and flashed a significant look at Channing. "Lot of good that would do," he said. "Mendicott laughs at sheriffs. They don't even know where his hang-out is up there. From what you've told me the outlaws could pick off a million men before the posses could get down that trail. What's more, Mendicott has friends scattered around to tip him off an' to lead his pursuers astray. An' he'll stand an' fight. He's smooth an' he hasn't ever learned what the word fear means. Isn't that so, Channing?"

"He's bad medicine," Channing replied shortly.

"He's all of that," confirmed Farman. "That's why I don't see that there's much use in my trying to hold on to the place. He's bound to get it some way sooner or later. There was some sense in that letter he dictated, at that."

"Why, Uncle," exclaimed Hope, "you're not considering selling Rancho del Encanto now?"

"It might be best," Farman answered, a look of pain crossing his face. "I hate to do it, but I can't buck Mendicott. If I stay on here, it's going to mean trouble from now on. I can see the hand-writing on the wall just as plain as if Mendicott had visited me an' told me so. I've got a bullet hole in my side to show he means business. I wouldn't let McDonald start into the hills after you, for I knew it would do no good. I had to wait. I hate to keep on waiting for him to make new moves."

"But, Uncle, if you feel that way about it, we could leave the ranch for a time and come back when matters adjusted themselves."

"Come back an' find him in possession," said Farman bitterly. "I'd have to sell all my stock to do that, an' the way the cattle are now, an' the market, I'd have to shoulder a big loss. I can't afford it . . . not only on my account, but on yours, Hope. I am going to look after you. There is no one else to do it. Don't shake your head! I can use my property to benefit who I please, an' leave it to whom I please when I die. I don't care so much about myself, but it isn't safe for you here. If we move, we move for good," he concluded sternly.

There were tears in Hope's eyes as she looked at Channing in appeal.

"I don't reckon I'd sell the ranch, Nate," said Channing.

"What am I going to do?" the rancher demanded with a helpless gesture.

"I'd wait and see what turns up," Channing suggested.

"An' maybe when it turns up, it'll be too late to slide out of it with anything," Farman pointed out.

"Just the same, I'd wait," said Channing, stifling a yawn. "I sure would, Nate."

Nathan Farman smiled. "You talk like a man who knew more'n he wanted to put into words," he accused.

Channing shrugged. "Maybe I do," he retorted coolly. "I'm not long on giving advice, but I'm giving you some just the same."

This seemed to irritate the rancher. "If you know anything about this deal an' are minded to be a friend of mine, it's your place to tell me," he flared out.

"If I had put in as much time and hard work as you have to build this place and make it what it is, I wouldn't let any man's first move, or second or third moves, run me off," said Channing crisply.

"But there's a girl . . . a blood relative . . . that I want to live with me the rest of my life," said Farman with heat. "I'm not going to keep her in danger."

"Then send her away," said Channing calmly, "and you stay here."

Hope looked at him thunderstruck. "I'll not go away!" she cried in indignation as soon as she found her voice. "Your first advice was good . . . that we wait, I mean. But Uncle nor anyone else ever could get me to leave here now. I'm going to stay!"

Channing smiled pleasantly. "You hear that, Nate? Miss Farman has spunk enough to stick it out. Why don't you do the same?"

Nathan Farman was frowning. He turned to Hope. "You've had a hard day, Hope, child," he said kindly. "Suppose you run upstairs. I think Missus McCaffy will have a bath ready for you soon. I . . . I want to talk to Channing."

"All right, Uncle," said Hope "but don't you decide to give up Rancho del Encanto or you'll break my heart as well as your own."

She kissed her uncle, said good night to Channing, and went slowly up the stairs. But she did not go to her room, although she walked to the door. She slipped quietly back to the head of the stairs on tiptoe and listened breathlessly.

"Channing," said her uncle slowly, "I want to thank you from the bottom of my heart for what you've done for Hope . . . an' me. I want you to know that I appreciate it. I . . . I can't tell you how much because I usually say thanks an' let it go at that, being no great hand with words."

"All right," said Channing easily, "let it go at that. Words are pretty much what you make 'em by the way you say 'em. I'm satisfied."

"I am not foolish enough to think you did this altogether on my account," observed the rancher.

"Eh?" said Channing. "What do you mean by that?"

"I'm an old man," said Farman, "but I'm not blind. An' I could always add two an' two."

"You may not be blind, but I reckon you're getting just a wee bit feeble-minded," said Channing coldly.

"No, I'm not, Channing. But we'll pass over that. You did us a favor an' I've thanked you best I know how. But I'm entitled to know something. How did you happen to be in that place of Mendicott's?"

"So you're angling for information," said Channing in a tone of ice.

"Exactly. Information I'm entitled to under the circumstances. I've heard some queer things about you, Channing, but I never paid much attention to them. I'm going straight to the point now. Was you a captive in there, same as my niece?"

"Whether I was or not has nothing to do with what I did," Channing evaded.

"But it has something to do with things as they stand now," said Farman stoutly. "I want you to tell me. Channing, are you mixed up with that Mendicott in any way?"

"That's slipping 'em in fast," was Channing's comment.

"If you haven't got anything to do with him, all you've got to do is say no," said Farman sternly.

"And if I don't say no, you'll think the other way," said Channing with a short, mirthless laugh.

"It doesn't leave me any other way to think," said Farman angrily. "If you're in with him, how do I know that this isn't all some kind of a trick? You seem to be happening along in the nick o' time quite regular. This is serious business. Are you going to answer my questions?"

"No," said Channing coldly, "I'm not."

"You're putting yourself in a funny light. I suppose you know that."

"I'm not dumb, if I am obstinate," snapped out Channing.

Nathan Farman considered. "There's no use in our arguing about all this," he said finally. "I've got to know where I stand, whether I decide to stay here or not. I'm not askin' anything unfair of you, Channing. I suppose you could be in with Mendicott an' still be friendly to us, but I can't see just how, knowin' what I do about that fellow."

"Then let it stay as it stands," said Channing.

"No, I can't do that," said Farman soberly. "I have big interests here an' it isn't just the ranch an' the stock. My niece is here. To tell you in so many words, it's a case of her being herded with somebody she hadn't ought to be associating with. I wouldn't want to hurt your feelings, but I'm her uncle an' I reckon you can see black from white."

For some time there was silence. At the head of the stairs Hope put her hands to her throat. It did not seem possible, after all that Channing had done, for him to be anyone but a friend. She thought her uncle was stretching a point too far. She was tempted to go down but restrained herself when she considered how her intervention might appear in Channing's eyes.

"I reckon I get what you're driving at," said Channing after a time.

"Well, then, don't you think it's your best policy to speak right out?" asked Farman.

"No, I can't say as I do," said Channing in a drawl. "I know my own business, Nate, better than you do, and I know a whole lot more about some things than you do in the bargain."

"That's just it!" thundered the rancher. "You know more'n you'll tell an' that leaves me in the dark. I've got to be sure, Channing. I've got to be sure of everybody that's around this ranch. If you can't talk free, you'll have to leave Rancho del Encanto!"

"I don't remember asking permission to stay," said Channing.

"If you do ask it, you won't get it till you've come clean!" shouted Farman. "You acted as if you figured on staying, an' I took it for granted. It looks mighty suspicious to me . . . the way you're acting, I mean. You're trying to lord it over me an' make me accept your advice without giving any reasons. You'll have to talk right smart or . . ."

"Or what?" demanded Channing.

"Or leave the ranch!"

Channing rose. Hope heard him walking to the front door, caught a glimpse of his face, stern and cold, as he turned toward Nathan Farman with his hand on the knob. "I sent word to Mendicott I'd be here," he said. "Good night, Nate." He opened the door quickly and went out.

Hope went down the stairs. Her hands were trembling and her eyes were wide with distress. She walked slowly to her uncle's bedside and looked down upon his stern features. He did not seem surprised to see her. He took one of her hands.

"How could you do it, Uncle?" she said with a catch in her voice. "How could you do it after . . . after . . . ?"

She dropped upon her knees and buried her face in the counterpane.

Chapter Twenty-Two

If Nathan Farman was sorry that his temper and his eager solicitude for Hope's welfare had gotten the better of him in his interview with Channing, he did not show it next morning. He greeted Hope affectionately when she came down and called cheerfully to Mrs. McCaffy to bring him a cup of coffee soon as it was ready.

McDonald appeared nervous at breakfast. Hope noted it and attributed it to trouble in connection with the work on the ranch. But she was nervous herself. Channing had gone. She had heard him ride away in the night, and her sense of security suffered. She regretted that her uncle had acted as he had. He had ordered Channing off the ranch because he wouldn't tell him all he knew. He hadn't told Hope, either. But he had kept his word with her and she felt, under the circumstances, that her uncle should have had more faith in him. Certainly he was for them and against Brood, so far as the former foreman was concerned. He had stopped the sale of the ranch. She wondered why she didn't tell her uncle of Lillian's declaration that Channing was the one man in the country Mendicott was inclined to handle cautiously. Even if he were associated with the outlaw chief, he could oppose him in this matter. His very refusal to talk seemed to indicate that such was his position.

After breakfast Nathan Farman called McDonald in and gave orders that the branding be held up a few days until all the cattle could be gathered on the mesa.

"I want every head of stock I own in here close," the rancher commanded.

McDonald promised to start the general roundup immediately.

"You're not getting them together with a view to selling them, are you, Uncle?" Hope inquired anxiously.

"I don't know," Farman confessed. "I'll have to wait an' see. But don't you bother about this business, Hope . . . don't worry. I'll take care of it."

Despite his confidence and his attempt to reassure her, Hope did not feel that her uncle was coping with the situation properly. Something told her it would require a vast amount of tact to deal with Mendicott and secure a satisfactory adjustment of the trouble. She could not forget the outlaw's eyes.

The rancher insisted on getting up this day and Hope and Mrs. McCaffy helped him into a rocking chair and pushed it to the open door leading to the porch. Here he sat, looking out over the lawn and hedges to the mesa where cattle were grazing peacefully.

Hope helped Mrs. McCaffy with the housework and in the kitchen.

"Your uncle's peculiar," the housekeeper confided to the girl. "He's always been quick-tempered. I heard him order that man Channing off the ranch last night an' somehow or other it seemed to me that Channing was holding a card up his sleeve. I can usually read these men pretty close. Anyway, it struck me that way."

"Missus McCaffy, do you believe Channing is an outlaw?" asked Hope.

"Laws, child, I don't know," replied the housekeeper. "Maybe he is. He comes an' goes. I ain't seen him often. He's mysterious, sort of. Now take that little shrimp of a Crossley. I can read him like a book. Everything he knows is planted right in plain sight on his face, but Channing's different."

Hope laughed at her reference to the little driver. "You and Jim don't seem to get along any too well," she observed.

"That's because he's sassy," said Mrs. McCaffy. "I won't stand sass. Lately he's got worse. Maybe it's because his arm bothers him. Well . . ."

The pound of hoofs came to their ears and Hope just had time to walk into the living room to her uncle's chair when two men flung themselves from their mounts and came up on the porch.

"What do you want?" demanded Farman without waiting for them to speak.

"We couldn't get the notary," said one of the men. "An' there didn't seem to be any need for him right away because Brood is on his back."

The speaker stopped talking suddenly as he caught sight of Hope. His eyes bulged and he nudged his companion who also stared.

"That's all right," said Nathan Farman sharply. "I don't reckon we'll need any notary now. You can tell Mendicott I said that."

Hope pressed her hand on her uncle's shoulder to caution him. The spokesman of the messengers found his voice and scowled. "You want me to tell the chief you ain't goin' to sell the ranch?"

"I'm not going to sell it at the present time." said Farman in a softer tone. "You can tell him that. I've got to round up my cattle and find out just what I've got. That'll take time."

"All right," said the man, turning to go. He hesitated with his hand on his horse's mane. "Maybe the boss'll take it into his head to come an' see you himself," he said with a harsh laugh.

The two of them mounted their horses and struck out for the trail leading into the foothills.

"That was a threat, Uncle," said Hope apprehensively.

"I know it," said Farman, "but he had to find out sooner or later."

"They'll go up there and tell Mendicott that I'm back at the ranch," said Hope in a worried voice.

"Maybe Channing's got there ahead of them," snapped out the rancher.

"No. I don't think so. He didn't ride toward the hills last night."

"Did you see him go?" asked Farman in surprise. "Was you watching?"

"Yes, I was watching. I couldn't sleep, it had all disturbed me so. I was at the window. He rode down toward the desert."

"A blind, maybe," muttered her uncle. "Swung back around probably. Things aren't all right with that fellow or he would have talked when I asked him to."

"Maybe he has reasons for not wanting to tell all he knows," Hope was quick to point out.

"If that's the case, he's hand an' glove with Mendicott," said Farman grimly. "I might have known it. It explains his comings an' goings an' easy life. If he was a prospector, he'd be packin' some tools, an' he'd be finding a likely lead once in a while like the rest of 'em. It's a wonder I didn't wake up to all this a long time ago."

Hope saw it was useless to argue with him, and she realized that she had no very sound foundation for any argument she might put up. But the thought of word reaching the outlaw that she was again at Rancho del Encanto worried her. She couldn't get the memory of those beady black eyes out of her mind. She could see him sitting under the lamp, looking at her; she could hear his smooth voice telling her that he had ordered a man shot. The sound of that shot still rang in her ears. And Channing was gone.

When she went back to the kitchen, Jim Crossley came to the rear door. "What'd those fellers want?" he asked Hope.

The girl quickly explained and Crossley shook his head doubtfully.

"Just like a game of checkers," he observed. "Farman's made the last move an' now it's up to the other feller. Thing is, who's got the kings."

"Jim Crossley, get out of here!" stormed the housekeeper. "You talk like the advance agent for a famine or drought or something. If you can't think of something cheerful to say, you stay away from this kitchen!"

Crossley retreated, but Hope turned to Mrs. McCaffy with a serious look. "Jim's right," she said. "And it wouldn't surprise me any if that man Mendicott came down here."

"He wouldn't dare!" exclaimed the housekeeper. "Somebody'd pot him. Why, even that skeeter of a Crossley might do it."

Hope shook her head. "He isn't afraid of anyone or anything," she said convincingly. "I could tell that without hearing it from anybody else."

At suppertime Nathan Farman gave explicit orders to McDonald. "Bring the men in to the bunkhouse," he instructed. "Bring 'em all in. You can work out on circle as far as you can in the daytime an' leave the stock that's on the desert an' in the hills till after. I want the men in here an' I want 'em armed an' ready in case anything should happen."

"They're pretty nervous," said McDonald, shifting his weight from one foot to the other.

"What do you mean by that?" Farman asked sharply.

"Seems like they've got more an' more uneasy lately," said the foreman.

"You mean you couldn't depend on them if there was trouble?" the rancher demanded.

"I couldn't be absolutely sure," replied McDonald, looking at him squarely.

Nathan Farman frowned heavily. "Well," he said at length, "I don't look for any raid on the ranch exactly. I believe Mendicott's too clever for that. He'll find a better way to drive me out of the country if he's set on doing it. But I want the men in anyway. Do what you can with 'em to spunk 'em up."

The night and the next day passed quietly. Things moved smoothly on the ranch and McDonald reported good progress in rounding up the cattle. Hope gained some small measure of her confidence and went about cheerfully, helping the housekeeper.

Next evening Nathan Farman insisted that he be moved out on the porch. It was a glorious evening, with the mountains and mesa bathed in a soft light after the sunset. Hope and Mrs. McCaffy were looking at the flowers. The men were squatting about the bunkhouse, talking idly. It was a peaceful ranch scene, soothing in its quietude, when the still air suddenly resounded to the clatter of hoofs on the foothill trail.

Hope saw some of the men start up, but they sat down again as a rider came into view around the barn. The horseman rode slowly toward the bunkhouse, holding the reins in his left hand and keeping his right at his side. His keen glance darted everywhere, and, as he passed the little group before the bunkhouse, he turned slightly so he could keep an eye on them as he rode on toward the porch. Hope hadn't needed a second glance to distinguish that lithe figure in the saddle. The riding costume, the polished boots, the lean, pockmarked face under the big black hat were all too familiar to her. Mendicott had come to Rancho del Encanto!

Chapter Twenty-Three

Mendicott rode leisurely to the steps, glanced casually at Nathan Farman, who was sitting in his rocking chair on the porch, checked his horse, and looked off over the mesa for several moments before he dismounted.

Hope hurried to the end of the porch and climbed upon it. She walked slowly to a place beside her uncle's chair, her eyes riveted upon the outlaw. Nathan Farman leaned forward, staring. His fingers picked at the quilt over his knees, then closed tightly against his palms. He spoke to Hope. "Go inside."

Hope hesitated. "Why can't I stay, Uncle?" she whispered.

"Go inside!" he ordered sharply.

She entered the living room, but stood just within the door where she could see out on the porch. Mrs. McCaffy came tip-toeing in from the rear of the house where she had entered. The two women did not speak, but watched the drama being enacted outside.

Mendicott tossed the reins over his horse's head and stood for a space, looking the animal over. It was a magnificent horse, a black gelding with a coat of satin, long-flowing mane and tail, the slim, strong, tapering legs of a racer—full of life, holding its head high, moving it impatiently. The saddle, too, was black, embellished with dull silver ornaments. But it was in good taste. The outlaw's gaze roved constantly to either end of the porch as he mounted the steps. There was still light, although the shades of the twilight were rapidly shrouding the mesa, and he caught sight of Hope, standing in the doorway. He looked at her steadily

149

for a brief interval, holding her eyes as if a spell had been cast over her. Then he nodded, and his teeth flashed in a quick smile. The smile was gone when he turned to Nathan Farman.

He surveyed the rancher at length, coolly and deliberately, as if studying him, reading his mind and classifying him in his own way. There was something sinister in the very presence of the outlaw, in his cool confidence and evident contempt, that struck the persons with whom he came in contact with a chill. His graceful movements, the aristocratic cocking of his head, his subtle swagger—implied rather than executed—his ease of manner, and his personal appearance all stamped him as different from the general run of unsavory characters who defied constituted authority and elevated him, in a way, while at the same time conveying the impression that he was exceedingly more dangerous than if he had been unshaven, adorned with many weapons, and violent of speech and vicious in manner. His quiet mien was disturbing and fascinating. His pockmarked face was neither repulsive nor brutal, the small, black mustache set him off well, and his hands were exquisitely shaped and well cared for. It was in the eyes that his brutal, ferocious, inexorable nature and instincts made themselves known. Cruel eyes they were, without a hint of sympathy or human kindness, hard, cold, unmerciful, unrelenting, and sanguinary—but never transmitting a hint of what was going on in the man's mind.

"I received your message," said Mendicott to Farman in modulated tones of voice that were in keeping with his manner.

Farman nodded. The rancher was visibly nervous and striving to appear calm. "Will you sit down?" he asked.

"Not out here," said Mendicott pointedly, with a look toward the door.

Farman understood. The outlaw had no wish to remain on the porch where he made an excellent target. Farman was not so stupid as not to realize that nothing could be gained by an attack on the man at this time. It was highly improbable that Mendicott had come to the ranch alone. Doubtless there were many of his followers secreted among the trees about the mesa. Farman called to Mrs. McCaffy and she and Hope carried his chair into the house, assisted by Mendicott himself. Mrs. McCaffy brought a lighted lamp and put it on the table in the living room. Farman and Mendicott sat opposite each other at the table. The outlaw had so placed himself that he could see both the front door and the door into the dining room and the stairway. Hope and the housekeeper retired to the dining room, where they stood in the shadows looking into the living room.

"You changed your mind about selling the ranch when you learned your niece was . . . was out?" asked Mendicott.

"Yes," replied the rancher firmly. "I'd have sold quick enough to get her out of your reach. But there are some matters, such as taking stock of the cattle an' other property, that I have to look into before I can talk sale or price."

Mendicott crossed his legs and drew out tobacco and papers. "I suppose there's something in that," he said, rolling a cigarette. "When will you finish and be able to state a price?"

"That I can't tell . . . at present," Farman evaded. "It'll take a little time. The stock's pretty well scattered, an' . . ."

"But you intend to sell, do you not?" interrupted Mendicott in a crisp tone that cracked on his listeners' ears like the snap of a whiplash.

Farman looked unsteadily into the outlaw's small black eyes bent upon him. "I am . . . considering it," he answered.

"You are considering it seriously?" asked Mendicott.

"Yes, but let me ask you a question," said the rancher. "How does it come that after all the years I have put in here, you suddenly decide you want this place? Rancho del Encanto represents my life's work. You wish to take it away from me on short notice . . . no notice at all, so to speak. Why do you want it?"

"That's a fair question," said Mendicott, holding the other's troubled gaze. "I guess you know that I've looked on this country in here as my territory for some years. Yours is the only ranch in here, and we want a ranch. Therefore we haven't any choice in the matter except to get this one. You can find many a ranch as good as this that'll do for your stock business just as well as this, but we can't find one so well situated for our . . . purposes. That's why we're set on getting this property. I take it you've got sense enough to see that?"

Nathan Farman realized to his sorrow that there was considerable in what the outlaw had said. Rancho del Encanto was ideally situated for Mendicott's purpose—as Farman understood that purpose. And it was the only ranch in that part of the country. Were it not for sentimental reasons, Farman would have been willing to part with his property under the circumstances.

"Now, there's another thing, Farman," said Mendicott in a sharper tone. "We're not asking you to shave your price. We're not trying to get something for nothing. We just ask that you put a price within reason, take your money, and leave. Of course we don't expect you to come back."

There was an unmistakable threat in the outlaw's last sentence. It was not lost on the rancher.

"I understand what you're getting at," said Farman. "If I sell, it'll have to be . . . for keeps, you might say. But I'll tell you as man to man that I don't know what this place is worth. I've got to round up my cattle an' take an inventory all around. If I sell the place, I want to sell it with everything that's on it, except some of the furniture and a few of the horses."

"You can find that out in a week or two," said Mendicott with a frown. "Otherwise, we'll make you an offer. I can tell you offhand pretty well what the place is worth as it stands, with all stock and everything else."

"You want it at your own price?" flared Farman.

"No," snapped out Mendicott, "but we don't propose to be all summer finding out what you want for it. We're ready to buy."

"It's an outrage!" stormed the rancher. "What would the authorities say about such a high-handed piece of business as the kidnapping of my niece?" He was forgetting the menace of the outlaw in his own indignation.

Hope, looking from the shadows of the dark dining room, saw Mendicott's eyes narrow. The outlaw snapped a thumb and finger. "I don't care that for what they think! I'm treating you pretty well, at that, Farman. I'm putting this up to you in a business way because you have been here such a long time. I'm . . ." He bit off his speech in a hiss as the sound of a man coming up the steps to the porch reached them. His right hand dropped below the table as the footfalls came from the porch. Then Hope felt an exultant surge of feeling as she saw Channing in the front doorway.

Channing hardly seemed to notice Farman; he looked steadily at Mendicott. The outlaw leader's eyes glittered as he waited for the newcomer to speak.

"Nice evening," said Channing as he advanced across the threshold. "Were you saying you had a business proposition here?"

The question was addressed to Mendicott, and the outlaw's face darkened until the pockmarks were white spots that gave him a fiendish appearance. It also took Nathan Farman by surprise, and the rancher stared at the visitor with a puzzled frown on his face. Hope sensed that Channing was now out in the open on their side and definitely against Mendicott. The situation appeared fraught with grave possibilities.

"Why do you come in here and ask such a question?" demanded Mendicott in a snarl. His vicious mood, precipitated by Channing's arrival, seemed to be getting the better of his customary calmness.

"Because I'm interested," said Channing. "If it has to do with the sale of this ranch, I'm quite a bit interested." He looked quickly at Farman, and his eyes were full of meaning.

The rancher wet his lips and remained silent, watching the drama between the two other men. It was now apparent to him and the two women who were watching, also, that Channing was one man for whom Mendicott entertained a certain respect, but it was apparent, too, that the outlaw leader was exceedingly angry.

"If you're so interested, maybe you can find out when this man is going to be ready to sell," said Mendicott with a sneer. "I came down here because he sent word he'd changed his mind. I got your message that you'd be here, but I only half believed it."

"Well," said Channing with a queer smile, "I'm here. And it'll be some little time, I reckon, before Farman's ready to say he'll sell and for what."

Mendicott rose quickly and turned toward the rancher. "Is that so?" he asked in a hoarse voice, his eyes blazing.

Farman saw Channing nod to him ever so slightly. He was puzzled by Channing's attitude, bewildered by his sudden entrance into the negotiations. But it was evident from Mendicott's manner that this wasn't a trick.

"I guess that's the way of it," he heard himself reply.

Mendicott whirled on Channing. But Channing made no move to back down by word or gesture. He returned Mendicott's gaze squarely. "You got your answer," he said grimly. "I'm half thinking of getting an option on this ranch myself, Mendicott. Brood overplayed his hand and isn't able to look after things. That leaves the way open for another buyer. I might take it into my mind to be that buyer."

For several moments the spectators held their breath. The outlaw leader seemed on the point of drawing his weapon. Channing, too, was alert, his hand poised above his gun, his gaze locked with Mendicott's. And then Mendicott's manner underwent a swift change. He actually smiled at Channing, turned, and smiled at Farman.

"This could be called a pretty frame-up," he said slowly, as if choosing his words with great care. "Maybe it is, but I can't see where it's going to get any of us. Of course, if you're taking an option on my behalf, that's different." He looked at Channing as he concluded.

"I hadn't looked at it in that way," said Channing.

"And that leaves me but one way to think . . . and act!" said Mendicott in a voice that was thick with rage. "You're playing with something that makes fire seem tame. I'm advising you both to do a lot of thinking . . . soon."

He strode to the door, turned for a single look that included both Channing and Farman, and slipped out into the night.

Channing leaped to the table and blew out the light in the lamp. A few moments later the echoes of a horse's hoofs came to them in the darkened room. After a short interval Channing again lighted the lamp. He stood looking at Nathan Farman grimly.

"I don't know why I'm doing all this, exactly," he said in a low, tense voice. "Maybe I'm just a plumb blamed fool. But I put the business to that fellow straight between the eyes. I reckon you better leave the matter to me by giving me that option."

"How do I know you're not workin' for Mendicott, after all?" cried Farman.

"You've got to let your common sense answer that, I reckon," said Channing.

Nathan Farman passed a hand over his eyes. "You better stay here tonight." he said, "an' we can talk things over tomorrow. It's too deep for me tonight. I . . ."

He raised a hand weakly and Hope and Mrs. McCaffy hurried into the room. Channing nodded to them and to the rancher and went out the door.

Chapter Twenty-Four

When Nathan Farman had been made comfortable in bed, with both Hope and Mrs. McCaffy fluttering about him, making him as easy as possible, Hope sat down at the bedside and talked to him in a soothing voice. The excitement had nearly proved too much for him after his wound and the weakening days he had spent on his back. Hope realized more than ever this night that her uncle was an old man, and that his life had been a life replete with hardship and worry and much responsibility. It was all too apparent that he was not fit to cope with Mendicott, that the outlaw would go to any length to achieve his ends, that it didn't tend to ease her uncle's mind one way or the other to be possessed of this knowledge. But she was glad that Channing had returned.

"I knew he'd come back," she told her uncle. "He has been somewhere nearby expecting this visit from Mendicott. It'll help you to sleep, Uncle, to know that I have every faith in Mister Channing because all his actions from the time I first met him have been in our interests."

Then, while Nathan Farman listened with his eyes closed, holding one of her hands in his, she told him of the meeting between Channing and Brood in the outlaws' rendezvous, and of Brood's evident astonishment and obedience to Channing's command to go back into his cabin. She told him, too, something of what Lillian Bell had said to her in the mining camp. She stressed what Lillian had said about the two of them, Channing and Mendicott, having an equal number of friends, and of Mendicott's having more respect for Channing than any other man in that part of the country. "Tonight's events have proved it," she concluded in triumph. "Anyone could plainly see that Mendicott was furiously angry. Why, once he was on the verge of drawing his weapon. And it made him all the more angry to see that Mister Channing wasn't afraid of him. You said it would take a brave man to face Mendicott," Hope pointed out to Nathan Farman. "And you've seen him faced tonight. We've got to turn in some direction, Uncle, we've got to trust someone. Something . . . oh, I don't know what . . . tells me we should trust Channing."

"I'll talk to him in the morning," muttered Farman, patting her hand.

She turned the light in the lamp low and sat with him until he slept.

Mrs. McCaffy tiptoed into the room and beckoned to her to come out into the kitchen.

"Something's going on out there by the bunkhouse," the housekeeper whispered. "I guess it's the men. They're afraid for their lives with that devil of a Mendicott, an' his coming here this way tonight has made them all the worse. I can't say as I blame 'em, the way things look,"

Hope hurried to the kitchen door. She arrived there just in time to see two men standing before a group of others in the starlight before the men's quarters.

"There'll be no leaving here at this time," came a voice she recognized as Channing. "The quicker you men get it into your heads that you're going to stick it out, the better. That's plain talk, and McDonald and I mean it. Here, you, get back there with the bunch!"

Mrs. McCaffy had joined Hope in the doorway.

"It's that slippery little Mexican, Mendez," she said in an undertone.

Mendez had halted some little distance away from the group on Channing's side—the side toward the barn. "No, no," he said in a hissing voice. "I go, señor, I go."

"You mean you'll stay!" thundered Channing. "Get back there where you belong."

"You make me stay to get killed, maybe?" snarled out the Mexican.

"You stay or you'll probably get killed," was Channing's swift reply.

Mendez crouched and sprang to one side, his right hand darting up and behind his left shoulder.

Channing whipped his hat from his head and leaped backward. The spectators caught a gleam of flashing steel in the starlight—a white streak that struck the hat Channing brought across in front of him. Then Channing had the Mexican by the throat and threw him several feet to the ground before the other men. He picked up his hat, slipped the knife into a pocket, and bent over the Mexican.

"You know why you didn't stop a bullet?" he said fiercely. "You know?"

"I dunno," said Mendez sullenly.

Channing reached down and jerked him to his feet. "Because we need your rope for what's got to be done around here the next few days. We need your rope, and you'll use it like you're told or we'll hang you with it!"

Mendez slunk back toward the bunkhouse door. They could see his hands working at his sides. As he reached the bunkhouse door, there came an inarticulate cry, followed by an oath in Spanish. Then Mendez came from between the other men of the little group, bounding straight for Channing.

"Gringo dog!" he yelled in a frenzy.

Channing leaned forward and his right fist caught the Mexican on the jaw, stopping his rush and knocking him to the ground. He picked up the man and threw him back against the bunkhouse door, where he lay inert. There was a breathless pause. Then one of the men muttered something.

"Who said that?" demanded Channing belligerently.

There was no reply. McDonald moved a step toward Channing and stood with his hand on his gun.

"Who said that?" repeated Channing.

None of the men spoke or moved. "All right," said Channing. "That's the way we want it."

Mendez was stirring. He gradually got to his feet, fumbled at the bunkhouse door till he found the latch, lifted it, and staggered inside.

"Order 'em in there," said Channing crisply to McDonald.

"You heard him," snapped out McDonald, moving toward the men grouped about the door.

After several moments of hesitation the men began to move slowly into the bunkhouse. Channing and McDonald waited until the last of them, but one, was inside. The one remaining was Jim Crossley.

"Get a padlock an' lock 'em in," Channing told Crossley.

While Crossley went to the barn and presently returned with a padlock, McDonald and Channing stood close to the wall on either side of the bunkhouse door. Crossley lost no time in fastening the chain to the staple of the door and snapping on the padlock. Then the three men moved to the shadows of the trees behind the bunkhouse.

Hope had stepped back into the dimly lighted interior of the kitchen. Now Mrs. McCaffy followed her and found her standing by the table, her face white, her eyes wide with apprehension.

"What does it mean?" asked Hope with a helpless gesture.

"It looks as if Channing's sort of took charge around here," said the housekeeper. "Well, it had to be done, I guess. We've got to keep the men, an' they've got to be told what's what. An' they're afraid of Channing, that's sure. McDonald ain't had the experience, I guess."

"But that Mexican!" Hope exclaimed.

"Mendez is a sneak!" said Mrs. McCaffy emphatically. "You can't trust a Mexican like that. Why did he want to get away so bad? You can bet Channing knows. Probably a spy of Mendicott's . . . yes, more'n likely. Mendez is fixing to get himself hung. They won't fool with a Mexican like that up here. Your uncle would have let him go long ago, but he's a wizard with a rope, an' he needed him."

"Probably Mendez has had instructions to do something like this," said Hope in indignation.

"Likely so," confirmed the housekeeper. "I reckon we'll have plenty of excitement around here. Something tells me Nate Farman isn't goin' to lose this ranch, but there's goin' to be the devil to pay keeping it."

There was a rap at the kitchen door. Mrs. McCaffy hesitated for an interval, and, when it sounded again, more authoritatively, she opened the door cautiously. Channing was standing outside. He removed his hat and spoke to both of them.

"You women had better put out the lights and go to bed," he said shortly, but in a voice that was not unpleasant. "Jim Crossley will stay here in the kitchen tonight. McDonald and I will be outside. There's no reason why you shouldn't get a good sleep."

"Are you giving orders to the women, too?" asked Mrs. McCaffy tartly.

"I'm telling you what's best," said Channing with a frown. "It's the only reason I have for bothering you."

Hope went to the door. "Is there any real danger, Mister Channing?" she asked anxiously.

"I dunno," replied Channing bluntly. "But I don't 'spect so."

She caught the suggestion of a smile in his eyes.

"Anyway, you won't have to be warning me tonight," he said lightly.

"I am reposing a great deal of confidence in you," she said as she turned away.

He retreated as Mrs. McCaffy took up the lamp. He closed the door softly as they started for the stairs.

In her room Hope reviewed the events of the day calmly. It seemed to her that nothing could happen now to startle her. Her nerves and senses were numbed. She trusted Channing because of some reassuring quality about him, because of what Lillian Bell had said, because of the look in his eyes. She knew he could be terrible, as he had been for a brief time that night. She knew he could control men. And she realized, with a flutter of excitement, that he was not afraid of the arch outlaw, Mendicott. It seemed enough.

She sat down by her window. All was still outside. A faint, scented breeze was stirring in the trees. The hills were shadowy forms rearing into the star-splashed sky.

After a time she dozed, only to awaken with a start. There was a pungent odor in the air, a dull, red glow outside the window. She looked out and felt an instant tightening of the throat. Shouts came to her ears. She stared, unable to move. Flames were leaping upward from the roof of the bunkhouse!

Chapter Twenty-Five

Hope sat motionlessly at her window, looking down into the yard between the ranch dwelling and the bunkhouse that was illuminated by the glare of the mounting flames. She saw a form come into the square of light—the tall form of Channing. Then McDonald came into the lighted space, and he and Channing turned their attention to the bunkhouse. The men inside were smashing out the windows with boards torn from bunks and pieces of furniture. Evidently the flames had broken out simultaneously at both ends of the roof, for they were coming out both small windows at each end of the building above the main sleeping room. This indicated that the fire had been set by someone inside the bunkhouse, and Hope thought at once of Mendez. With the thought came recollection of the appearance of the girl, Juanita. Very much did it look as if there was some connection between these two, the trouble of the earlier part of the night, and the fire.

The men in the burning building were shouting hoarsely. Channing was putting the key in the padlock while McDonald stood back, shouting instructions to the men within. Faces, white with fear, appeared at the windows, and then, as Channing unlocked the door and stepped back, drawing his gun in event of an emergency, the men trooped out, carrying their meager belongings.

As soon as the door was clear, Channing leaped inside. The other men crowded back toward the barn with McDonald watching them. When he called to them and motioned to them to halt, they obeyed. The roar of the flames from the attic of the building attested to the fact that it would be impossible to save it. The ranch was without fire-fighting apparatus, and to fight a blaze with such a start with pails of water would be futility itself. The men stared dully at the tongues of flames licking at the roof and the smoke pouring from the windows. Hope's hands were at her throat. It had happened so swiftly. And where was Channing? What was he doing inside the smoke-filled, flaming building?

As if in answer to her question, Channing appeared. He was bearing a burden in his arms—the limp form of a man. He put the burden down on the end before the men. McDonald ran toward the house.

Hope left her window, hurriedly put on a dressing gown and slippers, and went out into the hall. There she met Mrs. McCaffy, attired in similar fashion, holding a lamp and appearing frightened. "It's the bunkhouse," said Hope in a matter-of-fact tone. "It's on fire. There's no wind to speak of, so I don't think there's a chance for this house to catch. Let's go down and watch where we can be near Uncle."

They went down the stairs and found the rancher was sleeping the sleep of utter exhaustion through it all.

"We won't wake him unless we have to," Hope decided.

They passed through the dining room, the kitchen, and the rear door where they looked out into the lighted yard and saw McDonald throw a pail of water on a form on the ground. A man sat up quickly and the dark, belligerent features of Mendez shone evilly in the flickering flares of the fire.

"There's the man who started this," said Channing, addressing the others. "He started the fire with newspapers and other rubbish up there in the attic. It got going too fast for him before he could get out, and the smoke fixed him. He's the tool of Brood's, and he'd burn every one of you to keep in with the gang he's with!"

The men muttered, then talked loudly among themselves.

"String him up!" came the cry from half a dozen throats.

Channing waved a hand for silence. "That's what you've got to be scared of!" he cried. "Somebody working behind your backs and not somebody that comes out in the open to fight. I'm here, to fight with you, not against you. We can hold this place, and, when we need it, I'll get help. I locked you in there to give you a chance to do some thinking, not to burn you to death."

There was a cheer at this.

"We can take care of this fellow later," Channing continued. "Right now we've got to see that the house and none of the other buildings burn. We'll have to form a bucket chain and keep the roof of the ranch house wet so the sparks can't set it afire. Morning will be time enough to come to an understanding. Are you going to help?"

There was another cheer, and the men hurried to put their belongings out of reach of the sparks that were falling in showers. Ladders were brought from the barn and soon men were on the roofs of the house and barn, putting out the flaming embers that fell there and wetting down the roofs with pails of water passed up to them by the men below.

Nathan Farman called from the living room and Hope hurried in to him. He insisted that he be carried to a chair in the kitchen where he could see what was going on. Once there, he called lusty orders to do things that were already being done under the direction of McDonald and Channing.

Mendez had been taken away somewhere, possibly to the barn, and there either tied or locked in a room or stall. There was need for only an occasional order, and these were mostly given by McDonald. But Channing was everywhere in evidence, watching the work of the men, helping them, calling an order now and then, superintending the work in general.

Nathan Farman watched him with a puzzled frown. Hope told him bit by bit all that had happened that night, and of his declaration to the men that he would fight with them, in the open, and get help if it should be needed.

"I reckon it takes one bad man to fight another," Farman concluded.

"But Mister Channing can't possibly be as bad as the man he's fighting," defended Hope.

Her uncle looked at her curiously. "You seem to be much interested in him," he said. "It's all I've heard since you got back."

"Because I believe he's acting squarely with us," Hope returned, her face flaming. "I wish you would not jump at foolish conclusions, Uncle."

Her uncle was silent, watching the scene outside the kitchen door.

As the bunkhouse burned lower, becoming a fiery caldron of leaping, trickling flame, sending showers of sparks aloft, and throwing off an intense heat, the men began spraying the window casings and porch of the stone dwelling. Not once did the fire spread to other buildings, although Channing, with two others, found it necessary to tear down a board fence corral near the barn. The tops of trees behind the burning bunkhouse caught, but the trunks merely smoldered. In a remarkably short time the fire had resolved itself into a heap of glowing embers and the men were sent to cut a path through the timber behind the ruin to prevent the start of a forest fire that might sweep up into the hills and impair the watershed.

It lacked an hour of dawn. Channing sent Crossley to the house to ask that Mrs. McCaffy make a pail of hot, strong coffee for the men. For once the housekeeper had no banter for the little driver. She made the coffee, and they saw Channing take the pail and the cup from Crossley and himself carry it to the men.

The kitchen and the mess room of the bunkhouse having burned, the Chinese cook who cooked for the men came to the kitchen.

"You can help Missus McCaffy," Nathan Farman ordered. "The men will eat in the house today."

At dawn a great breakfast was ready and Channing, McDonald, and the other men came trooping in. Spare leaves had been added to the dining room table, and the men, after a session at the wash benches, were ushered into the dining room. The women waited on them. Channing sat at one end of the table and McDonald at the other. Mendez was absent, and none of the house had the temerity to ask about him. The men seemed in a cheerful humor, more cheerful than they had been in days. They cast surreptitious glances at Channing, who ate moodily with only an occasional remark in a pleasant tone, always addressed directly to someone of those about the table. He went out with the hands after breakfast, but McDonald lingered at a word from Nathan Farman.

"He seemed to have 'em acting pretty sensible," said the rancher.

"They put a lot of stock in him . . . more'n they do in me," said McDonald.

"What's he doing?" asked, Farman crossly. "Is he taking charge?"

"If it hadn't been for him, I don't think there'd be a man left on the place this morning," said McDonald soberly. "I let him go to it when he butted in. Looked like I had to let the men go or shoot 'em down in their tracks."

The rancher was thoughtful for a spell. "This is the sort of thing we've got to expect in the course of getting rid of men of Mendicott's stamp," he said finally. "I reckon we're playing with fire both ways. I don't get this fellow Channing at all, but he seems to be doin' us a service. Can he handle the men like I want 'em handled, McDonald?"

"I reckon he can," said the foreman slowly.

"Then I'll put him in charge," decided the rancher. "The two of you ought to make it stick."

"Shall I send him in?" asked McDonald.

"Yes, send him in," replied Farman.

When McDonald went outside, he found the men in a group before the barn door. Channing was there with Mendez. He was holding the empty dishes that had been used to serve the Mexican his breakfast. Mendez was scowling, and the attitude of the men was plainly hostile.

"I reckon we'll put you on a horse and give you a chance to get out of the country," Channing was saying. "You'll go south, understand? Not into the mountains, nor east to the desert, but south, out of the country."

Mendez bared his teeth in a snarling grin.

"Get his horse," Channing said to no one in particular.

Two of the men went for the Mexican's mount. The others grumbled and threatened the man with what he could expect to happen if he ever came back. When the horse was brought and the Mexican's saddle cinched on, the group broke away. Channing and McDonald moved to one side. Nathan Farman and Hope were watching from the kitchen door.

"Don't forget your directions!" called Channing, as Mendez drove in his spurs.

The Mexican leaned to the right as he shot past. There was a flash of light at his boot leg, and Channing dropped on a knee. McDonald stepped back with a little cry and reached to his shoulder. He pulled out a knife smeared with crimson. Mendez had missed Channing and struck McDonald.

A howl of rage went up from the men. Then came a cheer. Jim Crossley had stopped the Mexican at the porch of the ranch house by tripping his horse with a rope in a left-handed throw.

"I expected it!" Crossley cried as the men rushed for the Mexican.

In a trice the ranch hands, infuriated by the memory of their narrow escape from the fire and by Mendez's second attempt to kill with a knife—the hated weapon of all cowmen—had the rope around the Mexican's neck and were leading him away on his horse.

Channing made no move to interfere. Hope looked on in horror as she realized what that grim-visaged procession meant. Then she ran to Channing as he turned toward the kitchen.

"What are they . . . what is he . . . aren't you going to stop them?" gasped out Hope.

He looked around casually at the departing men. McDonald was approaching. He, too, was making no move to deter the men from their purpose.

"Give 'em a chance to take it out on somebody and you've got 'em," was Channing's laconic statement, addressed to Nathan Farman. "It'll help their nerve."

"But . . . they're going . . . to hang him!" cried Hope, aghast.

"He tried to kill a number of men here last night . . . and again this morning," said Channing coolly. "It'll be setting a good example."

"Uncle, will you allow this?" said Hope, appealing to Nathan Farman.

"I've just put Channing in charge of Rancho del Encanto," said her uncle, avoiding her eyes. "Is that wound very bad, McDonald? Better come in an' we'll take a look at it an' bandage it up."

Hope stared after the procession disappearing in the trees behind the barn. She could visualize that form hanging from the limb of a tall cottonwood, swaying in the wind. She turned and found only Channing outside the door.

"You may not understand all this, but it's necessary," he said gravely.

"Oh! Get out of my sight!"

And she ran for the house.

Chapter Twenty-Six

Hope hurried past her uncle, McDonald, and the housekeeper in the kitchen, and flung herself into a rocking chair in the living room. She could not get that mental picture of the hanging out of her mind. Nor did it seem right, for Mendez hadn't actually killed anyone, although he had undoubtedly tried to do so. He was likely a spy of Mendicott's as well as a tool of Brood's. It might be that he deserved hanging. But Channing's attitude in the matter had been too careless—or too vicious. Her whole conception of Channing had changed. The situation required sternness, a firm hand, authority, of course, but Channing had appeared too stern, too tyrannical. There seemed to be much of the brute in him, Hope thought, more than she had been led to expect. It did not occur to her at the time that Channing's moves might have been with a view to impressing the men—to win them over first by intimidation, then by catering to them. She knew nothing of the handling of such men as worked on Rancho del Encanto—men who were not of the best stock of the general run of ranch hands. She could think only of the look of terror on the Mexican's face, and the look in the eyes of his captors.

"It's plain murder," she said aloud. "What is the use of laws, of courts, judges so far as a country like this is concerned? They think they are above the law, while they are really below it. They are every bit as bad as Mendez . . . and the outlaws themselves."

In her heart Hope knew strict measures were required in a time like this. It was all right to use them on the men to keep them there and prevent Mendicott to frighten them away, but

169

the deliberate taking of a life was another matter. Hope did not even believe in capital punishment, and she had forgotten the day when she believed she could have killed Brood herself. She thought on these things for some time and was interrupted in their contemplation by Mrs. McCaffy.

"Somebody outside wants to see you!" the housekeeper called.

Hope rose with a puzzled expression and went out on the porch. She descended the steps and walked around the house, where she stopped suddenly as she saw a strange scene. The ranch hands were grouped around a figure on a horse—Mendez. He hadn't been hanged!

She saw Channing beckoning to her and approached with a look of relieved inquiry.

"They . . . didn't hang him?" she asked foolishly.

"No," said Channing. "They decided they'd just as soon humor a lady."

She saw the men grinning. Mendez's face was pale and his black eyes were fixed upon her with a pleading expression.

She turned to Channing. "It wouldn't have been right," she said.

She realized that Channing had hurried after the men, had explained to them that she didn't want this thing done on the ranch, had probably cajoled them into changing their minds while permitting them to think they were doing a chivalrous thing by her.

"Do you still think it would have been right?" she demanded.

"What do you want done with him?" Channing asked.

"Why . . . why let him go. Send him away as you were going to do in the first place."

Channing turned to the men with a faint smile. "You hear? She wants this fellow sent away."

The men took it good-naturedly. The one who was holding the rope about Mendez's neck motioned to the Mexican to take it off. Mendez slipped it over his head with shaking hands.

"Beat it!" called one of the men.

Mendez spurred his horse and galloped swiftly away as the men hurled advice after him as to the direction he should take and the length of time he should stay.

"But he won't go that way any great distance, and I reckon we'll see him again," Channing observed to the girl.

She knew what he meant. He suspected that the Mexican would take a roundabout way to the retreat of Mendicott. She hoped she would not be present if he were seen again by any of the Rancho del Encanto men.

Later when Hope chanced to be in the kitchen, Channing's voice came to her from the living room.

"There are reasons why I want that option, Nate."

"I can't see why it's necessary," parried the rancher. "I'm taking enough stock in you to give you charge here. That's doing a lot."

"You're doing it because you believe it's the one way out," said Channing. "Maybe it is. I want that option to make sure. When it's signed, Mendicott's got to do business with me, don't you see?"

"An' perhaps he will," said Farman sourly.

"In one month's time I'll return your option, if you want it," said Channing. "I give you my word on that. Will you make it out?"

There was a brief silence. "For how much?" the rancher said finally.

"Say a hundred and fifty thousand dollars," replied Channing.

"Why, I don't believe the place would sell for that," said Farman in a tone of astonishment.

"Maybe not . . . if you put the price on it," drawled out Channing. "But you aren't selling it, you're giving me an option. Do I get it?"

"Oh, I'll write it out," said Farman in resignation. "But, listen to me, Channing, if there's any trick about this . . ."

"You can sure blame me," Channing concluded for him.

The two women looked at each other in silence as the voices in the living room ceased. They could hear things on the table being moved, a drawer being opened and closed—sounds that indicated that Nathan Farman was writing out the option on Rancho del Encanto. For a few moments Hope experienced a feeling of panic. The price seemed high; $150,000 was a larger sum than she had ever thought the ranch with its stock could be worth. Perhaps Channing was purposely putting the price high because he intended to exercise the option. It was certain that if he so decreed, Nathan Farman would have to sell. And it gave Channing added power as far as the management of ranch affairs was concerned. Another startling thought occurred to her. Did Channing have that much money? It hardly seemed probable. Could he get it? If so, from whom? The answer was all too plain; there was but one other man interested in the ranch as a purchase, and that man was Mendicott. All this worried the girl. It was the supreme test of her confidence in Channing—a man of whom she knew little.

She heard her uncle speaking again. "For what length of time shall I make this out?"

"Ninety days," Channing replied cheerfully.

"But you said I could have it back if I wanted at the end of thirty days," said Nathan Farman.

"You can," Channing affirmed, "if you want it."

His manner of saying this seemed to convey a double meaning. It was as if he knew that the rancher would not ask for the option at the end of the thirty days. It was even possible that he meant Farman wouldn't dare ask for it. Hope felt another twinge of misgiving.

"What will I make the terms?" Farman asked after an interval.

"Cash," answered Channing.

"Cash!" exclaimed the rancher. "I reckon that's why you're sort of hinting that I won't ask for the option back in thirty days?"

Even Hope realized that $150,000 in cash was an alluring offer for Rancho del Encanto. It might tempt her uncle. Was it all a scheme to put an attractive price before Nathan Farman?

"You can think what you please," said Channing coldly. "But you can put the terms down as cash."

There was another interval of silence, then: "All right, there it is, all signed."

"We'll have to have it witnessed said Channing in a business-like tone. "Better call in Miss Farman and McDonald."

Hope answered her uncle's call and sat down at the table with the paper before her. She looked steadily at Channing, holding the pen poised for her signature. His face was inscrutable, like the face of a gambler or banker hearing a request for a loan. He looked at her frankly but there was a hint of the supercilious in his manner— a mocking challenge in his eyes. At last she signed.

McDonald came in at Mrs. McCaffy's call and he, too, looked at Channing as he saw what it was he was asked to witness. But his look was curious and puzzled.

"Just sign as a witness," Channing reminded him.

McDonald affixed his signature and rose awkwardly.

"I reckon that closes this business for the present," said Channing, folding the paper and stowing it in a pocket. "There's just one thing, Nate, I want you to remember. You've always sneered at the desert . . . hated it, I guess. But it's the desert that's going to do more for you than anything else." His tone and look were prophetic. He gave the rancher no opportunity to comment on this, but turned to McDonald. "Have the men fix up their quarters in the loft of the big barn," he ordered crisply. "Give 'em anything they want and treat 'em nice. We've got 'em in good humor and we want to keep 'em that way till somebody throws another scare into 'em." He frowned deeply. For some moments he was lost in thought while the others studied him. "Send two men to keep an eye on the cattle on the mesa," he continued. "Tomorrow we'll make a hard ride to round up most of the cattle outside, and keep two or three men out after strays. When we got 'em all on the mesa, I'm going to move every last one of 'em off the ranch."

Farman started to speak, but desisted when Channing looked at him sharply.

"Is that all?" asked McDonald quietly.

"That's it, for now," said Channing. "I'm coming right out there to keep an eye on things."

McDonald left the room to carry out his orders.

Channing turned to Farman. "Is there . . . any spare artillery around here?"

Farman nodded and pointed to a lower drawer of a clothes press.

Hope went out into the kitchen. A few minutes later Channing went out to the yard.

The men went cheerfully about the work of arranging sleeping quarters in the barn. Nathan Farman decided that the meals would be served in the house. Channing continued to preside at the head of the table, and it was noticeable at dinner that all were on good terms. Channing appeared to have imbued the men with a goodly measure of his own confidence.

This confidence impressed Hope and her uncle. It served to convey the impression that Channing was sure Mendicott would make no new move for some time. They did not know, nor suspect, how soon this illusion was to be shattered.

In the afternoon the branding of calves was resumed on the mesa. Only Jim Crossley remained at the ranch house. He was sort of looking after odd jobs and keeping an eye on the last smoldering embers remaining from the fire. As the day wore on a sense of normality gradually returned to those on the ranch. Prospects of further trouble appeared more remote. Nathan Farman sat in his chair on the porch and dozed and smoked his pipe. He had, to all appearances, given himself up to the new order of things.

This condition obtained at supper, with the men laughing and joking. There was a more tense feeling as night approached, and those in the house were aware of it as well as the others. But the night passed very peacefully.

In the morning the men were at breakfast before the dawn. Channing gave crisp orders at the table, and they were well received. The men, with the exception of Crossley, who was again left at the ranch house, rode away with the first light in the east to gather the cattle ranging outside of the mesa. Channing and McDonald accompanied the men. As they rode away, Hope heard Channing singing. It gave her something of a thrill. Evidently he was satisfied with matters as they were. It was certain that he knew exactly what he was doing, why he was doing it, and how to do it.

"Danged good cowman," was Nathan Farman's comment when she mentioned the fact to him. "Don't see why he ain't been at it all these years. He's had experience, an' he knows how to handle men. I reckon he just fell for the free life. The desert got him, an', when the desert gets 'em, they sometimes get a little queer in the head."

"You're not intimating that Channing is queer that way, are you?" asked Hope in astonishment.

"No," answered her uncle, frowning, "I'm wondering if he isn't too all-fired smart."

Hope helped the housekeeper, although there was little that Mrs. McCaffy would let her do.

The men returned late. Nathan Farman grunted in approval as he looked through his field glasses and saw the cattle being driven onto the mesa. "They've got most of 'em," he said in satisfaction. "I wonder where he figures on takin' 'em? Anyway, he's running things so comfortable that I'm going to keep still an' let him go ahead."

It was after dark when supper was served, and it was as good a meal as it was possible for Mrs. McCaffy to prepare. The men spoke loudly in its praise.

"I reckon we won't wait to brand any more calves here," said Channing after supper. "The weather's fixing for a change, and I'm going to move the stock out of here before the change comes. We're due for some rain, and rain'll wash away tracks."

Nathan Farman nodded assent. He did not bother to ask Channing where he intended to take the cattle.

Hope walked in the yard under the trees this night. It had been hot all day, but with evening a cool breeze filtered down through the stands of pine and fir. The stars were clusters of diamonds in the sky. As she walked along the hedge in front of the house, Channing approached.

"Good evening, Miss Farman," he said politely.

"Good evening, Mister Channing. Everything . . . is quiet?"

She noted with surprise that he was wearing two guns this night. So that was why he had asked if there was any spare artillery in the house. It gave her something of a start—the sight of those two ominous-looking weapons on his thighs.

"Everything is quiet," he said soberly. "Miss Farman, I'm going to trust you with something."

Hope was stirred. Was he going to divulge more about himself? She answered in a low voice: "You can do that, Mister Channing."

He drew an envelope from within his shirt and held it out to her. "There's an envelope addressed to you, Miss Farman. If anything should happen to me . . . anything serious, I mean . . . you open that envelope yourself. There's a communication inside."

Hope took the envelope wonderingly. Before she could make a reply, he had swung on his heel and was walking away. She turned the envelope over and over in her hands, thinking hard. If anything serious should happen to him. It was borne in upon her that Channing had assumed a risk—that he was in danger. It explained the two guns, perhaps. He had been serious enough, and he was trusting her to respect his wishes in this matter, trusting her above the others. Hope put the

envelope carefully away, thrilled at the thought that it constituted a sort of bond of confidence between them. She heard
him singing softly somewhere in the shadows as she went into
the house.

Chapter Twenty-Seven

The quiet of the night was destined to be short-lived. Channing had assumed charge of the cattle on the mesa in person, affording McDonald an opportunity to rest in the house. Half a dozen men were in the barn loft and others were with Channing. Jim Crossley was in the rear of the house, walking in the starlight. The house was dark, and everyone within was apparently asleep. It was Crossley who was first to hear horsemen coming from the foothill trail and its branches. The flying hoofs echoed dully in the night. He stood for a few moments, listening, then sounded the alarm by firing his gun in the air three times. Several men called to him from the barn loft and he shouted to them to come to the house. Then he ran for his horse that he had kept close by, saddled and ready for an emergency. He galloped around the house, leaped the hedge, and rode to notify Channing. Channing sent him back at once with orders for the men at the house to stay there.

Channing had already seen the night riders sweep out on the mesa from the cover of the trees at the edge of the foothills. He swore softly. It was plain he hadn't expected such an early demonstration on the part of Mendicott. The move was, doubtless, in the nature of another warning that Mendicott was in no mood for delay in gaining his ends, that he didn't intend to permit Channing to frustrate his plan to harass Nathan Farman into disposing of the ranch. With Channing leading them, the men riding herd on the stock on the mesa showed unexpected aggressiveness. They drew their weapons and followed Channing around the herd to the west side of the mesa in an effort to get between the herd and the approaching riders. But the herd was now up and milling about as the raiders rode in, evidently bent on stampeding the cattle from the mesa into the foothills or desert where it would take some time for another roundup. The raiders were shouting and firing their weapons, but they found it difficult to get the cattle started on the run in the darkness. They cut halfway through the herd, and then out the north side, converging at the north end of the mesa between the cattle and the house.

The people in the house were roused by this time and were up. Hope and the housekeeper, alarmed by the shooting and the shouts, were in the living room with Nathan Farman, who called in Jim Crossley.

"Get the men that are here out behind that hedge in front of the house." he ordered, "an' bring me my Winchester."

They did not light the lamp, and Mrs. McCaffy and Hope helped the rancher into his chair and at his repeated command opened the door to the porch and moved him to a place at one side just within the door. Crossley brought the rifle and a box of cartridges and went back to carry out his orders as Farman moved the lever of the gun, slipping a cartridge into place in the barrel of the Winchester.

Watching from the door and windows they saw the handful of men left at the house creep into position behind the tamarack hedge between the mesa and the ranch dwelling. McDonald came downstairs with his gun in his hand and took up his station near Nathan Farman. The raiders plainly were finding it difficult to accomplish their purpose on the mesa. The milling cattle refused to stampede, despite the firing and the shouts, and there were now Encanto men between the raiders and the cattle.

"What are they trying to do with the cattle?" Hope asked her uncle.

"Looks like they figured on stealing 'em," said the rancher.

"Oh, it can't be that!" Hope exclaimed. "They wouldn't attempt to steal them in such bold fashion as this."

Nathan Farman laughed harshly. "They're on this ranch where they don't belong an' they're molesting the stock," he said grimly. "I reckon any court in the country would put that under the head of plain rustling."

The watchers in the house now saw a stirring sight. One of the Encanto riders spurred his horse straight for the bunched outlaws. From either side of him came spurts of flame—the red flashes of his guns. The other ranch hands with the herd fell in behind him and began pouring lead at the raiders. Hope and the others needed no one to tell them that the leader of this bold charge was Channing. He was the only one of the Encanto men armed with two guns, and the figure he made on his splendid horse in the starlight was unmistakable.

"That's him," muttered Nathan Farman.

Hope held her breath, expecting to see him shot from his saddle. But nothing like this happened, and he came on with his men at his back, his guns blazing, his horse galloping like mad. The raiders scattered and rode toward the foothills in front of the house. A cheer came from the men behind the hedge, and they loosed their weapons, sending a hail of lead toward the invaders.

The stillness of the living room was shattered by the roar of the Winchester in Nathan Farman's hands. One of the raiders toppled from his saddle and the rancher shouted in fierce joy. McDonald leaped out on the porch and emptied his gun. Then the invaders began to fire in the general direction of the house as they swept past.

"We've got 'em on the run!" cried Nathan Farman in great excitement. "They got more'n they were looking for. I don't reckon Mendicott's with 'em, or they'd charge the house."

He worked the lever of the Winchester rapidly and emptied the rifle at the fleeing riders.

Channing jumped his horse over the hedge in an effort to cut them off while Crossley, McDonald, and the men by the hedge started for the rear of the house trying to keep within range.

Hope shared her uncle's belief that Mendicott was not with the men. There was no doubt in her mind but that the raiders were members of the outlaw band carrying out orders to harass them by interfering with the cattle. In this they had failed and were fleeing for the safety of the hills. Evidently they had no orders to attack the house, or were discouraged by the reception extended to them. By this time the pursuit had reached the edge of the timber on the west side of the mesa beyond the house, barns, and other outbuildings and corrals. Here it ended, and the firing ceased.

After a time Channing came riding back to the house with his men. He sent those who were mounted back to the mesa to look after the cattle, quiet them, and see about the men who had been shot from their mounts. He ordered the others to saddle their horses.

A lamp had been lighted in the living room and Channing entered. He found Nathan Farman, McDonald, Mrs. McCaffy, and Hope there and smiled at them gravely.

"They picked off a couple of our men, and I guess we got a few of theirs," he announced. "I don't think they'll be back," he added with his queer smile. He stared at the rifle that the rancher still held. Then he looked at Hope, and the girl felt that he had enjoyed the trouble they had just witnessed. Perhaps he welcomed trouble. "Anyway, it's sure put some spunk in our men," he said.

"An' showed that skunk up in the hills that we mean business," said Nathan Farman, scowling at him.

"Well, he means business, too, I take it," drawled Channing. "I'm wondering if this is a good place for the women."

"It's a matter for the county seat an' the authorities!" stormed the rancher. "I'll be able to travel in three or four more days, an' I aim to go in."

"You mean over the range to the county seat?" asked Channing, elevating his eyebrows.

"That same," said Farman, putting his rifle aside. "We'll take the spring wagon."

Channing shrugged and got out his tobacco and papers. "Don't know that would help any," he said.

"Look here, Channing," said Nathan Farman sharply, leaning forward in his chair, "you know the way to Mendicott's place in the hills, I understand. What's to stop you from leading a big posse up there?"

"Nothing but Mendicott," was the simple reply.

"Thundering rot!" exclaimed Farman. "He could be surrounded . . ."

"If you could get the men and knew how to surround him," Channing broke in. "It isn't so easy to get men way up there after a bunch like that. And whenever you start anything like that, you've got to finish it if you're coming out with any men."

"How would you figure to get him or break up his band?" Farman demanded.

"I haven't figured on that end of it so much," Channing answered easily. "When a man is sort of holed up that way, it might be better to draw him out."

It was the first intimation of any definite plan on Channing's part, and the others looked at him with fresh interest.

"It would cost every man an' every head of stock on the ranch to do it," said the rancher doubtfully.

Channing stepped to the door and went out on the porch for a few moments.

"We're going to have a little spell of weather and I'm goin' to start with the cattle in the morning," he announced when he returned. "With the cattle out of the way, maybe it would be a good plan to go to the county seat. Maybe I'll go with you."

Nathan Farman looked at the speaker suspiciously. Hope took the announcement as a point in Channing's favor. He had

182

no fear of visiting the county seat, then, and there was logic in
what he said about an attack on Mendicott's rendezvous. She
remembered the inspiring sight of his charge on the raiders. His
life had been in grave peril then. He had foreseen something
like this when he gave her the envelope. She wondered what it
contained.

"We can't do anything now, that's sure," Channing was saying.
"You all might as well have your sleep out. We'll be moving the
cattle at daybreak." He turned quickly on his heel and went out.

* * * * *

Breakfast was ready for the men before dawn. Hope was up
early and insisted on helping in the kitchen. She had been unable
to sleep. They learned from Jim Crossly that two of the raiders
had been killed and another slightly wounded. The last had been
captured. One of the ranch hands also had been killed in the
running fight and two others hurt, one breaking his leg when his
horse was shot down under him.

Hope could see that her uncle was much worried. But his
manner was more stern and uncompromising than it had been
the day before. If Mendicott was endeavoring to throw a bluff
into him—as the rancher put it—he would have his trouble for
nothing. It seemed to Hope that a certain stern and unyielding
side to her uncle's character had been brought to the surface by
the incident of the night.

It was now known that Mendicott had not been with the
raiders. The wounded outlaw had talked a little to Channing,
the latter disclosed. The object of the attack had been to run off
the cattle, but the wounded outlaw denied they had intended to
steal them.

"What'll we do with him?" Nathan Farman asked Channing.

"Turn him loose," was the astonishing reply.

"So he can have another whack at us?" asked Farman in
answer.

"So he can take word back where he came from that I have an option on this ranch," replied Channing. "That'll keep Mendicott thinking and planning for a few days while I have a chance to cache the cattle."

The rancher nodded, but did not appear convinced.

Channing turned on him with a frown. "I'm figuring that you'll begin to see after a time that I'm in this thing against Mendicott," he said slowly in an earnest voice. "I'm waiting for something. If I were to tell you what, you'd laugh at me. I don't aim to be laughed at if I can help it. I . . . don't like it. And I'm trying to play him at his own game. I reckon you'll have to guess what that game is for the present, Nate."

The wounded outlaw was released and rode away into the hills. Channing had been careful to see to it that he heard nothing of their plans for moving the cattle. He suspected they were being watched from vantage points in the hills, and, when he drove the cattle away at dawn, they proceeded in a southeasterly direction, across the ridge separating the mesa from the desert.

Hope watched them go with an anxious expression on her face. They were left alone on the ranch, except for Jim Crossley and the two wounded men. If Mendicott now wished to attack the ranch house, it would be an excellent opportunity. Again she thought of the envelope Channing had entrusted to her. Would it be all right, she wondered, to open it in such an emergency? But he had said to open it only if something serious were to happen to him. She felt it within her blouse. It revived her confidence. She waved her hand impulsively as the last Encanto rider disappeared over the ridge.

Chapter Twenty-Eight

The day passed quietly enough at Rancho del Encanto. The Chinese cook had gone with the wagon accompanying the cattle, which seemed to please Mrs. McCaffy. The housekeeper's spirits rose steadily. Jim Crossley attended the wounded men who were made comfortable in the improvised quarters in the barn loft. The rancher was up and walking for the first time. He sat on the porch during the afternoon.

With the approach of night Channing's prediction came true, and a rain storm swept down from the northwest.

"It'll cover the tracks of the cattle," the rancher explained to Hope. "I guess he's hiding 'em in the desert. He ought to know where to put them where they can get feed an' water for a while, anyway. Well, I'm trusting him with the works, it seems like."

"He hinted that the desert would in some way prove our ultimate salvation," Hope pointed out.

"He's desert crazy," her uncle returned. "I've always been afraid of it," he added with a shrug. "An' I've always been leery of them that's stuck to it. I've seen 'em come an' go too many years."

"But, after all, you never knew very much about Channing," Hope remarked.

"An' I know less now," said Nathan Farman.

It rained hard all through the late afternoon and during the early evening. The night settled fast with the sky overcast with clouds and the rain still falling. They had finished supper and were sitting in the living room when Crossley came in with an impressive announcement.

"Channing's back," he said.

"What's that?" asked Nathan Farman in surprise.

"Rode in to be at the house tonight," said Crossley. "Aims to be on hand, I take it, if there's any more trouble. He's getting some sleep in the barn."

Farman muttered to himself as Crossley left. Hope experienced a feeling of relief from her worry because they were virtually alone on the ranch. It was a strange sensation, she thought to herself, this sensation of security in the nearness of this man. She cheered her uncle with her animated conversation, mostly one-sided this night. But she said nothing of the envelope that had been entrusted to her care. Later she went to her room and slept soundly through the night. When she awoke, it was day, and the sun was again shining.

She dressed hurriedly and went downstairs. Channing had left to rejoin the men with the cattle before dawn, not waiting to take breakfast at the ranch or see anyone.

This day also passed with no untoward incident. Nathan Farman walked about and commented cheerfully on the beneficial effects of the rain on the growing oats and hay. While Rancho del Encanto was under irrigation, any additional moisture helped and rain is far better than artificial watering for crops.

Channing did not return that night, and Crossley was scouting most of the day in the hills.

"He's got the cattle in the desert without bein' followed as near as I can make out," said Crossley that night. "He'll hide 'em where they'll have a hard time gettin' to 'em without bein' seen, I'll bet on that."

Although those in the house did not feel so easy this night, with Channing gone and few men on the place, there was nothing said to indicate their real feelings. Each was beset by the thought that, if Mendicott did not know that the stock had been moved, another raid might result, in which event it was likely that the outlaw chief would himself lead his men to see that his purpose was accomplished. His expeditions, led in person, were notorious for their success and the ruthless cruelty attending them. But, in the past, these raids had been on towns with plunder or revenge as the objective. In the present instance it was apparent to all concerned that Mendicott was engaged in a systematic campaign to obtain possession of Rancho del Encanto. What effect the knowledge that Channing had an option on the place would have, Hope and her uncle could only conjecture.

But the night passed without disturbance and another day brought renewed hope that the outlaw was holding back until he could arrange his plans, as Channing had predicted. What these plans might portend, however, was a source of worry.

Late in the afternoon, when Hope and her uncle were sitting on the porch enjoying the cool breeze from the hills, they heard a dull, rumbling report, like distant thunder, in the mountains.

They looked at each other in wonder. "That's queer," said the rancher. "Sounds like blasting. I didn't know there were any prospectors working back up there an' there's no work of any other kind I know of goes on in these hills."

He had hardly finished speaking when the echoes of two more reports rolled down on the wind.

"That's dynamite, sure as shooting!" he exclaimed. "There must be somebody working up there. It's a rock blast. I can tell that much by the sound, although I'm no miner."

They walked to the end of the porch and looked up at the foothills, but could see nothing.

"Well, we don't care, do we, Uncle, if somebody is prospecting around here?" asked Hope. "It doesn't seem so strange. Didn't you say prospectors worked in these mountains?"

"Yes, they do," he agreed. "But they usually come in from this side, an' lots of times they stop here overnight on the way in. Still, they could come in over the range, I reckon."

"That's probably what they did," said Hope. "We don't care how much they prospect up there. It seems good to know somebody is around besides that Mendicott and his crowd. I'd like to hear some more blasting. It sounds good to hear something."

But her cheerful words could not drive the puzzled frown from her uncle's face. He walked slowly back and forth on the porch while she sat and sewed.

An hour later they were startled by the pound of hoofs on the foothill trail behind the barn. They hurried to the end of the porch in time to see Jim Crossley gallop into view. He came down the trail at a perilous pace and rode up to the porch.

"They've done it!" he cried, flinging himself from the saddle.

"What's the mater, Crossley?" called Nathan Farman.

Crossley was breathing hard and was greatly excited. He pointed to an irrigating ditch near the hedge in front of the house.

The water!" he exclaimed. "They've stopped the water!"

"What do you mean?" cried the rancher, his face growing pale. "Speak up, Crossley, an' make yourself clear."

"They've blown up the dam, that's what," said Crossley, removing his hat to wipe his forehead. "I was scouting around up there an' heard the shots. It rained fine rock an' cement clear down to where I was at, an' I took to cover. Then I saw the water in the big ditch go down an' water came shootin' down the hill, an' I knew they'd blowed up the dam."

Nathan Farman stepped to the edge of the porch and turned a white face toward the ditch. Hope looked, too, and it needed no second glance to see that the water had gone down. The supply had been cut off. This explained the mystery of the thundering reports of explosives in the hills behind the ranch.

Her uncle went back to his chair and dropped into it with a gesture of despair. "I might have guessed it when I heard the shots," he said wearily. "You say pieces of cement fell, Crossley? An' water came down the hill? It was the dam all right." As Crossley nodded, the old man pounded the arms of his chair in a rage. "That's it!" he exclaimed, his face darkening. "It's

Mendicott's latest move, an' his worst. He's shut off the water an' let it go at the same time. We couldn't rebuild that dam in time to save the crops from burning up even if it would fill in time after it was built. That means I'll have to sell the cattle whether I want to or not. There won't be enough water for all the stock. I'd be lucky to have enough for the horses alone. An, it'll mean a scarcity of winter feed." He groaned. "It'll spoil the mesa."

Even Hope, ignorant as she was of technical matters concerning stock raising in that country, realized that this was a serious blow. She saw disaster reflected in the faces of Crossley and her uncle. And suddenly it was impressed upon her more than ever that it was the water that made Rancho del Encanto so valuable; it was the water that kept it green and beautiful. And now the water was gone.

"But we have the spring left," she said hopefully.

"Just enough for the house," declared her uncle. "Enough to drink for ourselves an' maybe the horses. It was the water rights to that stream that caused me to buy this place. I harnessed the creek and built the dam, put in the ditches, an' the laterals. An' Mendicott undoes it all with three shots of dynamite. By the heavens over this country, it's too much!"

He rose and stood shaking with rage, while Hope tried in vain to quiet him.

"Did you notice any water running in the big ditch at all, Crossley?" he asked.

"Just a little, sir. I figured what was in the ditch was just part of the stream that was still runnin' into it. Of course they can ruin the ditch quick enough." He hesitated as he saw the look on Nathan Farman's face.

"I know what you mean!" roared the rancher. "But they don't have to bother with the ditch now that the dam's gone with all the water in it. That stream'll be almost dry in a month!" He sat down again and put his face in his hands. "If I hadn't been flat on my back from the day this thing started, Crossley, an' so slow getting around since, I'd have gone after that fellow up in the hills myself!"

"It maybe won't get him so much as he thinks," said Crossley in an effort to cheer the rancher. "I'll bet Channing knows where there's water an' plenty of feed in the desert to carry the stock through if you want to keep 'em."

"But I've got to fatten the beeves," said Farman. "I've always fattened 'em in here on the mesa. They've got to carry good weight out of here to be in any sort of shape when they get to the shipping point. It's . . . it's . . . ." He swore roundly under his breath and looked at Hope. "This wasn't the kind of a time I planned for you out here, child," he said bitterly. "Maybe you would like to go over across the mountains an' down into southern Californy. Maybe we'd better go."

"No, Uncle," said Hope with a sober smile. "Let's stick it out. I'm getting something out of this . . . oh, I don't know what, but I feel different . . . more as if you . . . all of us amounted to something in the world. I'm beginning to understand what it means to fight for things."

"Then fight it is!" cried Nathan Farman. "An' I'm going to carry the fight to the man who's trying to ruin us. I'm going to the county seat an' put it up to the sheriff!"

He rose and called to Crossley, who was moving toward his horse. "Crossley, get the spring wagon greased an' bring in the grays. We'll start for the county seat in the morning."

Crossley acknowledged the order with a nod and led his horse away. "Uncle," protested Hope, "you are not going to start on this trip until Channing gets back, are you?"

"We're going tomorrow," replied her uncle sternly. "Channing only has an option on this ranch, an' with the dam out it isn't worth a fraction of the price that's named in the option. That lets the option out an' Channing with it. If the sheriff won't take a hand, I'll offer my cattle as a reward for Mendicott's scalp . . . an' I'll get it!"

He went into the house leaving Hope standing on the porch looking wistfully toward the ridge that shut off the desert.

Chapter Twenty-Nine

Hope found at suppertime that her uncle had meant what he said. His determination to carry the whole business to the authorities was unshaken. It seemed to have lent him strength, or it might have been the natural result of his recovery from his wound. It was a peculiar fact that he did not once refer to Brood in a vindictive way. If he entertained the wish to be avenged, so far as his former foreman was concerned, he did not so express himself in word or manner. It was evident that he blamed Mendicott for all the troubles that beset him. He inquired of Jim Crossley if arrangements had been made for the trip to the county seat and learned that the spring wagon was in shape and the horses ready in the barn. His manner of making the inquiry banished any last doubt of his intention that might have lingered in the minds of the others.

After supper Hope asked Jim Crossley if she could have a horse to ride. He said she could have his pony and in a short time he brought the rangy little bay to the porch. When Nathan Farman saw what was going on, he instructed Crossley to take the bay away and bring Firefly. Firefly proved to be a sleek, black gelding a little smaller than the big horse belonging to Channing.

"That's the prettiest and best horse on the ranch," Jim Crossley whispered to Hope, and Hope saw that it was, indeed, a beautiful, spirited animal. "Do you like him?" asked the rancher.

"He's as pretty as Black Beauty must have been in his prime," replied Hope, rubbing Firefly's nose—a procedure that the horse did not seem to mind.

"He's yours," said her uncle. "I've been saving him for you. You could have had him long ago."

Hope ran to her uncle, threw her arms about his neck, and kissed him.

"I've learned to love to ride since I've been out here," she told him. "I never realized it could be such fun."

"Better not ride him too hard at the start," her uncle cautioned. "Just a little canter, child. He's been on the grass. When he gets hardened a bit, you can ride him to your heart's content."

"I won't go farther than the ridge, Uncle," she promised.

Firefly took her in a flying spur across the mesa, and she turned him up the road to the top of the ridge beyond. When they reached the crest, she stopped and looked for a long time down into the desert. The sunset was flaming above the mountains, hurling its banners into the high skies gilding the peaks with gold. The air was cool after the heat of the day, but now and then a breath of wind would steal up from the desert and it was like the hot blast of a furnace. Hope surmised that summer had come on the heels of the transient storm.

She saw no sign of life anywhere in the great waste space that reached out to eastward. The sea of sage and greasewood was laved in a soft, pink glow and streamers of blue and turquoise hung on the far horizon, punctured by rose-colored cones of the lava hills. Somewhere in the north was Arsenic Spring; in the northeast was Ghost Wash; in the southeast was Bandburg. Strange what memories these places held for her. She remembered how she had ridden from the railroad far in the south and had imagined that one could never associate definite spots in that land of desolation with real happenings—with life. Yet now she was looking into it, dreaming, recalling incidents that seemed a part of some previous existence. Was she beginning to love the desert? She knew one could come to love it, but she did not believe that anyone not born to it could come readily to the resignation of living upon it.

She sat her horse, looking into it until the twilight had fallen and the land was bathed in purple veils. Then she turned back to the mesa and the portal of Rancho del Encanto. How long, she wondered, would it remain the Ranch of Enchantment with the water gone? More and more she understood her uncle's love for the place; more and more she thought she understood why Mendicott wanted it—was determined to have it. She did not like the idea of leaving for the county seat across the range until Channing had returned. And why didn't he return? Had he not had time to hide the cattle near some water hole and get back to the ranch? Had something happened to him? Would it be reasonable for her to assume that something had happened to him and open the letter? She decided not. She found herself thinking that nothing could happen to Channing.

When she rode back to the house, she saw a rider coming in from the mesa, and recognized Jim Crossley. She smiled, knowing that he had been watching her movements—standing guard over her at a distance.

Mrs. McCaffy was in a fluster when she entered the kitchen after turning her horse over to Crossley.

"Wants me to go to town," scolded the housekeeper. "Why should I go to town? I'm not afraid to stay here. Somebody's got to stay. Besides, there'd hardly be room for all of us in that wagon."

Hope was willing to be cheered, and Mrs. McCaffy's blustering way of talking and practical view of things in general never failed to amuse her.

Jim Crossley came in while the discussion was under way. "Why, Missus McCaffy," he bantered, "you know you've been complainin' about not havin' a chance to go to town forever to get some finery to dress up in. This is your chance."

"Jim Crossley, you shut your face!" exclaimed Mrs. McCaffy, growing red. "An' who would I dress up for around here? Sure not for the likes of you!"

"Oh, you can't tell," replied Crossley. "I might appreciate it."

"You're too fresh, an' you're getting worse," said the house-keeper, her hands on her hips. "It takes a little runt like you to think up lots to say without it meaning anything."

That night, as Hope sat by her darkened window, looking out into the star-filled night, she thought of Channing, and began to wish he would return before their start in the morning. She remembered Lillian Bell's quotation of his saying: Words are what you make them. It rang in her ears. And Lillian had said: We're all outlaws. Just what did she mean by that?

Hope was trying to adjust herself to an order of things that she never dreamed could possibly enter into her life. What she did not recognize was the fact that she was witnessing a country in its transitory period. It was like the thunder and lightning of a storm at its most violent height, just before the break.

Morning came with no sign of Channing, and, true to Far-man's word, they started immediately after breakfast on his order. Jim Crossley and the rancher sat in the front seat, Crossley han-dling the lines with one hand and Farman spelling him at driving. Hope sat alone in the rear seat. Mrs. McCaffy remained at the ranch to care for the two injured men.

"Channing will likely be back in a day or two," Nathan Farman told the housekeeper.

"I'm not scared none," said Mrs. McCaffy stoutly, pointing to the rifle in a corner near the stove. "I'll shoot the first suspi-cious character that comes nosing around an' ask him questions afterwards . . . if he can talk."

So they took leave of Rancho del Encanto, driving over the ridge to the road that led southward where the foothills met the desert. Once more Hope found herself viewing the wasteland at close hand. It was fearfully hot, but there was no wind and but little dust. They had to go south almost to the railroad before they reached the road leading west over the mountains. Thus she saw again the fantastic Joshua trees, the yucca, juniper, paloverdes, mesquite, and the giant cactus; the saffron-colored patches of baked earth, the unending gray sage and dull green greasewood; the painted buttes and cones with their mineral stains of red and green; the bare, forbidding hills clothed in purple haze; the burning ball of the sun shining mercilessly from a cloudless sky.

They turned west in the late afternoon and stayed that night at a roadhouse in the hills. Next day they crossed the range, and at sunset they stopped at another diminutive hotel with the burning valley of the San Joaquin below them. The following day they descended into a land of orchards and vineyards, where the heat waves simmered almost as fiercely as those of the desert, and in the latter part of the day arrived in Kernfield, the county seat.

Hope was left at the hotel, and Crossley drove Nathan Farman directly to the sheriff's office before he put up the team.

Farman found the sheriff in—Roscoe Kemp was his name. He was a large raw-boned man with sandy mustaches, a long face, and piercing gray eyes. He motioned the rancher to a chair at his desk and listened while Nathan Farman introduced himself and stated his errand.

As the rancher proceeded, becoming more energetic in his manner of speech as he outlined the happenings at Rancho del Encanto, the sheriff frowned and tapped his desk with a pencil stub, looking out the window into the hot street.

"Just why do you come to me?" he asked when Farman paused and mopped his brow.

"Why?" said the rancher in surprise. "You're the sheriff of this county, are you not?"

"I am," admitted Kemp. "But you seem to have just found it out."

"What do you mean by that?" demanded Farman with a scowl.

"I mean that you fellows over there have had a way for a long time of settling things to suit yourself without consulting this office," replied the sheriff. "Now that you're up against a boomerang, you come here for help."

"It isn't a boomerang," said Farman hotly. "It's a case of out-and-out desperadoes an' bandits, rustlers an' killers, with the worst man in the state at their head."

"We've been after that man more than once," said Kemp calmly, "and we never got any help from you fellows over there. We've tried to raise posses and couldn't get enough men to go out on the trail."

"That's because they were afraid to go, an' Mendicott has lots of friends in those little desert towns an' camps," Farman interrupted.

"Sure. Exactly. Then how do you expect me to raise a posse now?"

"You can take men from here," said the rancher, "an' you can get some over there. In a case like this you could even call out the state guard."

"Not in my county," said the sheriff, shaking his head decisively. "Not on your life. An' the governor would laugh at me."

"I'll go to Sacramento an' see the governor!" cried Farman.

Sheriff Kemp waved a hand. "That's up to you," he said quietly. "Do you think a troop of soldiers coming up into those hills could catch this bad outfit? They'd know they were coming days in advance. They'd scatter and hide. They'd pot the militia from safe spots all through those hills. It would take men who knew the mountains and desert . . . natural-born trailers . . . to catch Mendicott and his men. You know that."

"Then you mean to say you don't intend to do anything about this?" demanded the rancher.

"I'm not making any promises. Why didn't you report it when you were first shot?"

"Because I didn't think it would do any good," said Farman, glowering.

"Then why do you think it's going to do any good now?" asked Kemp.

"Because it's more serious!" cried Farman, striking the table with his fist. "It's got to a point where my property is being destroyed, my niece has been kidnapped . . . our lives aren't safe over there."

"Property has been threatened before . . . and stolen," the sheriff pointed out. "Mendicott has raided more than one town and we haven't been able to raise a posse in the very towns he raided. There hasn't been any co-operation with this office from that part of the county. Right now you have a man working for you, or have given him an option on your ranch, who doesn't seem to be right. We've asked this man Channing to help us on one or two occasions and he turned us down. He seems to be with you. He's run hog wild through the desert towns, I hear, but you're trusting him."

"He rescued my niece," said Farman "an' he helped drive them off the other night."

The sheriff laughed. "And now he's gone off with your cattle and got an option on your ranch. Ever think very hard about that?"

Nathan Farman was silent. It was true Channing had the cattle and the option. He had expected him back to the ranch before they left. Had Channing taken the stock? Had the option been a blind and the raid a trick? Would Mendicott really pay $150,000 for the ranch?

"Here's another thing," continued the sheriff. "The men on your ranch came around all right after this Channing took charge, didn't they? And in quick order? Doesn't that look peculiar?"

"The men seemed to have confidence in him," Farman defended doubtfully. "An' don't forget there were men killed in that raid the other night, Sheriff. That don't look like it was a trick . . . like Channing an' Mendicott were in together."

Again the sheriff laughed. "You know Mendicott wouldn't think anything of sacrificing a man or two to gain his ends. And what does Channing care about the men working on your ranch? Look at this thing from my standpoint. What am I to think?"

"You can find out," declared Farman

"I can arrest Channing . . . if I can find him," said the sheriff, frowning. "But what he's done seems all regular, thanks to you. And I can't make him say what I want him to say."

Nathan Farman rose with a gesture of disgust. "Then I've had my trip for nothing," he said angrily.

"I don't know that," said Sheriff Kemp. "But I'm not making any promises one way or the other. That's final."

Farman stalked out of the office. He hadn't proceeded a block along the street when he saw a figure slip into a resort. He knew the man instantly. It was Mendez, the Mexican. He hurried into the place after him, but he had disappeared, and he couldn't find him or obtain any information about him.

Meanwhile, Hope had remained in her room. She was lying down with the shades drawn against the heat of the dying day when there came a tap at her door. When she opened it, she found Crossley.

"There's a party in town that wants to see you an' me down the street," he said. "This party says it's important that we come along pronto, an' I don't think he wants anybody to know he's here."

Hope put the question with her eyes although she felt she knew the answer.

"It's Channing," said Crossley. "Will you come?"

Hope hesitated for an interval of bare seconds. Then she quickly put on her hat and hurried out with Crossley.

Chapter Thirty

Jim Crossley led Hope down the street to a large building that housed the post office on the first floor and numerous offices on the upper floors. They entered the post office and found Channing in a corridor on one side of the building. Hope noted at once that he appeared weary and worn. His clothes were covered with dust, and there were perspiration streaks on his face and neck. But his smile was bright and reassuring when he saw her. He walked forward to meet them.

"How did you get here so quickly?" asked Hope, extending her hand.

Channing took it in a warm pressure and shrugged. "I rode pretty hard," he confessed. "It's a good thing I had a good horse. I got back to the ranch the night after you left and came right on. I'm here on business, and it concerns you folks first. I had to come anyway, and I was coming with you folks. I knew your uncle was set to come in, Miss Farman." He looked keenly at the two of them and drew some papers from his pocket. "Can you keep something to yourselves?" he asked, looking at each of them.

"This seems to be the season for secrets," Jim Crossley commented.

"I guess we can keep silent, Mister Channing," said Hope decisively.

"Maybe he's here to rob the bank an' get that hundred an' fifty thousand," said the little driver.

Channing halted the persiflage with a look. "This is important," he said crisply, "and I have a good reason for not wanting it to get out at this time. I promise you it's nothing out of the way, Miss Farman."

"Then I guess we can promise, too," said Hope with a smile.

Channing tapped the papers he held. "I want you two to go up to the Land Office upstairs with me and file on two desert claims," he said seriously. "You both have your rights left, and anyway these ain't exactly land claims. If you can trust me that far, I'd like to have you go right ahead and file without even looking at the papers. I'll pay the fees."

Hope gazed steadily into the gray eyes of the tall, bronzed man who was speaking. She liked those eyes, she told herself, and recovered with a start as Crossley spoke.

"It's up to Miss Hope. If she says it's all right, it's OK with me. I'm follering her lead."

Channing looked at Hope in eager anticipation of her decision. She decided almost on the instant.

"All right," she said.

"Then we'll be moving," said Channing, leading the way to the stairs. They visited the office and made the filings without trouble. It was a mere matter of routine with the clerk, although he did take notice of Hope's looks and hair and favored her with his best smile.

When they came out of the office, Channing put the papers in a long envelope and sealed it.

"I'll let you take charge of this," he said, drawing Hope aside. "Keep it under the same conditions as the other envelope I gave you. Open it only if something happens to me."

She took the envelope and stowed it away. Here was absolute proof that he not only trusted her implicitly, but, after asking them not to be particular about ascertaining the full nature of the filings, he gave them to her and she could obtain the information if she wished by merely opening the envelope. It greatly strengthened her growing faith in him. "I'll keep it," she said, looking up at him.

It was a fact that Channing looked worried as well as tired. Evidently he had much on his mind. But he had no desire to show it. "There's another thing, Miss Farman," he said, looking about to make sure they were not being overheard. "I'd like for you to carry a message to your Uncle Nate. You'll see him, of course, at supper. The chances are I won't get to see him. I have something to attend to here."

"I'll be glad to tell him anything you wish," said Hope.

"Then tell him I said to go back to the ranch and not try to do what he's trying to do here. Tell him I said it would not do any good. Tell him it might make things worse. Tell him for me, to take my word for it, and tell him the cattle are safe."

Hope nodded in consent. It was evident by Channing's manner and the tone of his voice that he was in deadly earnest, and he looked into her eyes without flinching as he conveyed the message. She touched him on the arm. "Mister Channing, regardless of anything my uncle may think, or try to do, I know you are endeavoring to help us," she said in a low voice. "I can't see it any other way. I . . . I trust you."

He removed his hat and smiled down at her. "That's nice to hear, ma'am," he said. "There's those that wouldn't trust me farther'n a steer can fly."

"I can't say I just see why you are doing it, though," said Hope with the trace of a puzzled frown. "And I know you are in danger."

"Danger and me are not strangers," he said with a quick smile.

"But it's all so mystifying," pouted Hope.

Channing laughed softly. "That's because I have a hankering for surprises," he told her. "And because I have to . . . to protect myself." He looked at her gravely. "And because a bunch of people can blunder an' spill the beans easier than just one. And because I hate being laughed at."

"But why should anyone laugh at you?" she asked.

"Because I'm half laughing at myself," he said vaguely. "I reckon we better separate, Miss Farman. I'm going on upstairs. Crossley is waiting for you."

Hope delivered Channing's message to her uncle at the supper table.

"The devil!" exclaimed Nathan Farman, dropping his knife and fork. "He was here? An' beating it right out without seeing me? Tells me to go an' quit doing what I'm trying to do? The sheriff's right. That fellow is wrong, I'd bet my ranch. Sneaking around women with his messages."

Hope knew her uncle was wrong with regard to this last, but she had given her word and she could not tell him why she and Crossley had come to meet Channing and what they had done. She bit her lip in vexation at her uncle. "You can think what you wish," she said quietly, "but I am putting my faith and trust in Mister Channing. And remember, he said the cattle were safe."

Nathan Farman stared at her, "You're stuck on him," he accused.

Hope's face flamed, and she looked at her uncle angrily. "That is an unfair thing to say. Can't a woman trust a man without being . . . stuck on him, as you say?"

"Maybe so," growled out Farman, "but he's a good-looking devil, well set up, an' a sort of romantic cuss. You girls always fall for a man that's supposed to have a past or be mysterious or . . ."

"Uncle! Don't you give me credit for having any brains?"

"There, there, child, we'll let it go at that. I reckon I was put out, sort of, an' went too strong. I know you've got too much common sense to let a man like Channing get your goat . . . turn your head, I mean. I am going back to the ranch because I don't see how we're going to get anything done here. The sheriff didn't promise, but maybe he'll do something when he gets around to it. He's a queer cuss. Let's finish our supper an' go see a show an' forget about everything for a little while."

It was all said so contritely that Hope's smile returned. But it set her thinking. Was Channing helping them on her account alone? Did he perhaps think—but no! Never by any word or act had he shown that he entertained any feeling toward her except that of a friendly interest. True, he trusted her. But wasn't that a natural result of their association? He had spurned the talk of desert gold. Doubtless he had other views on making money. But Hope did not believe he intended to sell the ranch. She was convinced he was trying to block Mendicott's plans, perhaps because he had a grudge against the outlaw.

Hope went to a show with her uncle that night. It wasn't much of a show, but neither of them cared, for they had much on their minds. Nathan Farman was thinking of the look Mendez had given him as he slipped into the resort. It was because of that look that the rancher wanted to see the Mexican. It had been a look of hatred mixed with triumph. It gave Nathan Farman pause because he could not understand what had prompted it. And he had been greatly surprised to see Mendez in Kernfield. Evidently the Mexican had friends there, for he had been unable to find a trace of him after he disappeared within the resort.

They started home next morning. All of the spare space in the wagon was filled with supplies. Nathan Farman had tried in vain to hire some ranch hands in the town. A second visit to the sheriff had found that official still noncommittal. As a result the rancher was not in good humor and most of the remainder of the day the trio rode in silence behind the grays.

It took them three days to return to Rancho del Encanto and they met few people on the road. When they arrived, they found everything quiet. Mrs. McCaffy said there had been no visitors except Channing. He had returned late the day they left for the county seat and had started after them next morning. He had gone up to inspect the dam, she said, and had brought back the information that it was shattered and the water wasted. The big ditch was dry, and there was no water in the smaller ditches of the laterals on the mesa. Channing had returned the day before and was out somewhere on his horse.

It was suppertime before Channing returned. He listened while Nathan Farman told him what had happened in town. Farman also mentioned seeing Mendez, but Channing paid scant attention.

"I could have told you all that before you went, but I didn't know you were going so soon," said Channing. "I expected to be back before you started. When I got back and heard you'd left for Kernfield, I trailed right after you. I expected to go in with you when you went. I had my reasons for wanting to go." He directed a significant look at Hope, and the girl remembered the filing of the papers,

"The sheriff doesn't seem to hold you in any too good a light," said the rancher. "I mean he didn't exactly give you a recommendation, an' he hinted I'd made a mistake in trusting you at all."

"A county official isn't any too well supplied with brains," drawled Channing in reply.

Even the rancher himself smiled at this sally, although it was not altogether an endorsement of Channing's viewpoint.

"I'm going to tell you this much," said Channing to Farman. "Mendicott doesn't want this ranch for cattle or anything of the kind. He wants it for the water rights. I happen to know that."

"What does he want with the waters right if it ain't for cattle?" asked Farman in astonishment.

"That's what would make you laugh if I told you," replied Channing. "And I'm not sure yet, anyway. In a short time I ought to know."

They were interrupted by Jim Crossley, who entered the house with an envelope. He held it out to Channing. "A man just rode in from the desert, an' said this was for you."

Channing took the envelope eagerly and tore it open. He drew forth a sheet of paper and read to himself: The glory hole loses its glory tomorrow, Pap. He smiled almost affectionately at the others in the room. "I'm riding tonight," he said cheerfully, "but I'm not saying where."

An hour later they heard the pound of his horse's hoofs as he galloped across the mesa toward the desert beyond the east ridge.

Chapter Thirty-One

Channing sent his big bay flying down the east side of the ridge, turned a point into the south, and cut into the trackless desert. His mount struck into a swinging lope and the smooth-moving muscles and tossing head showed it could maintain this pace for miles and miles over the hard, sun-baked earth. The twilight shroud over the land was deepening into the soft velvet of the night. Already the stars were blossoming overhead, although there still remained faint glimmers of pink on the tips of the lava hills. The intense heat of the inferno was rapidly being tempered by a light breeze from the west where the black ramparts of the mountains traced their shadowy outlines against the sunset's fading sheen.

Night came suddenly—completely—an intense, brooding darkness, with the stars low-hung. There were no friendly lights of campfires or house windows, no sounds save the low murmur of the vagrant wind in sage and greasewood and the regular hoof beats. Yet Channing seemed strangely exultant. As he rode—a perfect figure in the saddle, easily and naturally—he sang. His horse threw back its ears as his fine tenor voice caressed the breeze in smooth-flowing cadences.

Hour after hour he rode until he reached the water hole where they had stopped on their return to the ranch from Bandburg. Here he halted, watered and rested his horse and himself, and smoked a cigarette. Then he was in the saddle again and on into the desert, across washes ghostly white in the starlight, over ridges capped with granite, up into the tumbled miniature hills, and at last down into the town of Bandburg, with its dim lights, its early-morning hilarity that constituted the dregs of the night's revelry, and its Yellow Daisy Mine—ravaged of its treasure.

He put up his horse in the livery barn at the lower end of the street. Next he proceeded directly to the Bluebird resort. He found only a handful of men in the place as it was nearly dawn, and the music and dancing had ceased. He ate some breakfast at the lunch counter and sat in at a game of stud poker to pass the time until daylight. There were only two games running, which was unusual even at that hour. He noticed, too, that the players did not appear as enthusiastic as usual. He wondered if the news he had received was generally known.

After an hour of play he left the table. It was broad day, and the camp was stirring. He made his way to the little assay office at the lower end of town and knocked on the door. He had to knock several times, but finally he was rewarded by seeing the assayer.

"What you got . . . banker's hours, Pap?" asked Channing cheerily as he entered. "Here it's morning and getting late, and you're still hibernating."

The old man blinked at him as he led the way into the rear room—a combination workshop, sleeping, and living room. "You get my note, eh?" he said, with a yawn.

"Last night. Left the messenger at the ranch to get fed and some sleep and came right on. She's done, is she, Pap?"

"The Yellow Daisy is gutted for keeps," said the assayer. There was a note of regret in his voice. "It'll be a long time before they stick a pick into another glory hole like that was."

"When are they going to quit?" asked Channing.

"This morning. The day shift'll be turned back."

"That'll make everybody feel good," said Channing, rubbing his hands.

"You act like you was glad of it," said the assayer in a tone of resentment.

"Oh, these gold grubbers!" exclaimed Channing. "Most of 'em think the desert hasn't got anything in it but gold. I'll tell you, Pap, gold is a small item compared with what's under the roots of the greasewood hereabouts. No, I'm not glad the Yellow Daisy's petered out. But as long as it had to peter out, I'm glad it happened just when it did. It's going to throw a lot of 'em out of work, eh?"

"It's going to kill the camp," said the old assayer sadly.

"So far as I know there aren't any of 'em got much saved up, have they?" asked Channing.

"You don't have to ask me that," replied the other with a scowl.

"No, I don't," Channing agreed. "I know. And I know where it went to. I had a hint this was coming soon because I was talking to Turner and Wescott over to Kernfield the other day. This mine has made 'em a lot of money, but they're willing to make more, I take it. Are they here?"

"Both of 'em," the old man answered with a nod. "I reckon they'd sell their holdings in the Yellow Daisy pretty cheap this morning."

"Means the end of the mine," said Channing. "They sank a shaft sixty feet or so below the floor of the hole, I understand, and got no promise. They're through."

"You seem to know a lot about it," the assayer commented. "What makes you so interested?"

"That's something else again," said Channing, rising. "Well, Pap, I'm going out and let you get the rest of your sleep."

Channing spent two hours circulating about the town. He stopped for a few cheerful words with every man he met who he knew. He talked longer with those who were evidently friends. And before 8:00 he went to the office of the Yellow Daisy Company, where he found the principal owners of the mine, Turner and Wescott. He was closeted with them for nearly half an hour, and, when he came out, he was smiling grimly. Then he walked slowly up and down the one main street of the camp.

It was 8:30 when the men began to come back from the Yellow Daisy. The day shift, which had reported for work at 8:00, streamed down the worn trail from the glory hole, the line of men appearing from below like a long, twisting, brown snake against the yellow flank of the hill. Many members of the night shift, which had quit work at 4:00 that morning, were still about, and they stared in wonder at the returning procession of miners and muckers. They hurried to meet them. Then the general word went out: "The Yellow Daisy is done." Back and forth they whispered it, shouted it, repeated it with incredulous and amazed expressions on their faces. "The Yellow Daisy is done."

The rapidity and thoroughness with which the news was passed until it had permeated every business place, resort, cabin, and tent in the camp was marvelous. Soon the main street was thronged. The bright desert sun glinted on scores of lunch pails, for the day shift was too startled to think of going home or changing clothes or anything save the message conveyed to them by Turner, part owner and manager of the mine. He had explained that it was unexpected—this sudden failing of pay dirt. The assays had shown the operations profitable until a week before. They had kept on working in the hope that the ground would show promise again, but it had failed. The great glory hole of the Yellow Daisy was divested of its gold. A shutdown was the only alternative. And the principal owners, Turner and Wescott, were leaving town at once.

Slowly it dawned upon the men that it was all true, and then they began telling themselves that it had to come, that they had expected it, that such a treasure hole could not last forever. They flocked to the resorts in droves; lunch pails littered the dirt street and were kicked about; men sought to drown their worry as to the future in the fiery liquor that was sold across the bars.

Channing mingled with the crowds. He spoke a word or two into the ears of his friends. He asked casual questions. And he waited. He knew it meant the end of the camp for the time being.

The Yellow Daisy had been the mine that had kept the town alive; all other enterprises were its offspring; all the prospecting excitement was based on its tremendous yield. As long as the Yellow Daisy glory hole was paying, men would come and search for and promote other glory holes whether they paid or not in the hope of duplicating its success. Now all development talk—all talk of big strikes and glowing prospects automatically ceased. It was the end. The miners knew it. The prospectors knew it. And more than anyone else, the promoters and hangers-on and parasites knew it. And they joined in a common orgy of talk and drink.

In the early afternoon Channing went up to the cabin occupied by Lillian Bell. He knew as soon as she admitted him that she had heard the news. But she did not appear excited. She had known boom camps before.

Channing's look was part doubt, part curiosity, part admiration, as she welcomed him. There was no talk of the failure of the glory hole at first. Lillian asked about Hope and affairs at the ranch, and Channing told her what had happened.

Then: "Lillian, what are you going to do?" he asked casually.

"Oh, I'll have to do a little thinking, I guess," she replied lightly.

"This is going to be a wild night," he said, "and probably Bandburg's last one. You going out ahead of it?"

The girl shook her head. "No, I'll stick to the joint till it shuts up shop. I'm always in at the death."

They talked some more on general topics, and then Channing said: "Lillian, there's liable to be another camp near here . . . a different kind of a camp. You want to keep in touch with me and remember, if you should want me for anything tonight . . . need me . . . I'll be hanging around." He rose to go, and at the door he turned and asked one question: "Has Brood bothered you? I know he's up and circulating."

"He'd have a chance to bother me . . . that fellow?" she exclaimed scornfully

211

Channing patted her on the arm as he left, and she watched him until he was indistinguishable in the crowds in the street below. Then she went in to dress for the evening.

With the coming of night the orgy swelled. The crowds of men became mobs. They fought and quarreled, split the reeking air with shouts and curses, settled old scores—spent what was left of their money. Channing stayed in the Bluebird resort—the largest of its kind in town. Here was the biggest, most boisterous and dangerous crowd, and scattered among the men were his friends. He kept an eye on Lillian Bell, who sang as usual. The celebration—if it could be called such—gradually grew until it assumed proportions that constituted a menace. A man—his money gone—demanded that the house buy a drink. He was refused pointblank with a sneer. It was the last night, and the proprietor knew it. No cause to coax future trade by acting as host.

"They've got all our money an' they're turning us down!" cried the man.

Then the trouble started in earnest. The attention of the maddened workers was directed from their own misfortune to the place that had taken their earnings. The place became an individual in their minds. The proprietor and his men were grafters! There was no law, and the camp was gone. The natural result was riot. The men surged behind the bar, and the proprietor and his assistants were too wise to use their guns. Bottles were confiscated, opened, and passed about. Glasses were hurled against the ceiling in frenzied glee, and the shattered glass rained down upon the heads of the mob. Mirrors were broken. Men pushed down into the cellar to loot it. There was no stopping them. The proprietor and his men, the gamblers and wheel operators and tinhorns, fled in terror for their lives, taking the money from the safe and leaving the place to the rioters.

Channing fought his way to Lillian Bell. The orchestra had fled, and she had taken refuge on a balcony. As he took her arm and led her down, for an instant he caught sight of Brood's face, black with hatred, in the mob below. Channing fought his way through the milling crowd to the rear door, keeping the girl close to him. When they were in the open air, he spoke. "Hurry up to your place, Lillian. Keep off the street. Go around. Get what things you want to take with you together, and be ready to go. The piano and furnishings can be sent for afterward. Do as I say, and don't open your door to anyone."

The girl promised and slipped away in the darkness. Channing knew she could defend herself if necessary. He knew she carried a small, pearl-handled revolver and that she could shoot straight to the mark. He turned back into the Bluebird, surged into the crowds, on the alert for Brood.

Meanwhile the word of what was going on in the Bluebird spread, and the result was a concerted attack on every resort in the camp. In an hour the men were in charge of all the places and everything was free to those who could get it. The riot became a debauch, and the uproar was terrific as the mobs streamed from the wrecked and looted resorts into the street. Soon they were marching up and down the street. Scores staggered out of line and collapsed. The air was filled with flying debris. Only the strongest of the men could stand this pace and keep on their feet.

Then came a first reaction in the early hours of the morning. The marching gradually ceased, and the men collected in a great crowd at the lower end of town. What was to become of them? How were they to leave? It was time for them to think of what they were going to do. This proved to be the moment for which Channing had waited. He leaped on the box of a dry water trough and shouted for attention. Scores of the men knew him, and the crowd was liberally sprinkled with his friends. They gave him a cheer on general principles. They wanted and needed a leader.

"Listen, men!" he cried in a ringing voice, "I know what you're all thinking about. You're wondering what you're going to do. Every last man of you that wants a job can have it. I'll give it to you!" His voice was drowned in cheers, and it was some little time before he could continue. He held aloft a paper and waved it before their eyes. "Here's an order from the Yellow Daisy for teams and ore wagons and powder and tools. There's a place up here in the hills to the west we want to bombard and open up. It'll mean work for all of you who want it, and your wages on this first job are ten dollars a day guaranteed by Turner and Wescott over their signatures. How many of you want to go?"

He waved another paper before their eyes, and they stared silently for several moments. Mental vision of another glory hole in their brains invited them. But the thought of having something to do at once—of work without the necessity of hunting for it—was the thing that impressed them most. A huge, red-faced man stepped forward and took the papers from Channing's hand. He was the former boss of the day shift, and Channing knew him well. He examined the papers and turned to face the crowd.

"It's all right, boys," he shouted, "we'll go!"

A great, tumultuous cheer from scores of lusty throats rose on the still desert air as the first rays of the morning sun slanted over the hills and stained the Yellow Daisy glory hole the color of fool's gold.

Chapter Thirty-Two

Channing got down from his perch on the water trough and the men swarmed about him. He picked out the big foreman of the day shift, Sam Irvine, and several others to take charge and gave his orders crisply. His lieutenants then went about the work of getting things ready for the trip out of Bandburg.

While Channing went to two of the stores to arrange for food supplies, tobacco, and other commissary needs for the men, and quietly bought a number of rifles and other firearms and a quantity of ammunition, Sam Irvine superintended the getting out of the teams, ore wagons, tools, powder and fuse, and other requirements of the expedition.

Channing strolled casually about the camp when he had finished making his purchases, which were charged to Turner and Wescott of the Yellow Daisy.

"Is it another glory hole?" he was asked by several men.

"No, boys, it's not a glory hole . . . not the kind you mean," he said, smiling. "It's hard-rock work for a short spell, and then it's any kind of work for a long spell. But it's sure better than sticking around here broke or beating it out of the desert to look for work . . . and work's scarce."

It satisfied most of the men. But there were scores who were not fit even to think about work, and there were others who were going out on the stages and on horses. The women had practically all gone. Channing wisely estimated that he would have about one hundred men for his undertaking when it came to the actual start—these in addition to a score of friends, most of whom, with the exception of Irvine, had been working at the gaming tables or at other occupations in the resorts.

As the morning advanced, two or three of the resorts reopened. But the majority of them remained closed, or, rather, open but abandoned. The stock of liquor had been mostly consumed, and what remained had been cached in spots remote from the main street. The Bluebird and other big resorts did not reopen for business. They were deserted by their proprietors who, knowing the camp was dead, had fled with their profits to new fields. Bandburg was a sorry-looking sight. In days to come some fresh boom might revive it, but there were no indications of such a revival this morning.

The heat descended, and the men sought the interiors of business places and the few reopened resorts. Some crawled away to their cabins or tents to get a wink of sleep. The ones Channing and Irvine depended upon helped with the preparations to leave.

Channing went up to Lillian Bell's cabin. He found her with a pack made up and two suitcases ready.

"All ready to go?" he said cheerfully. "Well, I wasn't sure just how it was going to pan out, but everything seems to be coming around all right. We're taking some wagons, so we can take all the stuff along you want. I guess we can even take the piano."

"What's this I hear about you giving the men work?" asked Lillian.

"My, news travels fast," Channing said with a pretense of surprise. "How in the world did you hear that so soon?"

"Now don't be stalling me, Channing," the girl reproved. "What're you fixing to do?"

"I'm fixing to go downtown and get some breakfast if I can't get anything up here," said Channing with a mock scowl.

Lillian sighed and shrugged. "You're past me, Channing," she said. "You like to keep folks in a fog. I believe you want people to think you're mysterious. I don't suppose there's any use in me

216

asking where we're going. Well, I'm willing to take a chance . . . with you." She looked at him quickly.

"You're not taking any chance with me, girl," he said, putting his hat on the table.

She turned away with a disappointed look in her eyes. "I'll get you . . . us some breakfast," she said. "Maybe you'll loosen up when you've hung on the feedbag."

Channing laughed and went into the kitchen, while Lillian prepared a hasty breakfast that was mostly bacon and eggs.

"Did you say something about wanting to know where you were going?" he asked. They were sitting down to breakfast.

"Has it affected you already?" she said with a lift of her brows. "I guess it's the smell of the coffee. Oh, I'm not so particular, so long as you're along as my knight gallant. You did tolerably well last night, and I suppose I should be grateful."

"We're going to Rancho del Encanto," Channing volunteered.

Lillian stared, incredulous. "You taking this big outfit there?" she asked in genuine astonishment. "Is there a mine on that ranch, for goodness sakes? You struck gold there?"

"Maybe," said Channing vaguely. "Oh . . . er . . . it'll be white gold I'll be mining, if any. No use, girl. I won't tell you about my business . . . yet. But that's where we're going, and we can take anything you want to pack."

This was as much as she could get out of him, and he left as soon as they had eaten, with the promise that he would return soon with a wagon.

When he left the cabin, he hurried to the Yellow Daisy property and there found everything in readiness. Soon the wagons, filled with supplies, tools, powder, and men, were proceeding down the road to the lower end of the main street. Channing had one of the teamsters drive up the street to where they could carry down the belongings Lillian wished to take. She was to ride in this wagon, on the seat with the driver. Channing was on his horse ready to start.

As they were going back to join the rest of the outfit, the old assayer hailed him from in front of his little office.

Channing rode over and leaned toward him.

"Brood an' some callers just rode outta town, goin' west," said the man in an undertone. "Thought maybe you'd be interested."

"Thanks, Pap," said Channing. "You figure on staying here? Why don't you trail along with us?"

The old man shook his head. "I'm through movin'," he said. "If this is goin' to be a ghost camp, I'm goin' to be one of the ghosts."

Channing reached down and shook his hand before he rode on.

Shortly before noon the teams and wagons streamed out the lower end of town, turned off the road that led south toward the railroad, and started into the desert in a direction west by north. Channing rode in the lead.

Those who had elected to stay in town, or who were going out of the desert by any means they could, watched them go. It was a queer procession—an exodus that hinted of the days of the pioneers. There was no road, no trail—only trackless desert and a blue-gray sea of greasewood and sage. The sun beat down with frightful ferocity, wreathing the water bags in misty vapor. Men tilted canteens and wet their foreheads and passed the last of the pilfered bottles against their better judgment. Streams of perspiration coursed through the thick dust on the flanks of the horses. And behind the wagons trailed a score of burros driven by a grizzled miner on a rangy nag.

The heat increased steadily as the sun mounted into the blazing sky. The horses walked slowly, picking their way behind Channing, who shrewdly selected the best passage through the scant vegetation. The men swore and suffered and drank immense quantities of water. Channing had seen to it that every water bag and canteen available had been filled and taken along. He would have preferred to make the trip at night. It would have been easier on the horses and the men—easier all around—but he did not want to risk another day in town. There was a chance that his plan would miscarry through a demand on the part of the men as to the nature of the work and other details. He depended upon Sam Irvine to hold them. They liked Irvine and had worked for him.

Channing rode back occasionally to see how Lillian Bell was standing the trip. She had a huge umbrella that had been commandeered somewhere, and it covered her and the driver on the seat beside her. There were no other men in this wagon. She always greeted him with a smile and a line of banter.

The sun swung overhead—a burning ball of fire. Mirages shimmered on level spaces in the distance. Even the soft, blue haze that draped the lava hills suggested heat. The western mountains, thrusting their grim heights above the purple veils that wavered about their shoulders, looked like the pieces of a picture puzzle stood on end. The dust rose in thick clouds and settled on the caravan.

It was mid-afternoon when they reached the water hole, Dick's Wells. Here they halted. The men crowded around the well and drank their fill. Then the water bags and canteens were all refilled. Next the muleskinners unhooked their teams and led the horses, one by one, to water. When this had been done, the water in the well was almost gone. It would take hours for it to fill again.

Channing had gotten out a basket containing cheese, canned beans, corned beef, canned tomatoes, and peaches, and these were handed out to the men with big slices of bread. But none had a great appetite. It was too hot to eat, too hot to think of anything but the everlasting heat. So, after an hour to rest the horses, they pushed on.

Through the balance of the afternoon they plowed through dust and heat while the sun slipped down the west arch of the sky. With the sunset, flaming red above the peaks, the air began gradually to lose some of its heat. It did not become cool, to be sure, but the absence of the sun lessened the impression of heat to a great extent. It was still hot when twilight fell, but it was heat that was endurable, and it seemed cool compared with the blast of the inferno by day.

They swung at last into the foothill road and turned north while the men gave a hearty cheer. The day over and a cool breeze creeping down the cañons from the mountains renewed their spirits. They cared little for what was ahead of them. They were out of the inferno for a time, anyway, and it was a welcome relief.

Night gathered its velvet curtains, strewed them with stars, and its wind voices whispered above the echoes of hoofs and the crunch of iron tires on the road. They swung over the ridge and into Rancho del Encanto. Channing led them to the space about the barns. Soon fires had been built and coffee pails slung. Horses were unhitched, watered, and turned into the stalls for oats and hay and rest. The men laughed and joked and sang snatches of song as they spread their blankets on the grass under the cottonwoods. They were in a good mood.

Channing had superintended all this, but first he had taken Lillian Bell to the house and turned her over to the astonished Hope.

"What does all this mean?" Nathan Farman had demanded.

"I've no time to talk now," Channing had said coolly.

But now that supper for the men was under way, the horses looked after, the packs of supplies opened, and camp made, he strolled back to the house and entered the living room, followed by Nathan Farman.

"Looks like you was taking charge of the place for fair," was the rancher's comment.

Channing saw Hope and Lillian peering down the stairs.

"I am," he said, turning to Farman with a smile.

"Whose men are those out there?" asked Farman.

"Mine," replied Channing crisply. "They're the best of what's left of the Yellow Daisy outfit. The Daisy's glory hole went broke yesterday morning, and they shut down. I was waiting for it, and I grabbed this outfit."

"But what're you going to do with it?" asked Farman, wrinkling his brows. "Oh!" His face lightened. "You're going to rebuild the dam!"

Channing shook his head. "Not now. Later sometime. Maybe soon."

"Then what are you going to do, Channing?" cried the rancher. "This has gone far enough. I've trusted you, halfway at least, an' given you everything you asked for. It ain't playin' square to keep me in the dark this way, an' I won't stand for it. You can't carry on in any such high-handed . . ."

"Wait a minute," Channing interrupted sternly. "You called me a tramp, you as much as said I was in with Mendicott, you drove me off your ranch . . . is it so? It is. Now I'll tell you something. Mendicott wasn't the outlaw you thought. He pulled lots of his thefts to keep his men good-natured and with him. It gave him a hold over 'em. He's bad, all right, but he's smart. He wanted this ranch because it carries the water rights with it . . . understand? I . . . we want it for the same reason, and we've got it. Oh, you won't have to move, you won't lose your ranch, but you're going to get down on your knees and bow to the desert, Nate, and you'll maybe bow to me . . . the tramp and the waster."

"He wanted . . . the water an' . . . you want it?" stammered Farman. "But if you're not going to fix up the dam, what's all this outfit for?" The rancher looked about in a daze. "What . . . what're you going to do?"

"I'm going to make this part of the country a safe place for women, and miners, and ranchers, and preachers, and gamblers, and everybody but the man who thinks he's got it roped and hog-tied," rang out Channing's voice. "I've traveled some with

Mendicott because I pretty near had to. I told him to lay off this deal . . . off this ranch and that water . . . and he laughed at me. I hate to be laughed at. Now I'm going to bring Mendicott to time, or I'll blow him and his gang higher than the mountains where they're hiding."

Chapter Thirty-Three

Lillian Bell sat in her room, in the soft glow of the shaded lamp, looking about at its quaint furnishings and tapping the table absently with nervous fingers. There was a light, puzzled frown on her face. Hope had received her with apparent joy; Nathan Farman had been most cordial. But Lillian felt she was intruding. It was the last place in the world she had ever expected to visit. Why had Channing brought her there? What had induced her to go with him when she had learned the destination? Her eyes became soft and luminous as she rubbed the old-fashioned, red-and-white fringed table cover. It was like entering a new world—or an old world she had long since left. After a time she went quietly to the door and slipped out into the hall. Hope and Nathan Farman also had gone to their rooms, and it was dark downstairs. She went down, out on the porch, and then walked on the soft cushion of grass in the front of the house. It seemed wondrously quiet to her—this beautiful spot where the desert and foothills met.

Rounding the corner toward the bunkhouse, she saw Channing in the starlight. She called to him softly, and he came at once. "Channing, what's the big idea?" she asked.

"Which idea?" he asked in mock surprise.

"Don't play the Willie with me," she said with a trace of irritation. "Oh, yes, there are two ideas. But first, what's the idea in my being here?"

"You didn't have no place in particular to go, did you, Lillian?"

"No, but I never would have selected this place."

"Well, this place is as good as any, and better'n most. I was coming here, and I didn't want to leave you back there with that mob. I've kind of looked after you, haven't I?"

"Yes, and I've often wondered why," said Lillian in a wistful voice. "I guess it's because you're always with the underdog."

"I wouldn't be putting it that way," said Channing. "I've always been interested in you. You're not like other . . . that is . . ."

"Oh, say it, Channing, old scout," she broke in. "I know what you mean . . . don't kick at the way I put it. But it is a rotten way to make a living. This place gives me the creeps. It's . . . it's too much like home . . . real home, I mean."

"I thought a rest in a place like this would do you good, Lillian," he said earnestly. "You'll have a place of your own someday . . ."

"Don't start pulling the sentimental stuff, Channing. You know I ain't that kind. Say, are you really going after Mendicott?"

"I sure am," he replied grimly.

"Well, you've got nerve," she said in a tone of admiration. "But I always knew you two would meet up one of these days. I guess it's come so soon because you want to help these people out. Channing, are you doing it just because they're the underdog in this case?"

He looked at her searchingly in the starlight. "What're you driving at, Lillian?" he asked.

"Oh, Channing, it's no use. You know what I mean. But I figure you'll play fair." The girl's tone was one of resignation. It even hinted of weariness. It subtly conveyed such an impression of loneliness as one becomes conscious of when the wind whines in the naked branches of the trees on a dreary day in late autumn.

Channing put his hands on her shoulders. "You need a rest, Lillian. Stop thinking so much. You're with friends here. Go up and go to bed and get a good sleep. The change from that mining camp is going to do you a heap of good. Maybe it'll start you thinking different."

"Maybe you're right, Channing," said the girl, turning to go. "In some ways you're sensible, and in other ways you're a regular devil. I guess I like the devil best."

Hope had been watching from the window of her room. She, too, had felt that peculiar sense of a strange loneliness when she saw them together. It was a feeling that was new to her. She could not analyze it exactly, but it suggested the desert wastes and the solitary figure of a man and horse, the man drooping in the saddle. She marveled at this mental picture. Then a fragment of Channing's words at the parting with Lillian came to her.

After Lillian had returned to the house, Hope stole down the stairs. A fragment of song came to her from in front of the house. Channing was singing.

Last night I was dreaming,
My love, dear, was dreaming. . . .

It was a song Hope loved, and he sang it beautifully—with fine feeling. She went out on the porch. Channing saw her at once and came to her. "Isn't it a little late to be up?" he asked, taking off his hat.

Hope remembered he hadn't removed his hat when talking with Lillian. She bit her lip. But, pshaw—Lillian and he were old friends. Doubtless the girl hadn't expected it. Very likely it wasn't the custom in Bandburg. But the copper-colored hair exposed in the light of the stars was a compliment to her. "I saw you and Lillian talking," she said, "and I was wondering if she . . . if everything was pleasant for her here. I . . . we will do anything to make her comfortable and happy."

"Oh, she's all right. Just wondered why I brought her here. I told her you were glad to have her. The rest will do her good."

"Yes, indeed," said Hope, "and we are glad to have her here. I want her to know that." She paused. "You were singing just before I came out," she said. "I like to hear you sing."

"Well, that's right nice, Miss Farman. But I reckon it's too late for a concert and, besides, I don't sing half good with an audience. I mean . . . I sing worse than ever with an audience," he stammered in conclusion.

"You don't sing half good at any time, Mister Channing. You sing real well. I like to hear you."

"Ma'am, you're plumb full of good words this night." He bowed quite low in acknowledgment of the compliment.

"Another reason why I came out," she said, "is I wanted to tell you how glad I was to hear what you said to Uncle tonight. But I knew all the time that you were not associated with Mendicott."

"Don't be too sure," he said, shaking his head. "Remember where you saw me for the second time."

"I know," she admitted. "It was at his place in the hills. But I believe you were there for other reasons than to help him in any of his schemes."

"You're right," he said after a pause. "I was there to talk and argue about a business deal against my will. But I could have gone there anyway . . . with no business at all."

"You can't mystify me any longer as to whether you're one of those bad men or not," she said, laughing softly. "As we say in the East, I have your number, Mister Channing."

He appeared puzzled for a spell. "You mean you're wise to me?"

"Exactly, so far as your relations toward us are concerned, anyway. No, you still mystify me in some ways. Your singing, your silences . . . I suppose you've inherited some of the desert's mystery."

"The desert has no mysteries if you know it, ma'am."

"But you can't readily explain its appeal, can you?"

"Shucks, you have to fight it to learn that, I reckon."

"Do you really like to fight, Mister Channing?"

"Why, in some ways . . . yes. Yes, I guess I'm just naturally cussed ornery thataway."

"I've come to feel something the same way," said Hope, laughing.

"Then you're coming to like this country, ma'am."

She started. "Why, I believe I am coming to like the country. But it could never take the place of my love for my native state."

"Of course not," he agreed. "But you would like this country in a different way. I was born in the desert south of here where almost every kind of cactus grows. There were lots of paloverdes and mesquite. The hills were green with desert cedar, juniper. Lots of water holes. Pretty as a picture. Here it's all sage and greasewood, and nothing else. But I wouldn't want to go back down there to live. I've been in here too long. But I like to think of that place down there and it's got to be with a sort of reverence, I guess you'd call it. It's hard to explain, I reckon."

She was astonished at his simple explanation that was nevertheless so clear. She could come to love this new country, and in time her memory of the green trees and flowers and still waters of her old home would take on the nature of a reverence. "I understand you," she said finally. "It's a new way of looking at it, original and convincing. But, now that I think of it, in all the years I lived back there I don't believe I ever heard one speak so feelingly and display such quiet, abiding pride in their country as you do in yours."

"It's my religion, ma'am."

She looked up at him, her eyes filled with wonder. The man was baring his soul, all naturally, unassuming, quite as a matter of fact. "I believe you have a good religion . . . of your own," she said.

"You've been very kind to believe in me, ma'am," he said in a low voice. "I've learned a lot since I met you, and I reckon it's all good."

"But you believed in me, too," said Hope, experiencing a little thrill because of the note in his voice. "You had to, to give me the envelopes."

"Why shouldn't I believe in you, Miss Hope?"

It was the first time he had spoken her first name. Somehow it seemed to draw them closer together. She remembered certain things Lillian Bell had said, and her uncle's hints. Her cheeks flushed. "I believe I'll go in," she said softly.

"I won't bother you with any more singing tonight, Miss Hope."

"You're trying to tease me," she accused at the door. "Well, you can't do it. You know I like your singing, and, besides, you were singing one of my favorites. It's called 'A Dream' . . . as you know . . . and this is a country of dreams, it seems to me."

"I know it is," he answered. "And it's getting more that way every day."

Hope hurried inside and up to her room. She stood at the window. The moon had come up, silvering the rugged landscape. His religion! Did she understand it? And, in understanding it, did she understand him and her own confused thoughts? Or was she merely bewitched by this land of desert and mountain and characters so new to her?

From the deep shadow near the window at the front of the hall, Lillian Bell stole silently to her own door and let herself in. She sat down in the chair in the soft glow of the shaded lamp, spread her hands upon the old-fashioned, red-and-white fringed table cover, and rested her face upon them.

Chapter Thirty-Four

The men were stirring long before dawn. Fires were started and preparations for breakfast under way while it was still dark. Channing himself had slept but two hours. The crucial test was soon to come, for the big majority of the men did not know the nature of the expedition. And Channing knew that Mendicott was probably already aware of the fact that some movement was afoot. Brood had ridden out of town with some companions, and it was safe to assume that he was headed for the rendezvous. However, Channing had not hinted of their destination before Brood had left Bandburg. Mendicott might assume it was to be an attempt to rebuild the dam at once. It was probable that he would laugh at the idea of the miners attacking his stronghold.

Channing conferred at length with Sam Irvine, erstwhile day-shift boss of the Yellow Daisy, and his score of friends, all of whom were his lieutenants. Irvine then singled out a score of powder men and miners and took them aside, with Channing, for a second conference. These men were seasoned, strong, fearless—hard customers, but nevertheless men who were opposed to open outlawry, as were most of the crowd for that matter. An offer of $100 was made to each of them for the work outlined, providing they were ready to engage in any fighting that might occur. Every man accepted. It was then arranged that these men should go ahead with Channing and his friends and Irvine was to follow with the balance. Irvine was to inform the men in his detachment of what was wanted with them after all preparations had been made.

Breakfast was soon over, the horses attended to, and the work of packing the burros completed just before dawn. The men in Channing's detachment were taken a distance up the foothill trail, and there provided with revolvers. Half of the rifles were packed on the burros. The other arms were in charge of Irvine.

Nathan Farman, who had been watching the preparations with excited interest, attempting to assist, but finding no opportunity to do so, now approached Channing as the latter came back down the foothill trail.

"Don't I get a hand in this?" he demanded indignantly.

Channing grinned and put a hand on the rancher's shoulder. "Listen, Nate, somebody's got to stay here with the women. Besides, you're not in any too good shape and haven't been for some time. I expect if Brood hadn't sneaked that shot at you, there'd have been the devil to pay around here long before this. You were always a fighter and still are, I reckon. But you're not in shape for anything like this. Besides, it's my party, and I want to run it my own way."

Farman took his hand and shook it warmly. "You're a go-getter, Channing, an' that's no mistake. I have been at a disadvantage an' that's a fact. They've had me down an' almost out. An' you can't blame me for being suspicious, sort of, the way things were sizing up. I'm still pretty much in the dark. You're not hiring these men, I know that . . . or I don't think you are . . . unless you've sold the option." He looked at Channing speculatively.

Channing shook his head with a smile. "No . . . not yet, Nate."

"Well, then, who in thunder is behind all this?" asked the rancher.

"Turner and Wescott, owners of the gutted Yellow Daisy, and . . . the desert. The desert's behind me, too, Nate, don't forget that."

Channing turned quickly as the sound of a horse, descending the foothill trail, came to them. A minute later little Jim Crossley rode up and got off his horse stiffly. He spoke in Channing's ear.

"Nothin' stirring on the trail yet," he said in a low tone. "I hustled up there right after you gave the word last night an' didn't see a sign of anything doin'. Looks like you have a clear trail."

"Good boy, Jimmy," Channing commended him. "Now do you think you can stand it to guide Irvine and his men to the divide after you've had some breakfast and a lot of hot coffee?"

"Sure thing," said Crossley quickly. "But I'll have to have another horse."

Channing turned to Nathan Farman. "See that he gets one of the best horses you've got," he instructed.

The rancher nodded, and Channing took Crossley to Irvine and introduced him. Then the little man went in the house to breakfast and Channing waved to the two girls, standing in the kitchen door. He took Farman's hand in his strong grasp.

"They say all ain't gold that glitters, Nate, but there're things that don't glitter that're gold . . . pure gold."

With this puzzling speech he mounted and rode rapidly up the foothill trail.

The sun was not yet up when Channing started with his detachment of forty-one men into the hills. He rode ahead, followed by his friends and the picked crew. The burros, driven by a grizzled prospector, brought up the rear. They proceeded slowly, in single file. For two hours they proceeded up the trail, and then turned into another trail leading to the right and started due north. This trail widened after a time, and they were permitted to travel two abreast. It led along the crests of ridges and through ravines and fragrant meadows, screened by pines and firs. It was a good trail, and they made good time. Almost imperceptibly it led upward.

Channing, schooled in hill sign as well as desert sign, rode well in advance. His was the gift of the sense of danger that is often the heritage and attribute of the man whose whole life has been spent following the trails of silence. This day he did not look so much for sign in the trail as for sign that they were being watched, or riding into ambush. He had little fear of the latter, however, for they were not following the trail to the rendezvous.

They were not molested, and saw no one during the morning, and a little after 1:00 p.m. they reached a large meadow where there was an old cabin. It was the meadow where Channing and Hope had stopped to get the burro and supplies the morning after Channing aided the girl to escape from Mendicott's stronghold. Here Channing called a halt. Look-outs were posted, horses unsaddled, burros unpacked, and the stock turned out to graze on the rich grass. Soon a meal was under way. The men were in good humor. After dinner they loafed for an hour, lying on the grass under the trees. It was during this interval that Channing explained his plan at length, outlining every move, overlooking no detail, providing for every possible contingency. The men listened attentively and nodded in approval.

They were a hard lot—those men. Hardy, strong-muscled miners; pale-faced gamblers, some, whose tapering fingers could close like lightning on the butt of a gun and send a bullet to its mark unerringly; grizzled prospectors who knew how to handle a rifle and had never known fear, save of the ever-present specter of the desert—thirst. The venture was not theirs for profit alone. The spirit of adventure drove them on, and they were natural fighters. Also they were respecters of fair play, and some had suffered through the wanton, ruthless deeds of Mendicott, who followed only his own wishes. They also respected Channing—and liked him. It was a friendly quality in his personality that drew them to him, as well as his reputation for fearlessness, for being an expert gun artist, for overlooking no chance to do another a good turn, for being a gambler who laughed in the face of a limit.

When he had finished, they saddled the horses and packed the burros. The second start of the day was made, and this time they took a trail that led them straight up the mountain. It was a good trail, but steep, and they proceeded slowly, for it was hard climbing for the horses. They went up and up, with frequent stops, until they reached a great, natural shelf just below a high divide. Here they stopped and unsaddled the horses.

"We'll have to make it the rest of the way on foot," Channing said. "But I reckon we can take the burros."

They climbed over the high ridge, leaving the horses in charge of four of their number, and descended to a rocky, miniature plateau on the crest of the junction of three ridges. Proceeding across this, they climbed again, and on the top of the next ridge Channing called the final halt.

"There she is," he said with a grim smile.

They saw a hole in the rock formation. It was the exit Channing and Hope had used in getting out of the cave and subterranean passage in the escape from the rendezvous.

As a first move the burros were unpacked. Then ropes were secured to trunks of the gnarled, wind-blown pines and lowered into the dark depths of the great cave. Men were sent to cut young fir trees on the sides of the ridge and drag them to the hole.

Channing pointed out the necessity for working fast as the day was nearly done, and it would be impossible to light a fire on the ridge without it being seen in the rendezvous, which was situated beyond the ridge—a cup in the shoulder of the peak of which the ridge was a spur.

He was first to lower himself into the cave, carrying a pine knot, rich in pitch, of which they had gathered many. Within the cave he lighted it, and thus aided several of the men followed him.

There was a long slope leading down from the hole in the roof of the cave to the floor far below. Next came the work of lowering the tools, powder, and supplies. The majority of the men were now in the cave, and they formed a line from the hole in the roof down the slope to the floor. The tools, sacks of powder, and fuse and supplies were passed from hand to hand until they were all on the floor of the cave. Then came the young fir trees, which were thrown down. These were followed by saplings, and then everything required for the work was in the cave.

The men each carried something as they started along the subterranean passage that led from the cave. The water flowing in the passage was less than a foot deep, for the snows had melted and the stream dwindled since Channing and Hope had been there. They splashed through the water, carrying their burdens, holding aloft the pine torches that lighted the way. And finally they saw a dim square of light ahead. Channing stopped them and ordered the torches put out.

"That's the hole in the rock wall where the stream runs out of the cup," he said. "It's the only way out of the place except by the narrow trail over the ridge down a piece from here. Mendicott and his outfit always use the trail. This place is mighty hard to get into when the water's high. The trail's just wide enough for a man on a horse. The hole at the end of this passage is just wide enough for two men to get out at once. So both places can be protected easily because a few men could pick off a million trying to get in either way. The end of the passage is probably watched, but as soon as it's dark we'll put the saplings across and pile up the trees for a screen so they can't see the light from our torches."

They piled the tools and supplies on the dry rock banks on each side of the stream and waited for the darkness. When the square of light was all but entirely blotted out, and they knew night had descended, they moved on with the trees and saplings, and soon the work of putting up the screen was completed.

Then the torches were lighted and Channing gave his final orders.

"Drill your powder holes on each side of the opening and above it. There's no danger of them hearing anything from in here . . . the trees and the ripple of the water'll drown what sound might leak out there. But if they should get wise, or start out this way, all you have to do is douse the torches in the stream and let 'em come. They can't come more'n two at a time, an' they'll be against what light there is while you'll be in the dark and can let them have it. Drill all the holes you can. We want to blow out the whole end of this passage, open it up wide."

Channing left in the hour after he had seen the work begun. He made his way back to the cave and climbed out. He hurried back to where the horses had been left, selected a horse other than Major, and started along a trail leading below the divide. He rode in the darkness between the trees for an hour or so, and then turned up on the divide. He followed this south for another hour and again took a trail leading below the high ridge. In this way he worked south, keeping close to the crest, and making steady progress without having to descend into the foothills.

Finally he came to where the going was easier, and here he pushed his horse. Soon he again turned up to the divide, lower now, and rode along its crest. His horse picked its way among boulders and rock outcroppings with ease, aided by instinct and the starlight. Thus Channing came finally to where Irvine and his men were stationed, having been guided by Crossley, who was with them. He ordered Crossley back to the ranch.

He led the others back up the divide, and then, at a point about a mile above the head of the narrow, perilous trail out of the rendezvous, he stopped them and gave his final instructions. They were going near the head of the trail and remaining on guard. They were not to attempt to go down the trail, but they were to stop anyone from riding out. This could be done as easily from the head of the trail as from below. After they had heard the explosions below, they were to await a signal indicating that the outlaws all were engaged in the battle in the cup, and then go down the trail. Thus the bandits were to be trapped and surrounded or shot to death.

Having given his instructions, Channing led them by the secret path to a point near the head of the trail, but sheltered from sight of a look-out there by a rock spur from the divide. He half expected a volley of shots, but none came. He was struck by the panicky thought that the gang might have left the rendezvous. Then he remembered that Crossley would have certainly spied their going on his scouting trip of the night before, and they could hardly have left during the day without encountering one of the two parties. Nevertheless, he could not shake off a feeling of uneasiness as he rode back to the shelf under the high ridge where the horses of the men in his detachment had been left. He hurried back up the high ridge and down into the cave.

When he reached the end of the passage where the men were working, he found that excellent progress was being made. The miners were working in relays, drilling the holes for the powder. They promised every hole would be drilled and loaded before dawn. They were the cream of the Yellow Daisy miners—this crew. Channing had trusted them to do their work well without directions from Sam Irvine, because they knew their business. He had left Irvine in charge of the other men because he realized that they would need a strong man at their head, and he had to be in the passage to direct the attack on the rendezvous. The miners were true to their word. It lacked half an hour of daylight when the last stick of dynamite was tamped in, with its cap and fuse ready to set it off.

Two men volunteered to light the fuses. The fuses were of different lengths, and the longest were to be lighted first, so that when all were lighted, they would be burning about evenly. There were four holes above the aperture, six on either side, two great holes at the bottom on either side where several sticks were to be exploded, and six holes in the roof near the opening. As the rock opened, or curved in on each side inside the aperture and the roof swelled upward, it was expected that the shots would tear the hole open to ten times its size, which would permit a dozen men to leave or enter the passage at a time.

Channing led all of the men, except the two who were to light the fuses, back to the cave. Here there were two strong currents of air, both circulating down the stream—a coincidence that showed that there was another opening somewhere in the mountain, but that Channing never had been able to find. The air currents would quickly sweep out the fumes and gases of the explosion.

They waited quietly, the great cave alive with shadows cast by the flaming torches, for the remaining quarter of an hour preceding the explosion. The fuses were in long lengths to give the men who set them off time to run back to the cave.

"They're coming!" one of the men cried. "I see their torches."

In another minute the men had joined the party in the cave. There was a breathless pause. Men stared at each other in expectancy, and crowded back toward the center of the big cavern. It seemed as though hours passed, but the time could be reckoned in seconds, actually. Channing stood nearest the stream and the passage that led toward the opening into the rendezvous. His eyes were slightly narrowed. One of the men drew his revolver. Channing shook his head.

"No need of that till you get up there. Now, men"—and he faced them all—"throw your torches in the stream when you get near the opening. They're likely to be there ahead of us, but we'll have 'em out in the light and we'll be in the dark. That gives us an advantage. But they'll drop back, and we'll have to fight it out in the open."

A low rumble came to their ears and gradually swelled to a roar that seemed to tear through the passage and the cave and lose itself in distant mutterings and reverberations. It came again and again, like the rolling of thunder in the high heavens. A pungent odor struck their nostrils as the sounds ceased. Thin smoke streamed past. And then suddenly the air was clear.

"All right!" called Channing. "Come on!"

They dashed into the stream in the passage and ran toward the opening. As they went on, the air again became rancid. Then they saw light ahead, and a rousing cheer went up that echoed shrilly in the passage. The opening was no longer small and square. It looked as if a great, jagged hole had been punched in the wall of rock. It was fully ten times its original size.

They threw their torches into the stream, drew their guns, and plunged on in the light that filtered in through the opening—the gray light of dawn. A vast quantity of rock had been loosened and was banked in the passageway. But this merely served as a bulwark behind which they could fire as if from a fort if they could reach it ahead of the outlaws.

When they had almost reached the fallen rock, several men appeared upon it. Shots echoed in the passage. A man stumbled and fell. The others turned loose their guns. The men with the rifles drew to one side, stopped, and took careful aim. Two of the heads behind the rock rampart disappeared. Then they reached the fallen rock.

Channing crawled up and cautiously looked over. He had a splendid view of the lower end of the cup. Men were running toward the opening. He motioned to the others to move up, and they turned their guns upon the outlaws.

Four men just below them threw up their hands. One was too late and fell forward on his face. Channing looked at the other three quickly and then turned his gaze on the clearing ahead. He was looking for a small man in riding pants and military boots. His brow wrinkled as he failed to see him among those who were running down the little stream from the cabins in the center of the rendezvous.

The men with the rifles began to fire. Two more of the outlaws dropped. The others stopped, and then they turned as of one accord and swept back to the shelter of the trees.

"Come on!" Channing yelled, and vaulted over the top of the rock barrier. "Hold those three fellows one of you!" he cried as the others swarmed over after him.

Then the invaders, cheering and yelling, swept out on the floor of the cup and started for the screen of trees behind which the outlaws had taken refuge.

Chapter Thirty-Five

Channing shouted and gestured to his men to take shelter behind the trees that grew in clumps about the cottonwoods along the banks of the stream. In the first excitement of the encounter they had forgotten their instructions. Now they remembered and began to run by twos and threes to the pines and firs around the edge of the cup. In this way they shut off the outlaws in the lower end so that they could not make a dash for the trail or the opening to the passage without being subjected to a withering fire.

Several men came riding down the trail, and there was firing above. Channing, with three others, ran for the lower end of the trail, but the riders evaded them and galloped on toward the cottonwoods.

"I reckon that's all that was up there," said Channing in a satisfied voice. "Now I'll go up myself and give Irvine the signal to come down. If they make a break for it, let 'em have it."

He hurried up the trail, and, when he was halfway up, he saw Irvine and his men. He waved to them and fired his gun three times. He waited until he saw they were coming down the trail, and then returned to the floor of the basin.

There were scattering shots, but evidently no damage was being done. Channing had estimated that there would be between thirty and forty men in the rendezvous. He wondered that Mendicott did not give the order to charge. It was probable, though, that the outlaws would race down on their horses. But Irvine and his men were coming down the trail fast, and the remainder of the detachment was concealed in the trees. Thus Mendicott had missed the opportune moment for a rush. If he charged now, he would but charge into an ambush.

When Irvine and his men reached the bottom of the trail, Channing sent them along the trees south of the creek.

"When you see me wave my hat, riddle the cottonwoods," he told them. "Just keep shooting into 'em and that'll drive 'em back to the cabins."

He ran around the lower end, taking advantage of every bit of cover, and saw that his men were all below the line of fire that would come from the south side. He issued the same orders to his own men. Then he waved his hat.

Bullets poured into the cottonwoods from two angles, subjecting the hiding outlaws to what was most certainly a deadly crossfire. At first there was a return volley, but the firing from the cottonwoods ceased almost as soon as it started. Then, in response to signals from Channing, the men on the lower end began to move forward, and those on the south came in until they reached the meadow. There they stopped, but Channing and his detachment moved on into the cottonwoods. The outlaws had taken up their stand among the cabins. But they had left several dead and wounded under the cottonwoods.

Channing stopped before a man sitting on the ground, his face pale, his left hand clasped about his right arm. The wounded man's jaw dropped as he recognized Channing.

"You're not mussed up much, are you?" asked Channing coolly. "Hit anywhere else 'cept in that arm?"

The man shook his head.

"All right, get up," commanded Channing, and he helped the man to his feet. "How many are in here?" he asked.

The man still appeared too bewildered to speak.

"C'mon, talk up," said Channing sharply. "How many? Forty?"

"Not more'n twenty-five or -six now, I guess," muttered the man.

Channing whistled softly. "Where's the bunch? Is Mendicott here?" The other shook his head.

"What's that?" cried Channing, grasping the man by his good arm. "You say Mendicott's not here? Don't lie."

"He went out last night," said the other, and Channing knew that he spoke the truth.

"Who was with him?"

"Brood an' half a dozen others," replied the man.

Channing's face froze into grim lines. For several moments he thought steadily. Then he loosened his grip on the other.

"You walk back there and tell that bunch we've got a hundred men here, and they're all aching to cut loose. Tell 'em if they don't march out on that meadow without their guns, we'll close in on 'em an' blow 'em to bits if it takes all week. We've got thirty rifles an' thirty men tied to 'em that know how to use 'em. Tell 'em who sent the message and tell 'em I'll give 'em five minutes to make up their minds. Now beat it."

The man hurried off toward the cabins, holding his arm, which was bleeding. Channing walked nervously back and forth under the trees. The quarry had escaped! Mendicott had gone! But it wasn't like Mendicott to leave the rendezvous and forsake his men. Channing laughed harshly at the thought. Little Mendicott cared for his men, save to use them to serve his own ends. No, Mendicott had had something in view. Channing suddenly stopped in his tracks and his jaw snapped shut; he pressed his lips tightly together. He heard a cheer from the men behind him, and through the weaving branches of the cottonwoods he saw the outlaws marching into the meadow holding their hands above their heads.

The invaders swarmed around the captives, and Channing, after a search of all the cabins, gave crisp orders to Sam Irvine to look after the wounded, take the horses in the rendezvous, send for the others, and proceed leisurely to Rancho del Encanto. He called to three men he knew, and the four of them saddled four of the outlaws' horses and rode up the trail out of the cup.

On the divide Channing hesitated. He wanted his own horse, Major. But Major was with the other horses on the shelf under the ridge near the hole into the cave. It would take time to go and get him.

"Can't do it," he muttered, and spurred his mount down the divide. They made excellent time, Channing taking chances that perhaps he would not have taken if he had not been in a hurry. He wanted to get to Rancho del Encanto as quickly as possible.

"Tough luck," he told one of his companions over his shoulder as they were climbing a hard bit of trail, "not finding Mendicott, I mean. Had a hunch he wasn't there when we didn't get a rise out of 'em on the divide last night and when they didn't come at us pronto in the basin this morning. But he hasn't left. He's not that kind. He'd quit the rest of 'em if it suited his purpose. I know him."

The sun had barely journeyed halfway in its climb to the zenith when they reached the ranch. Channing slung himself from his horse and breathed a sigh of relief when he saw Nathan Farman come to the kitchen door. As the rancher came out, the two girls appeared behind him.

"Missed him!" Channing ejaculated. "I was afraid he'd come here."

"Who you meaning?" asked Farman. "Oh . . . you didn't find Mendicott? You got into his place?"

Channing nodded. "Mendicott and Brood and a few others that don't count were gone. Went out last night. They were clever enough to slip around Crossley. I wonder . . ." His face clouded and his brow wrinkled for a moment. Then his jaw squared again and his face grew stern. "I have an idea," he said, looking at first one and then another. He smiled at Hope, who looked radiant in the morning sun with her hair of gold and her white dress. Lillian looked beautiful, too. She nodded at Channing with a languid air.

Then Channing looked again at Nathan Farman. "He wouldn't leave," he said slowly, with a peculiar glint in his eyes. "He wouldn't leave until he'd seen me. Mendicott's no coward. And he's wise. He's seen the game is up. He's figuring on handing us one more wallop and beating it for good. But first he'll call on me. I can bank on that call, I reckon, only I'm going to beat him to the front door."

He called to Crossley to look after the horses. Then they went out to the corrals and procured fresh mounts. Channing picked the best. He did not see Hope's horse, Firefly, which was in the stall.

Hope came out to him. "Wouldn't you like to take my horse?" she asked. "It's supposed to be the fastest on the ranch. It's in the barn."

Channing's eyes glowed as he looked at her. "Nope. I can't be riding no woman's horse on this trip. It might kill him."

"Are . . . are you going far?" she asked. His insinuations about a meeting with Mendicott had not been lost upon her. She was struck now by the cheerfulness of his manner. Did he know where the outlaw chief was? Was he deliberately going to meet him? Did he welcome that meeting? Her eyes fell upon the butt of the gun on his right thigh. She shuddered and turned away.

She felt his hand upon her arm. "Don't worry," he said in her ear. "And remember those envelopes." He turned to his work of saddling the horse.

Five minutes later he rode away from the ranch with his three companions.

"Uncle!" Hope exclaimed. "There's going to be trouble."

Nathan Farman put his arm about her shoulder. "He can take care of himself, child. Don't worry."

"That's . . . what . . . he said," Hope said with a catch in her voice. "But he said something right afterward that makes me think there's . . . cause to worry." It was his remark about the envelopes. If Mendicott should kill him, she would have to open them. It was a disturbing thought—the thought of Mendicott as the probable victor.

Nathan Farman held her off and looked at her. His own eyes held a strange light. "There, there, child, go in the house an' take his advice an' mine an' don't worry."

It was from Lillian Bell that she received the most comfort. "Don't worry, Hope," she said. "If he's going after Mendicott, and I guess he is, he's going as a different person than you know. Mendicott won't have no more chance with him than a jack rabbit." She finished in tones that snapped.

Hope looked at her in surprise. "How do you mean he's going different?" she asked, although she believed she knew.

"He's going after him a singing devil," said Lillian fiercely. "That's the way I like him." Then, to Hope's amazement, the girl burst into tears. Hope put her arms around her, but Lillian brushed her away. "I'm silly," she said with a light laugh. "I've always been that way about men . . . when they've been devils. Come on, kid, let's go out and water the flowers."

The pound of hoofs came from the entrance to Rancho del Encanto, and a number of horsemen swept up the road to the house. Nathan Farman met them.

"Why, it's Sheriff Kemp from Kernfield!" he exclaimed, as the official dismounted. "I reckon you're too late, Sheriff."

"Oh, he's beat it, has he?" said the sheriff with a frown.

"Guess he has. They blew up his place up there in the hills this morning an' didn't find him."

"Who are you talking about, Farman?"

"Why, Mendicott, of course," replied Nathan Farman, surprised.

"Well, I want that man Channing first," said the sheriff, scowling. "I've a warrant for him, an', when I get him good an' tight in jail, I'll think about the other fellow."

Hope was listening in startled amazement. The sheriff wanted Channing? He was going to put him in jail? And then she saw

a pair of evil black, beady eyes looking at her and recognized
Mendez, the Mexican, among the sheriff's men.

"I think there's some mistake, Sheriff," Nathan Farman was
saying coldly. "I've no complaint against Channing. You wouldn't
do anything when I asked you to, but he took hold of things an'
did do something."

"No doubt," said the sheriff wryly. "Where is he?"

"I don't know," answered Farman truthfully.

The sheriff frowned and looked at the girls and Jim Crossley.
"None of you know?" he questioned.

There was no answer.

"All right, men, we'll tie up here a piece to rest the horses an'
get something to eat, if Farman here'll offer us his hospitality,"
said the sheriff.

Nathan Farman nodded, his face dark as a thundercloud.

The men rode on toward the barn.

Suddenly the Mexican wheeled his horse and rode back to the
front of the house where the sheriff was standing on the porch
with Nathan Farman.

"Channing, he ees maybe gone to Ghost Wash, where he
took the cattle," Mendez suggested.

The sheriff looked at him thoughtfully.

"He maybe ees goin' away with them, or . . . somet'ing,"
continued the Mexican.

"There might be something in it," pondered the sheriff.
"Where is Ghost Wash?"

"I show you," said the Mexican eagerly.

"All right," snapped out the sheriff. "We eat an' rest first."

Hope had hurried to the front of the house and had heard
what Mendez had said. How had he known? A slip of the tongue
of one of the men, of course. Yet Ghost Wash would be a practical place to hide the cattle. It was some distance away, protected
by ridges, and there was grass there, and white sage, and there
was water. She went into the house, stole up to her room, and

put on her hat and riding clothes. She had been riding often of late, and no one would think anything of it. The sheriff was after Channing! Somehow she could not bear to associate the word jail with Channing—he who was so essentially of the great outdoors. Channing—and jail.

Her heart beat fast as she went down the stairs and out to the barn. Jim Crossley saddled Firefly willingly and hung the usual canteen of water on the saddle horn. She rode away from the house on her usual route, which led to the top of the ridge across the mesa. There she was accustomed to dismount and pet her horse and think. This morning she did not dismount. She guided Firefly down the ridge and struck north along the edge of the desert toward Arsenic Spring and the black lava hills.

Chapter Thirty-Six

There was but one consuming thought in Hope's mind as she headed north. Channing must know the sheriff was coming for him. She did not stop to reason what the sheriff wanted him for, or what it was that prompted her to ride forth to warn him. Her Puritanical instincts of convention were submerged in some instinct more primitive and more powerful. She had acted on impulse—an uncontrollable impulse. She was excited, eager, glad. As she left the ranch behind, the hot breath of the desert smote her. It was veritably a blast from a furnace, for the desert now was the fiery inferno of summer. She turned her head away with a little gasp, but the heat did not deter her. She thought of it only for a moment and pushed on.

Firefly went ahead at a swinging lope. She had learned the horse's gaits—learned to ride like a man in the saddle, and learned to love the feel of horseflesh under her. The baked earth was firm, and Firefly had no trouble in picking a path between the clumps of sage and greasewood.

Hope remembered that Channing had ridden out of the entrance to Rancho del Encanto, and that was positive proof that he was going into the desert. She had no doubt but that Ghost Wash was his destination. Channing had mentioned something about Mendicott's taking one last wallop at them. What other blow could he deal now than to attack the men with the cattle and possibly steal them? It was logical. There had been logic in Channing's voice, cool conviction in his eyes. But he must know about the sheriff. Did the sheriff want him for something about

MAN OF THE DESERT

which Hope knew nothing? For some deed of the past? For—perhaps—murder? Hope tossed her head. She did not care, she told herself—she did not care! And the realization gave her a thrill.

She took up the canteen and unscrewed the cap, but she drank very sparingly. She would have to conserve her water. Perhaps, though, she could overtake Channing. If he should see her, he would certainly turn back to meet her. He must have gone that way. It was the way they had gone the day after the escape from the rendezvous. Straight east from Arsenic Spring, that was it. She would hurry to Arsenic Spring and turn east—away from the mountains. She remembered he had pointed out a small pyramid or cone of rock on the far horizon beyond Ghost Wash, which he had called Button Butte. He had used that as a mark. She could use it as a mark, too. And she could take a mark behind her, as he had done, and thus keep in a straight line.

The heat weighed down upon her. It was almost stifling. It was even more severe for one like herself who was not accustomed to it—who was braving it alone for the first time. But the purpose of her mission gave her courage. At last she saw the ghastly waters of Arsenic Spring. The burning ball of the sun was almost directly overhead, and she was miles from the ranch. She looked into the spring and shuddered. What a mockery in this waterless land for one dying of thirst to find this water, a few swallows of which would cause death. But perhaps it would be a more merciful death than to die of thirst. Instinctively she unscrewed the cap of her canteen and sipped.

She turned east. Through the shimmering heat waves she thought she saw Button Butte on the dim, hazy eastern horizon. She looked behind and selected a high peak as another mark. She must keep riding toward the butte with the peak directly ahead. In this way she could make Ghost Wash, and there—she had no doubt—she would find Channing.

She rode on, buoyed up by the thought. The horse now proceeded at a walk, and its head drooped. Heat, heat—heat! The sun hurled it upon the desert and the desert threw it back in a burning glare. Hope pulled her hat down over her eyes. The lava hills to northward were bathed in a slimy-appearing haze, and haze hung in streamers to southward and draped the mountains behind; it seemed in the very air except close at hand, where everything was clear-cut and brilliant, dazzling in its brightness. Hope saw something move, and screamed. Then they had passed around it—a long, blunt-nosed lizard with a pointed tail, yellowish-pink, ugly, repulsive, death dealing. It was the first time she had seen one, but she recognized it instantly by the descriptions she had read and heard—a Gila monster.

For the first time she wavered. But she soon forgot the incident. It seemed she could think of nothing but the everlasting heat. The air was on fire with the scorching rays of that brazen sun in its glassy sky. She looked for the butte on the eastern horizon and sat up suddenly in the saddle. It had disappeared! She wiped her eyes and looked again and again. No use. Her mark to eastward was gone. She looked around at the mountains. They appeared to have changed, assumed new aspects; she could not for a certainty distinguish her peak—her marker. There was no trace back there of Arsenic Spring.

She halted Firefly. Her first thought was of water. She took a little. Oh, if she could only drink the whole canteen! She felt she could drink several canteens of water—barrels of it. Tears came to her eyes. She would have to turn back. And Firefly was acting as though dead. The horse wasn't a desert horse, perhaps. Of course not! Her uncle had no use for the desert, did not go upon it, did not rear horses for it. She would have to turn back. She reeled in the saddle. This brought her sharply to her senses. She would have to use all her will power to endure the heat for even the ride back to the foothills. She marveled that they should appear so far away.

Then she turned back. There seemed to be thought now only of the heat—of getting back. But she hadn't proceeded far when she saw horsemen approaching from the southwest. Her interest was awakened. Who—why, the posse, of course! And they were on their way to get Channing.

Hope halted her horse and waited for them. Firefly drooped and seemed to sleep. The heat waves danced. Already the sun had begun its dip to the west. But Hope had made a resolve. She would go with the posse if it killed her.

Sheriff Kemp was in the lead, and to her surprise Hope saw that her uncle was with him. She caught a glimpse of Mendez's leering features, and bit her lip.

Her uncle appeared stupefied. "Why, child, what are you doing out here? Did you get lost? You shouldn't ride out on the desert like this. I wouldn't dare do it myself. One of the men'll take you back. You . . ."

Hope managed to laugh while the sheriff looked at her suspiciously.

"This is nothing, Uncle. I've been farther out than this. I often ride on the desert. I was just turning back as you came along, but now I'll go along with you."

"No, indeed," said Nathan Farman sternly. "You'll go back, young lady."

But Hope was obdurate, although it required all her strength, and her uncle stormed to no avail.

Finally the sheriff broke in. "If she wants to go, let her," he said crisply. "We're losing time."

This settled it, and Hope rode on with the posse, which was guided by the Mexican. And now that she was with someone who knew the way, she felt better. The presence of the others gave her confidence. She did not believe she felt the heat so much, although it was there—and it was terrible. She knew now why Channing had laughed when she had spoken of that light heat the time they had ridden together from Arsenic Spring to Ghost Wash.

The sun was well down in the west when they finally came in sight of the white surface of Ghost Wash from the crest of the west ridge that hemmed it in. It was deserted.

"The wrong hunch!" cried the sheriff, looking angrily at Mendez.

The Mexican shrugged, and keen disappointment shone in his eyes.

The sounds came to them from beyond the ridge on the other side of the wash—the sharp staccato of pistol shots. Hope looked northward and saw cattle running toward the white lake that Channing had called a deposit. She cried out and pointed.

"They're runnin' 'em off!" shouted the sheriff. "I thought so."

He spurred his horse across the wash with the others following. Hope smiled to herself. So that was what the sheriff thought. He surmised that Channing was stealing the cattle. She laughed aloud as they plunged up the opposite ridge. From its crest a strange sight met their eyes. The cattle were scattering everywhere in the north. Riders were hurrying after them. But there were other men who were lying prone on the ground, and several horses were down. There had been a fight. And there were two other men. Hope cried out again when she saw them. The sheriff swore, and Nathan Farman reined in his horse with a jerk. In a shallow wash or cup in the desert just ahead, the two men were walking slowly toward each other—one from the west, one from the east. They were some distance apart, and were walking slowly, cautiously, each keeping his eyes upon the other. They were not walking as men walk up to each other to extend greeting. On the rim of the cup in the east was a horse with reins dangling. Hope knew that horse. And she knew the man who was walking from the east, with the light of the dying sun in his face. It was Channing. She did not need to look closer at the other man. His horse, too, stood on the rim of the cut—in the west. She knew it was Mendicott.

The outlaw's last blow had been struck at the cattle and now the two rivals of the lightning draw were walking slowly to their last meeting—it would mean death to one of them, perhaps both.

Nathan Farman said something under his breath. The sheriff looked at him and shook his head.

"No way to stop it . . . now," said the official. "Maybe it's just as well this way."

Channing's hat was pulled low over his eyes to shade them from the rays of the setting sun. He slowly began to circle toward the north. As he did so, Mendicott circled toward the south. Even Hope, inexperienced, realized the significance of this. Channing respected his adversary too much to give him the advantage of having the sun at his back, while he, Channing, was looking into it.

A breeze had sprung up from somewhere. It blew its hot breath in the anxious faces of the watchers on the desert ridge. And it brought the notes of a song. Hope's hands flew to her bosom. Channing was coming toward his enemy a singing devil. And he was singing her song—the one she had told him was one of her favorites. She could almost see his eyes—she imagined—cold, glinting, narrowed eyes, locked with those of his enemy. His clear tenor rode sweetly on the breeze. Mendicott seemed to hunch his shoulders, yet he walked almost jauntily, with just a hint of swagger. Channing was singing a song of love when swift moments would surely bring death from smoking guns. She could see the white pockmarks on Mendicott's face, his fierce, black eyes, his sneer—the look was burned into her memory, even though she could not see his face. The men were walking more slowly. They were much closer. They seemed to measure each step. The sun made the cup a bowl of gold. Closer. The wind changed and took away the notes of Channing's voice.

The watchers on the ridge held their breath. The men were barely thirty feet apart. Mendicott stopped. Channing took a step—another. Mendicott's right hand darted down in a move swifter than the eye could follow. Hope saw it and gasped with a pain of fear in her heart. A loud report came up to them. She saw smoke at Channing's hip. There was smoke at Mendicott's hip. They must have fired together.

Mendicott leaned back. The gun at his hip spoke again, but Channing stood still. Then Mendicott dropped to a knee. He fired again and fell forward on his face. Channing suddenly went to the ground in a heap.

With a choking cry Hope spurred her horse down into the cup, rode madly to where Channing was lying, flung herself from the saddle, and gathered his head in her arms.

Chapter Thirty-Seven

It was Nathan Farman who first spoke to the sobbing girl when the posse reached them. He talked to her soothingly as she held Channing's head against her breast. A stain of red slowly widened on her dress.

"Let's look at him," said the rancher. "He isn't dead, child. Come, he must have attention."

Nathan Farman and Sheriff Kemp made an examination of Channing's wound. Hope looked on with wide, dry eyes. The others stood about them. Once she looked away from the head in her lap and saw the crimson banners of the sunset flying above the western peaks. Once before she had looked at the sunset from this place—or nearby—and Channing had watched with her. Now . . .

"He's hit over the left ear," she heard her uncle say as if from a distance. "But I don't believe it's very deep. It's bleeding a lot, naturally, but I don't think it's serious. Looks to me like he's just creased."

"Well, we better get him over to that cabin where there's water," said the sheriff. "Come on, some of you, an' help us carry him."

Hope walked behind them, holding Channing's head with her handkerchief over the wound. The linen soon was stained a deep red.

"It was that last chance shot of Mendicott's that hit him," the sheriff said. "Channing popped him over the heart first crack. He knew it an' wouldn't shoot again. It's a wonder to me how Mendicott managed to stand long enough to shoot twice afterward."

Mendicott was dead then, Hope realized dully. But what of it?

They spread saddle blankets on the bunk in the cabin and rested the inert form upon it. Hope, cool now, helped them wash the wound with water from the spring.

"Just as I figured," said Nathan Farman in tones of satisfaction. "It's a crease. Just deep enough to knock him out for a time. He'll come around all right. That boy's good for many an' many a hard year yet, I'll say."

Hope's heart gave a great bound. It appeared to be true. Already the bleeding was checked. She bandaged the wound herself. Then she sat by the side of the bunk while the men prepared a meal from the emergency provisions that were in the cabin.

Then came the long, desert twilight—and a lessening of heat. Hope ate a little, but refused the hot coffee they urged upon her. Nathan Farman came in and sat down on the bench. He smiled at her with a fatherly look in his eyes. She was bathing Channing's temples with water. His eyes were closed, the bronzed features immobile, but occasionally his lips twitched as if he were going to speak, yet no word came.

And suddenly Hope remembered the letters. She felt of the bosom of her dress to make sure they were there. He had said to open them if anything serious happened to him. Should she open them? Wasn't this serious? She thought for a few moments, and then told her uncle.

Nathan Farman was surprised, and he, too, thought for a time.

"Well," he said finally, "it might be that there's something we should do while he's out of business. Maybe that's what he meant. I guess it'd be all right to open them, Hope."

He lighted some of the stubs of candles he found on a shelf, and Hope drew out the envelopes. She opened the first one he had given her. It contained the option on Rancho del Encanto and a note that read:

> If anything happens to me give this option to your uncle and tell him to take it to Turner & Wescott in Kernfield. They will know what to do. I am hiding the cattle at Ghost Wash.
>
> Channing

Hope handed the option and the note to her uncle with a smile of joy. Nathan Farman recognized the option with a start of astonishment. Then he read the note and jumped up from the bench.

"Hey, Sheriff!" he called. "Come here . . . hurry up!"

When the sheriff hurried in with a look of concern on his face, Farman handed him the option and the note. "Square as a die!" he exclaimed. "Gave the option to my niece in case anything happened to him. He must have got it for Turner an' Wescott, accordin' to that, an' from what he said the other day, what they want are the water rights, or part of it. Tells there what he was going to do with the cattle. An' you thought he was tryin' to steal 'em! Square as they make 'em, Sheriff, an' a danged, all-fired good friend of mine."

"I guess you're right, Farman," the sheriff agreed. "What's that other envelope you've got, young lady . . . if it's any of my business."

Hope quickly told them about the mysterious filings the day they were in Kernfield, when Channing had taken Crossley and herself to an office in the federal building.

"Let's look at 'em," suggested the sheriff.

Hope opened the envelope and handed him the papers.

"Why, these are potash claims!" he ejaculated. "Potash claims on this deposit right up here north. I wonder now if Turner an' Wescott are interested in that lake . . . an' what good is it? Too far from a railroad an' it'd soon be worked out. Can't understand it."

A great light dawned on Hope, and she smiled happily. She told them of the time Channing had brought her to the cabin after the escape from the rendezvous, how she had mentioned the gold of the desert, and he had flared up and told her how many other things there were in the desert besides gold. She had asked him what the lake was, and he had said it was a deposit of potash, borax, and salt. She remembered now there had been a sparkle in his eyes when he had looked at the white lake. "And that's what it is," she finished in triumph. "It's something about that lake with the potash and salt and borax. It must be that Turner and Wescott are going to develop it some way, and that they need the good water that Rancho del Encanto owns. And that must be why Mendicott wanted the ranch. He knew about it and probably wanted to get control of it and sell it at a big price. I'll bet that's why Channing was up there in the first place, to talk to him about it. Remember he said Mendicott laughed at him?"

The question was addressed to her uncle, who was sitting dumbfounded. Nathan Farman nodded open-mouthed.

"And that's why Channing put such a big price in the option," Hope continued. "He wouldn't tell you all about it, Uncle, because you know you didn't believe in the desert, and would have made fun of the idea. Why, he told you once he wouldn't explain because you'd laugh at him. Remember he said he hated to be laughed at?"

Nathan Farman smiled wryly. "The end of Mendicott proves it," he said. "Well, girlie, it all sounds sensible enough . . . don't it, Sheriff?"

"It does, sure enough," agreed the official. "And what's more, he's benefiting this country in here if he puts over whatever deal he's got on. I should have known better than to listen to that confounded Mexican's story about Channing planning to steal the cattle."

Hope laughed. Then she put a hand on Channing's forehead and began to cry softly. But they were tears of gladness. The rancher and the sheriff went out.

Night settled down and the desert cooled under the stars.

The men of the posse had been sent north by the sheriff to help gather the cattle. The sheriff now rode north himself. He returned near midnight and told Nathan Farman and Hope that their surmises had been correct. Mendicott and half a dozen of his men, including Brood, had attacked McDonald and the other men with the cattle. McDonald had shot down two of them before he was killed himself. They had stampeded the herd north, and then Channing had arrived. He had gone into the fight and routed the outlaws, all except Mendicott. Then had come the meeting between them. All the raiders had been killed or wounded except Mendicott and Brood. The latter's horse had been shot down under him, but he himself had disappeared.

"But we'll get him," said the sheriff convincingly. "An' Channing's shooting of Mendicott was mighty good riddance . . . a service to the state."

"I was afraid they'd get McDonald sooner or later," said the rancher soberly. "He was marked from the time he shot that man at the ranch. I reckon he knew it, the way he acted at times."

Hope was sorry to hear of McDonald's death, but she had little time to think of it. Channing was stirring and muttering, evidently in delirium. She laved his temples with the water and fanned him. All night she sat at his side. He quieted down in the hours of the early morning, and Hope dozed in her chair.

When she awoke, she saw the first faint light of dawn through the open door of the cabin. Her right hand was lying on the bunk. She felt a light pressure upon it, looked down at it, and saw that it was covered by Channing's hand. Then she looked at him. His eyes were open, and he smiled.

"You're . . . you're better?" she said wonderingly, hardly able to realize that he had regained consciousness.

"Good's ever 'cept for a headache," he murmured. "Is . . . there any water . . . handy?"

She hurried to get him a drink and spread the good news. The men had returned with the cattle and the wounded, and her uncle and the sheriff were already about. They hurried into the cabin after her.

"Take it easy," Nathan Farman warned. "No, don't try to sit up yet. We've got to dress that head again. I reckon you'll part your hair over the left ear after this. He creased you plenty."

"Last shot," said Channing faintly. "Didn't think . . . he could get in another."

Farman nodded. "You'll have to quit talking, too. Take it easy a few hours . . . all day . . . till we get a chance to move you to the ranch."

But Channing improved so fast that it was impossible to keep him quiet. He insisted on eating something and drinking two cups of strong coffee. His wound apparently had had no effect upon him except to knock him unconscious and leave him with a severe headache when he came out of it. He appeared cheerful, and by noon was sitting up and talking.

He listened while they told of opening the envelopes and what they had deduced from the contents.

"You're about right," he affirmed. "I've had a claim on that lake up there, and the rest of it was held by some of my friends and Brood and Mendicott. I got Turner and Wescott interested in the proposition for a potash mill . . . potash, borax, and salt are the products . . . and they were agreeable to take a chance if I could hand over claims to the whole lake and get some of your water. Mendicott got wise to it and that's why he wanted the ranch. He couldn't have made it stick, but I wanted to put the deal over myself, anyway, so I went into it. I'd have stuck to Rancho del Encanto anyway after . . . after meeting Miss Hope, here." He smiled at Hope, and she flushed as red as the desert dawn. "I didn't explain to you, Nate, because I wanted to surprise you, and then I didn't want to give you a chance to laugh at me. I wanted to prove everything first." Channing laughed in delight while the rancher put his tongue in his cheek. "Those filings of Miss Hope's and Crossley's are on what was supposed to be Mendicott's and Brood's claims. But they never recorded them, nor even staked them out. They were too blamed sure of themselves to take the trouble. Turner and Wescott'll do business now. I knew they would when their Yellow Daisy glory hole petered out. I couldn't get the men an' supplies till that happened. Then I got the men and stuff from Bandburg. They'll give you an' interest for some of the water, and I believe I know how to get into that stream that flows out of the basin where Mendicott had his headquarters. That'll about double the supply and give Turner an' Wescott enough for drinking water and such for the mill, and you enough for your stock and crops. Anyway, we're going to have the mill. If Mendicott could have gotten the ranch, he'd have had the water rights with it, of course, and could have asked almost any price."

The sheriff rose and stood over the wounded man.

"What do you want, Sheriff . . . my gun?" asked Channing. He made a move toward his empty holster.

"I don't want your gun, darn it," sputtered the sheriff. "I want your hand."

* * * * *

They started back in mid-afternoon. Channing had insisted on getting up, and the others realized that his superb physical condition and iron constitution had mitigated the seriousness of his wound. He complained only of a headache. Instructions were given to the Encanto men to drive back the cattle. The seriously wounded were men left in the cabin, with two others to look after them. The spring wagon was to be sent to take them to the ranch in the cool hours of the early morning. A man was given careful instructions as to the trail, and was dispatched to Bandburg for the doctor, who was believed to be still there.

The sheriff, Nathan Farman, Hope, Channing, and two others were in the party that started back for the ranch. Mendez was found missing that morning, but none commented on the fact.

The sun was down behind the western mountains, and the peaks were running red when they came in sight of Arsenic Spring. They checked their horses of one accord and stared ahead.

A figure was reeling in the desert, falling, rising, clawing at the air—the figure of a man.

"It's Brood," said Channing calmly. "Tried to make it on foot, lost his way, and the sun got him . . . the sun and the thirst. He's been digging at the ground. I can tell by the way he acts. He's tearing off his clothes. It's the last stage."

It was indeed Brood. All recognized the big form of the man even at that distance. And he was tearing off his clothes—staggering, clutching at the air, feeling of his swollen, blackened tongue, croaking in his dry throat, no doubt—always getting back at his clothes.

They rode on at a faster pace. Brood's coat was gone, so were his shoes and shirt and hat.

"Doesn't know what he's doing!" Channing called. "Delirium . . . it's the end."

There was no malignity in Channing's tone, no hatred or contempt—only pity for one who could not fight his battle with the desert and win.

"He's making for the spring!" cried the sheriff.

They all saw that he spoke the truth. In his delirium, Brood's feverish gaze had caught sight of the mocking water. Reason was gone. He fell upon his knees and crawled—crawled inch by inch.

They shouted in an effort to divert his attention and increased their pace. But they could not cover the distance in time. Brood wriggled on the hot floor of the desert till he had gained the edge of the stream, and buried his face in the ghastly water flowing from Arsenic Spring. As they reached him his body gave a convulsive shudder, and was still.

Chapter Thirty-Eight

They were mistaken in thinking that Channing had success-fully shaken off the ill effects of his wound. He was swaying in the saddle before they reached the ranch, and that night he tossed and talked incoherently in the throes of a wild delirium.

The doctor came from Bandburg in the morning and attended him and the wounded men who were brought to the ranch shortly after daybreak.

Sam Irvine had brought the captives and wounded from the rendezvous, and the former Yellow Daisy men made camp in a big meadow below the shattered dam, according to orders that had previously been given by Channing. The sheriff and his dep-uties remained at the ranch all that day and that night. Mendez had disappeared—gone for good, it looked like.

Both Hope and Lillian Bell watched over Channing. All day the fever raged and that night it subsided as quickly as it had come.

"Reaction as much as anything else," the doctor grunted. "He'll be up and around as good as ever in three days. Lucky that bullet didn't cut an eighth of an inch deeper."

Quarters for the wounded were arranged in the barn, and the doctor remained at the ranch. Next morning the sheriff started for Kernfield with the prisoners. He carried a message to Turner and Wescott dictated in a weak voice by Channing.

Lillian Bell announced her intention of going to the county seat in one of the wagons conveying the less seriously wounded of the outlaws. Hope opposed this vigorously, and so did Channing.

"No use, folks," said Lillian, "it's too dull for me here. I've passed the home, sweet home stage. I've got to be looking around for a new location."

"But there's going to be a big camp here," Channing protested. "We're going to rebuild the dam, and then the work on the buildings for the potash plant will start, and . . ."

"Not my kind of stuff, Channing," said Lillian with an impudent shrug. "I've got to have pay dirt in mine . . . gold . . . that's me. I've lived in the camps too long."

Channing caught sight of her face in the mirror and motioned to Hope to leave the room.

"Lillian, I know why you're going," he said slowly. "And it isn't necessary, girl . . . don't you see?"

"Yes, I see, Channing," she said, going to the bedside. "Only you don't see. I . . . I couldn't stay here. I love her, Channing . . . and you've got it coming to you. You're square." There was a quaver in her voice. Then she threw back her head and laughed recklessly. "I'm going to find me a fighting devil, Channing, that stays a fighting devil all the time."

When he started to speak again, she bent over him suddenly and kissed him. Then she went quickly out of the room.

She found Hope in the hall.

"Listen, girlie," she said, putting her arms about her. "You've got yourself some man. He was dead in love with you from the time you went out to warn him that Brood was in Bandburg . . . remember? That got him. I saw it. He'll stick to you till they're mowing grass on the desert, and I reckon that'll be sometime. Me? I'm going to get me a fighting devil that stays put. I've got no use for 'em when they tame down. Good bye."

She kissed Hope and hurried down the stairs. But Hope knew she had not spoken the truth at the last. She ran after her with a tightening of the throat. But Lillian, laughing gaily and bantering with the men, was already in a wagon with her belongings and calling: "¡Adiós!"

Hope went back to the room where Channing lay. He called her to the bedside and took her hand. Hope was both sad and happy—almost in tears.

"Remember what I said about things not glittering being gold . . . pure gold?" he said whimsically. "Lillian's that sort . . . only she didn't understand, dog-gone it. She couldn't."

His arm stole about Hope's shoulders and brought her lips down to his.

* * * * *

In three days, true to the doctor's prediction, Channing was up and about. He took full charge. The cattle had been driven back to the ranch and up into Forest Reserve range, where there was plenty of feed and water. The camp below the ruined dam bustled with activity. Frank Turner, of Turner & Wescott, visited the ranch and announced that the Yellow Daisy Company would develop the potash deposit, build a huge mill, and a narrow-gauge railroad from the main line in the south.

Nathan Farman was paid a large sum for control of his water rights with the understanding that he was to have enough water for his stock and fields. Engineers came and found that Channing's surmise regarding the outlet of the water from the cup that had been Mendicott's rendezvous was correct, and that the water could be run into the Rancho del Encanto dam by blasting and tunneling into the ridge below the former hiding place of the outlaws. They found, too, that he had been correct in contending that the deposit in the potash lake was a seepage and that they could pump thousands of gallons of brine out of the lake daily without diminishing the supply. From this brine was to be extracted the potash and salt and borax by improved methods.

The claims of Channing and his friends and Hope and Crossley were taken over, and good-size blocks of stock in the potash company given in exchange. Channing was made assistant manager of operations. Thus Rancho del Encanto, while still preserving its beauty and individuality, became a quiet spot on the edge of a hive of industry.

There came a day in the early autumn when Nature lavished all the contents of her paint pots on the foothill landscape. The leaves of the cottonwoods were flakes of gold. The berry bushes scattered rubies in the wind. The sky was a laughing blue.

Channing and Hope rode together in the sunset to the crest of the ridge that shut off the desert. There they dismounted and stood looking into the east, across the throbbing waste of the lava hills, girdled with flowing scarves of pink and purple.

"I've been pretty busy lately," said Channing, without looking at her.

"And you've accomplished wonderful things," said Hope in a low voice.

"I'm going in to Kernfield in a day or two," he said.

"Yes? You have to make so many business trips."

"But I didn't figure on this being a business trip."

A covey of desert quail flew past with a musical whir of wings.

Hope didn't speak. She looked up at him, standing close to her, the rays of the sunset striking copper fire from his hair, his eyes soft and luminous with a light that struck an answer in her own as she turned them away.

"I figured you'd go along, Hope," he said softly, taking her hands. "Do . . . you . . . want to go?"

"Why?" she murmured. "Why, Channing?"

"Because I love you, Hope. I always knew the desert would bring me something sometime better than its gold . . . better than all its treasures. I reckon that's you, sweetheart."

266

She put her arms about his neck and raised her lips. "I never knew what the desert would bring me," she whispered, "but I'm glad, dearest . . . I'm glad."

The desert twilight flung over them its robes of royal purple as the sky blossomed into stars.

THE END

About the Author

Robert J. Horton was born in Coudersport, Pennsylvania. As a very young man he traveled extensively in the American West, working for newspapers. For several years he was sports editor for the Great Falls Tribune in Great Falls, Montana. He began writing Western fiction for Adventure magazine before becoming a regular contributor to Street & Smith's *Western Story Magazine*. By the mid-1920s Horton was one of three authors to whom Street & Smith paid 5¢ a word—the other two being Frederick Faust, perhaps better known as Max Brand, and Robert Ormond Case. Many of Horton's serials for Street & Smith's *Western Story Magazine* were subsequently brought out as books by Chelsea House, Street & Smith's book publishing company. Although virtually all of Horton's stories appeared under his byline in the magazine, for their book editions Chelsea House published them either as by Robert J. Horton or by James Roberts. Sometimes, as was the case with *Rovin' Redden* (Chelsea House, 1925) by James Roberts, a book would consist of three short novels that were editorially joined to form a "novel." Other times the stories were serials published in book form, such as *Whispering Cañon* (Chelsea House, 1925) by James Roberts or *The Prairie Shrine* (Chelsea House, 1924) by Robert J. Horton. It may be obvious that Chelsea House, doing a number of books a year by the same author, thought it a prudent marketing strategy to give the author more than one name. Horton's Western stories are concerned most of all with character, and it is the characters that drive the plots rather than the other way around. It is unfortunate he died at such a relatively early age. Many of his novels, after Street & Smith abandoned Chelsea House, were published only in British editions, and Robert J. Horton was not to appear at all in paperback books until quite recently.